THE FIST

TIERRE FORD

Disclaimer

This is a work of fiction Name, characters, places and incidents either are the product of the author imagination or are used fictitiously. Any resemblance to actual persons, living, or dead, event or locales are entirely coincidental

ABOUT THE AUTHOR

At just 12 years old, I started selling drugs in the 6th grade—following the blueprint I saw in my own home. My father was both a dealer and a user, and by the 7th grade, I had bought my first car, was paying my mama rent, and buying my own school clothes.

That same year, the school system labeled me as "slow." They placed me in a remedial reading class—embarrassed me, honestly. I was ashamed. But I still kept my swag, my gold chains, my Starter jackets, and my game face. I was one of the most popular kids in school, but truth be told, I had stopped learning. I was only there to show off.

Then one day, my reading teacher—who I'll never forget—looked me in my eyes and said, "You don't belong in this class. You're smart. Don't let them label you." Her words stuck with me, even though my CRT test scores said otherwise.

At age 12 years old I became my neighborhood's youngest drug supplier. I started with 10 dollars, and I flipped that all the way to over $500,000. Me and my Dad link up dealing together supplying the market. I dropped out of high school in the 10th grade. I bought my mother a house with a pool in the backyard, purchased luxury cars, before I was locked up at 19.

At that point in my life, I had never read a full book. Not one. But my father always told me, **"The mind is the most powerful tool in the universe. Street sense and book sense together? That's unstoppable."**

So I gave books a chance.

It started with street fiction. Then history. Then business. Then biographies about powerful and wealthy people. I started seeing myself in those pages—not always in their polish, but in their ambition, their boldness. Then I read **Think and Grow Rich and As a Man Thinketh.** Those two books changed my entire mindset.

That's when I met my friend Cool Harris. I saw some of his writing on a notepad, and it rocked my world. I realized I had something to say, too. From that moment on, I picked up the pencil—and I've never looked back.

I earned my GED, took business and college courses, and started studying resilience. I discovered that, back in the day, Black people were once forbidden to read. There's even a saying: **"If you want to hide something from a Black person, put it in a book."** That became my fuel.

Now, I write both fiction and self-help books, covering everything from mindset and mental toughness to financial strategy and spiritual growth. I pour my soul into every page with one mission: to light a fire inside someone who's ready for change.

To everyone who's followed my journey—thank you. Let's set the world on fire with truth, with courage, with knowledge. Let's break every chain and every myth that says we don't read.

Peace—And Keep The Faith.

TIERRE FORD

Chapter 1

Checkmate

In the heart of the city, where buildings leaned like old men and hope wore scuffed sneakers, there was a neighborhood known as *The Bricks*. Concrete walls carried bullet holes like birthmarks, and the air tasted like metal and struggle. This wasn't just a place—it was a proving ground. And anyone who made it out deserved not just a medal… but maybe a bulletproof vest too.

The sound of shouting pierced the afternoon stillness. A man in a dingy white tank top argued loudly with a woman outside a faded apartment building. His voice cracked with frustration, hers with fury. The subject? Her EBT card—stolen, again. Nearby, children paused their games, half-amused, half-accustomed. This was normal. Just another day in the Bricks.

Kids scattered across cracked pavement, chasing dodgeballs like their lives depended on it. Girls double-dutched with the intensity of Olympic hopefuls. On a nearby stoop, two men argued over a five-dollar debt as if it were a matter of national security. Amid the chaos stood a crew— young, sharp, and hungry.

T-Money -10 . Tom Tom -11. Bay-12. Dee -12. Kareem-11. Eddie B-13. Ash-10. D-Bo -12. Buck-13. And White Boy-10.
Ten names. Ten hustlers-in-training. Ten reasons the system didn't sleep.

SIDEWALK – WALKING TO KROGER – DAY

T-Money, strutted ahead like he owned the street.

"Y'all ready to hit Kroger?" he asked. "Money ain't gonna make itself."

Tom Tom laughed. "What you waitin' on? An invitation?"

Someone tripped. Nobody stopped. In the Bricks, even gravity had competition.

KROGER PARKING LOT – DAY

They split up with the precision of a practiced hustle. Buck and Eddie B offered help loading groceries. Kareem and Bay offered to fix a stranger's flat tire. Inside this world, every gesture had an angle. Every act, a hustle.

T-Money and Tom Tom played a game of their own: "Kroger Bingo"— scanning the lot for the best cars.

A sleek black Benz rolled into view.

"**Bingo!**" T-Money shouted.

"Boy, shut up. I saw it first," Tom Tom replied, but he was smiling.

"That's Big John. That's who I wanna be like."

Big John stepped out in slow motion, shades on, gold chain gleaming, confidence pouring off him like cologne.

"What y'all little hustlers up to?" he asked.

T-Money didn't miss a beat. "Tryna turn a nickel into a dollar. Carry groceries, changin flat tires, —whatever pays."

Tom Tom chimed in. "We tryna be like you, though."

Big John chuckled. "Naw… be better than me. I got two baby mamas and a bad back."

He handed each boy a crisp ten-dollar bill. Game recognize game.

KROGER PARKING LOT – LATER

A prehistoric car rolled in, coughing up black smoke like it had lung disease. The kids stared.

"**Bingo!** That's Kareem's car when he grows up," Ash joked.

Kareem frowned. "Ain't NO WAY I'm drivin' that."

The car squealed to a stop, doors creaking open like haunted house hinges. Sammy emerged, shirt stained, sandals crusted.

"Ayy, I need two of y'all to cut some grass," he said.

The crew looked at him like a negotiation panel.

"How much?" asked T-Money.

"Thirty-five dollars."

"That's all?" D-Bo asked, unimpressed. "Man, my sweat is worth at least fifty."

"You cuttin' grass, not buildin' mansions," Sammy snapped. "Thirty-five or nothin'."

D-Bo sighed. "Fine. But I'm takin' three water breaks."

T-Money and D-Bo climbed into Sammy's car, which sputtered to life before the muffler dropped to the pavement. Everyone burst out laughing.

KROGER PARKING LOT – MEANWHILE

Buck scanned the lot like a hawk. "We need another customer."

Eddie B nodded. "People tip real good when they desperate."

A brand-new car pulled in. Sparkling. Tempting.

"**Bingo**," Bay whispered.

"Dee. White Boy. Inside job," Buck instructed.

Inside, Dee and White Boy "accidentally" bumped into the lady by the water aisle, asking way too many questions. Outside, Buck, Bay, and Eddie B slowly let the air out of her tire.

Minutes later, the lady returned.

She stared at her tire. Sighed.

Buck approached with the fake concern of a seasoned actor. "Aw, man. Flat tire? That's really unlucky. But we just so happen to be experts."

They fixed it quickly. She handed them a twenty—biggest score of the day.

Then—**screeching tires. Sirens.**

KROGER PARKING LOT – MOMENTS LATER

A cop car rolled up. The boys froze.

The officer stepped out. Not smiling.

"I hear y'all boys out here soliciting."

No one moved. No one snitched. The street code was older than all of them.

Eddie B finally spoke. "We just tryna make money legally, officer."

The cop didn't budge. "Doesn't matter. Leave. Now."

Silence.

Then someone yelled—**"FUCK THE POLICE!"**

Chaos exploded. Kids bolted like lightning. Over fences. Behind dumpsters. Past shopping carts. It looked like a heist scene—except this was real life, every damn summer.

The officer stood still, shaking his head like he'd seen it all.

Because he had.

In *The Bricks*, every kid learns fast: the world doesn't wait, and time doesn't blink. Hustle too slow, and you're food. Hustle too loud, and you're a target. But in the cracks of broken systems, young kings were being formed. Not in palaces—but in parking lots, in the shadow of patrol cars, under the heat of summer hustle.

And this? This was just the beginning.

Chapter 2

The Hustle Or The Haunting

The woods behind The Bricks weren't on any map—but every kid from the neighborhood knew where to find them. It was where secrets got buried, hustles got planned, and running from the police turned into strategy sessions. The makeshift clubhouse—just an old shed half-covered in graffiti—stood crooked, like it was holding on to its last breath.

Inside, the crew regrouped after their wild chase from Kroger. Out of breath but laughing hard, their lungs burned, their legs ached—but their spirits? Still undefeated.

T-Money wiped sweat from his brow and leaned against a tree.

" Man Sammy grass was taller than me. We might need to invest in some lawnmower his neighbors just as bad ," he said.

Tom Tom, never one to miss a beat, threw his arms up. " Or car washes?"

Eddie B rolled his eyes. "Sounds like y'all have money to fund the ideas."

Buck grinned like the devil just whispered in his ear. "Hold up—I got it. We steal candy from the store and sell it at school. Hundred percent profit."

Kareem shook his head. "Man, we gon' eat all the profit."

"That's a start," Buck shrugged.

Ash stared off into the woods. "Something gotta give."

The laughter died down. A beat of silence. Each of them suddenly became aware that their dreams were bigger than their surroundings—farther than their arms could reach.

T-Money looked up at the sky, barely visible through the canopy of leaves. "My dad said supply and demand make the world go round. We just gotta figure out what people want."

And just like that, the clubhouse wasn't just a hideout anymore—it was their boardroom.

APARTMENT COMPLEX – NIGHT

Street Lights flickered like broken promises. The air was thick with Southern humidity and leftover barbecue smoke. A group of teens—boys and girls—hung out on the pavement, their laughter echoing through the complex. Bottles clinked. Music from a nearby unit bled into the night.

Eddie B grinned. "Let's play Hide and Go Get."

T-T rolled her eyes, lips curled in a teasing smile. "Eddie, you always wanna do something nasty. You better find me first."

The group erupted in laughter.

Buck counted down. "Alright, twenty-five seconds. Y'all go hide. Whoever gets found… owes a kiss, a hunch, or whatever your preference."

The girls scattered behind parked cars, giggling in the shadows as the boys closed their eyes and counted like it was life or death.

Farther down the block, just outside the circle of teenage games, the real business was being whispered.

Big John leaned against a rusted car, speaking in low tones with Gus, Bud, and Bear.

Gus scrolled through his phone. "Man, I heard they picked up about ten people on the Westside."

Big John nodded, sunglasses still on even in the dark. "Yeah… Feds thick right now. Homies snitchin'. Streets feel off."

Bear shook his head. "I'm tellin' y'all—we need to switch lanes. Rap game's where it's at."

Bud spat on the ground. "I keep hearin' the rap game will suck you dry."

Big John smirked. "Heard they rob you blind without a gun. I'll stick to what I know."

The teens played just yards away—laughing, chasing each other, alive in their innocence. Unaware the wolves were watching. Unaware the fire was coming.

Gus checked his phone again. "Man, I'm headed to Blue Flame."

Big John cracked his neck. "I'm right behind you."

T-MONEY'S HOUSE – NIGHT

T-Money stepped into his apartment. The living room reeked of old takeout and weed smoke. A few bodies lay slumped on the couch, eyes glazed, barely moving. One man nodded off mid-sentence, lips twitching like he was still chasing a high.

T-Money ignored them all. He walked straight to his room, closed the door, and locked it behind him. Silence wasn't peace. It was survival.

TOM TOM'S HOUSE – NIGHT

Big Tom sat like a shadow came to life, bottle in hand, TV flickering in front of him.

"Where yo' momma at, boy?" he slurred. "Is she out there cheatin' on me?"

Tom Tom stood at the doorway, hands in his pockets. "I… I don't know, Dad. Thought she was with her sister."

Big Tom's eyes narrowed. "Boy, you're lying' to me."

He stood up too fast—then dropped like dead weight onto the floor.

Tom Tom didn't flinch. Just shook his head and stepped over him. He didn't cry. He didn't even go to check if he was okay. He just closed his bedroom door behind him and sat in the dark.

D-BO'S HOUSE – NIGHT

The sound of the TV was a whisper compared to what echoed down the hall. Moaning. Beds creaking. A woman screaming. His younger sisters watched cartoons like none of it was happening.

D-Bo marched to the TV, grabbed the remote, and turned the volume all the way up.

A bedroom door opened. Two teenage boys strolled out, shirts off, guns tucked into their waistbands.

Tutu laughed. "Boy, we had her in a preze."

Fat Head added, "WWF action. Tag team."

He looked at D-Bo.

"What's up, D-Bo?" he asked, mockingly.

D-Bo didn't answer.

Tutu shrugged. "Ain't personal, lil' homie. Just business. You'll understand when you get older."

They walked out like it was just another night.

D-Bo didn't move. Just clenched his fists and stared at the wall, his jaw locked, his eyes hard. Rage lived there now.

ASH'S HOME – NIGHT

The living room looked more like a trap house than a home. Ash's mom sat at the table counting crumpled bills. His dad handed out baggies with the precision of a bank teller. The door barely stayed closed with the traffic.

Dope fiends came and went like clockwork—eyes darting, hands shaking, desperate for that next hit. A little girl, no more than five, slept in the corner with a teddy bear under her arm.

Ash stood in the hallway. Watching. Breathing it in. Already calculating how not to end up like them.

The Bricks didn't raise boys. It forged survivors. Between the police, poverty, addiction, and pain, childhood was a luxury—one none of them could afford. Each house held its own horror. Each soul carried its own scar. And while most kids dreamed of basketball courts and birthday parties, these kids dreamed of escape… or revenge.

Some ran.
Some hustled.
Some just endured.

But all of them knew one truth: the world wouldn't hand them anything.

They'd have to take it.

THE NEXT DAY

SCHOOL BUS – MORNING

The bus was a jungle on wheels—engine growling, gum stuck under every seat, windows streaked with finger-smudged graffiti. Laughter bounced off the metal walls, mingling with the sound of backpacks thumping the floor and sneakers squeaking on the rubber mat.

T-Money sat in the middle row with a girl beside him, lips closed as they whispered and giggled. The kind of moment that made a broke kid feel like royalty for five minutes.

Behind them, Mona—the queen of gossip—leaned forward with eyes wide and hungry.

"Somebody got kicked out!" she announced, voice slicing through the noise.

Jeff, always ready to add gas to the fire, leaned into the aisle with a grin. "Damn, who?! Somebody's mama got high and forgot to pay rent again?"

As if summoned by cruel timing, the bus slowed to a crawl and stopped in front of a sidewalk crowded with a sad parade of furniture—couch cushions slouched like tired bodies, baby toys spilled across the curb, milk crates full of clothes stacked like they'd been tossed by a storm.

T-Money's eyes locked on the scene.

There, in the sunlight, stood his mother and little sister. Eyes red. Faces raw. Desperately trying to figure out what to save and what to abandon.

Mona pointed and shrieked, "Ohhh, it's T-Money! You got kicked out?!"

The bus exploded in laughter. Kids doubled over, slapped seats, howled like wolves. Some banged fists on the windows, while others held up invisible cameras like it was a show.

But T-Money's crew didn't laugh.

Tom Tom. Buck. White Boy. Dee. Ash. They sat still, jaws clenched, eyes locked forward like soldiers waiting on a command.

The air on the bus changed.

The doors hissed open.

T-Money shot up and darted down the aisle. He didn't look at anyone. Didn't speak. Just ran—full speed—off the bus and down the street like his life depended on it.

"T-Money!" his mother cried out, dropping a box. "Baby, come back!"

His little sister called after him too, voice cracking—but he never looked back. The pain was too big for tears. It ran in his blood now.

Tom Tom and White Boy jumped off the bus and chased after him, pushing past startled kids and ignoring the driver yelling at them to get back inside.

Meanwhile, Ash and Dee climbed down slow and steady.

They didn't say a word. Didn't try to comfort anybody.

They just bent down and started helping T-Money's mom and sister gather what they could. Lifted boxes. Stacked bags. Picked up a framed picture of T-Money as a baby—cracked, but still smiling.

Nobody told them to help.
Nobody had to.

In the Bricks, heartbreak didn't wait for weekends or weather forecasts. It hit you on Tuesday mornings, in front of your whole school, while your pride burned to ash in your chest.

And still, the world moved on.

Because the hood had a cruel way of teaching boys that manhood wasn't a matter of age—it was pain measured in silence, loyalty measured in action, and love buried beneath layers of armor no one could see.

T-Money ran that afternoon —not just from shame, but from the feeling of being *seen* too deeply.

But in that moment, as boxes were lifted and friends stepped in, something unspoken wrapped around him and his crew.

Brotherhood.

A currency more valuable than anything they'd ever hustle for.

Chapter 3

The sun hung low like a warm secret, painting the sky with streaks of gold and purple. In the backyard of a modest but well-kept home on the Eastside, balloons swayed, red cups clinked, and the bass from a speaker vibrated deep in people's chests. A big banner stretched across the fence: **"WELCOME HOME, EDDIE B!"**

Smoke from the grill curled into the sky, blending with the smell of meat, seafood, weed, and cologne that was just a little too loud. It was a celebration—but not just of freedom. It was a reunion. A reminder that some bonds could outlast time, prison bars, and bullet wounds.

At the grill stood Dee—bigger now, beard thick, apron loud: **"KING OF THE GRILL"** in bold red. He flipped ribs like he was born to do it, nodding to the beat of old-school trap music. Nearby, Sugar stirred a seafood boil with a big wooden paddle, eyes closed like she was saying a prayer over the pot.

On the patio, T-Money and Bay sat locked in a chess match, eyes sharp, fingers twitching. The board sat between them like a sacred battlefield. Tom Tom and White Boy stood over their shoulders like sports commentators.

Kareem was off to the side, whispering into Savannah's ear, making her smile like she was still in high school. D-Bo and Shan danced in a rhythm known only to them—offbeat, off-tempo, but completely in sync with each other's joy. They looked ridiculous. They looked free.

Inside the kitchen, Ash stacked deviled eggs with militant precision, muttering counts under his breath. Buck came out of the bathroom looking like he'd just survived a hurricane—and proud of it.

Kids jumped on a trampoline in the corner, nearly colliding with a football that zoomed dangerously close to the hot grill.

"You lookin' real nervous, T," Bay said with a grin.

T-Money didn't flinch. **"Man, nervous? The only thing shaking is your queen—and she just got taken."**

He moved his knight like a surgeon, cool and calm.
 Checkmate.

Bay stared at the board like it had betrayed him.

White Boy erupted in laughter. **"Bay's queen has been in witness protection for three moves!"**

Bay threw his arms back. **"Aight, run it back. Best of five."**

"Best of five?!" White Boy laughed. **"Man, you playin' a season opener while T just won the championship!"**

BY THE GRILL

Dee wiped sweat off his forehead.

"Man, this grill is hotter than my ex's temper."

Summer . **"You need some iced water baby? "**

"naw a cold beer"

Laughter rolled through the yard like good weather.

THE DRINK TABLE

Buck poured a drink and raised his cup.

"To my Dogg, Eddie B! Finally free!"

The whole backyard echoed back: **"FREE!"**
Cups clinked, shoulders bumped, grins stretched.

"Been a long time—no wood. I'm overdue," T-T said, sipping her drink.

"Eddie B gon' send you straight to urgent care," Egypt shot back.

"**She gon' need a wheelchair by the end of the night!**" White Boy added.

The whole crowd cracked up. T-Money nearly choked on his drink. Ash peeked from the kitchen, chuckling.

D-BO & SHAN'S "DANCE FLOOR"

D-Bo and Shan danced like they were arguing with the music—and losing.

Bay shook his head. "**Somebody cut the music off. They are out here violating the beat.**"

"**That ain't dancing. That's cardio,**" said T-T.

White Boy added, "**Nah, that's a crime. Call the cops.**"

More laughter.

THE BIG ANNOUNCEMENT

Ash stood on a chair, holding a giant plate of deviled eggs like a trophy.

"**Aight, listen up! Before my man Eddie B walks in, let's get one thing straight—these deviled eggs are the best in the city.**"

White Boy pointed. "**Too late! Bay done had three already!**"

Bay shifted, the lumps in his throat obvious.

"**Mind ya business.**"

Another wave of laughter crashed over the yard.

Then—**a car pulled up.**

The music didn't stop—but the people did. Heads turned. Drinks froze mid-air. A few kids climbed down from the trampoline to get a better look.

The car door opened.

Out stepped Eddie B—chains glinting, smile wide, arms open.

"**I'm HOME, baby!**"

The backyard erupted.

Cups flew. Music surged. The grill flared up like it knew the moment mattered. Kids ran. Women hollered. And T-T sprinted straight into Eddie's arms.

"Boy, you got five years of work to put in tonight!" she laughed, holding him like the years had just folded in.

Cheers rang. Ash held his deviled eggs up like Simba. Someone turned the music all the way up.

The party had officially begun.

The Chessboard.
The black king rocked gently in check.

T-Money moved his piece with quiet confidence. **"Checkmate."**

V.O. – T-MONEY (REFLECTIVE)
Fifteen years later, and the crew came a long way from flattening tires and helping' old ladies with groceries. Now? Now they call themselves The Fist—something Old raggedy car Sammy inspired.

I remember Sammy watching some documentaries. Wild Kingdom or somethin'. Wolves, ants, bees—all moving together, unified. That's when it hit me—five fingers slap, but a fist knocks you out.

FLASHBACK – APARTMENT – NIGHT

A young T-Money sits beside Sammy, eyes glued to the flickering screen. A pack of wolves moves like one organism. Ants carry impossible weight. Bees build like engineers.

BACK TO PRESENT – EXT. BACKYARD

Tom Tom tipped his king over, finally conceding.

"One day, I'll get you."

T-Money smirked. **"One day."**

They both looked toward the grill where the rest of the crew laughed, danced, and toasted.

V.O. – T-MONEY (CONT'D)

When we formed The Fist, we made a pact—pool money, flip weight, keep each other whole. If one took a loss, the rest carried the load. That way, pressure never crushed just one man.

FLASHBACK – INT. BASEMENT – NIGHT

A dark room. One table. Cash being counted, weighed, sorted. Rules spoken. Hands raised.
No woman-hopping. No snitching. No gambling against each other. Disputes? Handled like men.

BACK TO PRESENT – EXT. BACKYARD

Smoke curled into the night sky. The beat of old records rolled under the stars. T-Money and Tom Tom sat side by side, kings without crowns. Behind them, a team laughed loud enough to make the world forget how hard it had been to get here.

V.O. – T-MONEY
For eight years, the plan worked. Flawless. Damn near perfect.

But the thing about plans? They don't bleed.

People do.

Chapter 4

The Cost Of Coming Home

The bedroom was quiet, dim, and heavy with something unspoken—lust, pain, time. The lamp cast a golden glow over two glasses and a half-empty bottle that caught the light like temptation in a bottle.

Eddie B stood in the doorway, five years of federal time trailing behind him like smoke off the barrel of a gun. His eyes had changed—older, sharper, burdened—but tonight wasn't about the weight. Tonight was about release.

T-T stood by the bed, barefoot, lips parted. She looked like a memory he'd been holding onto since the day they cuffed him.

"I missed you, baby... so bad," she whispered.

She didn't have to say more.

They collided like thunder meeting fire. Kisses turned violent. Clothes hit the floor like confessions. Her back found the bedpost, his hands found her waist. Every touch was a scream, every moan a hymn. Years of need poured out in a language only their bodies understood.

"Oh, Eddie... I love you... I need you..."

He gripped tighter. Deeper. The room turned humid, breathless, timeless.

The bed creaked under reunion. The lamp flickered with rhythm. Eddie trembled, the past slipping from his shoulders in a single groan. He collapsed onto the mattress, chest heaving. She curled up beside him, fingers tracing patterns only love—or lust—could write.

"**Damn... worth the wait,**" she grinned.

Eddie smirked. "**Hell yeah.**"

They lay tangled in sweat, in silence, in survival.

GAS STATION – DAY

The midday sun beat down on the blacktop. Cars lined up like soldiers waiting for orders. Bay leaned against his ride, calm, clean, and low-key—like always. His shirt hugged his arms just right, chain subtle, eyes scanning like a seasoned vet.

Two young boys—Slime and Chubby Kid—walked up, too confident for their age.

"**Hey, you tryna buy some weed?**" Slime asked casually.

Bay looked at them sideways. "**Shouldn't y'all be in school?**"

"**We just tryna eat, man,**" Slime said.

Bay nodded slowly. "**I feel you. I been there before... Keep your weed, but here—**"

He reached into his pocket for some cash.

That's when **two guns** kissed his face.

"**Say one word, you dead,**" Chubby hissed.

Black van. Screech. Doors open.

Four masked men snatched Bay so quickly it looked rehearsed. Tossed him in the back. Slammed it shut.

The boys jumped in Bay's car and sped off.

People watched. Nobody moved.
That's just how the city works.

THE OFFICE – NIGHT

Inside the condo, the air buzzed with electricity. Money counters whirred like machines in a casino. Two bulging bookbags sat on the couch. Weed smoke hovered like a fog of war.

T-Money sat at the head. D-Bo, Tom Tom, Buck, and Eddie B formed a loose circle—tight-knit but alert.

"How long before Cuz pull up?" D-Bo asked.

"Said he finished unloading twenty minutes ago," Buck replied. **"So he's twenty, thirty out."**

T-Money handed a bag to Eddie B. **"That's 100 racks from all of us. And we have each given you one solid buyer to help you build your team up. This gon' put you back on your feet."**

Eddie laughed in disbelief. **"The Fist strikes again! When I left, we barely had a hundred stacks total. Y'all really leveled up."**

"Ain't never gonna be a tighter crew," Tom Tom said.

"History in the making," T-Money agreed. **"Anybody heard from Bay?"**

Buck frowned. **"Straight to voicemail."**

"Same," T-Money said. **"That ain't like him..."**

Silence hit the room.

Then—**a garage door rumbled open.**

"There go Cuz," Buck said.

"Like clockwork," D-Bo nodded.

Cuz walked in, hoodie half-zipped, expression unreadable. They moved fast—loading up book bags, gym bags, vacuum-sealed bricks.

"Highway hot today," Cuz said. **"Saw like seven trucks pulled over."**

Buck smirked. **"When the hustling gods are with you, ain't nothing to worry about."**

ABANDONED SCHOOL – NIGHT

The walls peeled like dead skin. A flickering light struggled to exist. Bay sat zip-tied to a rusted chair, face swollen, lip split. Dried blood formed a crust along his cheek.

Five shadows surrounded him. Three were kids—**Slime, Chubby, Rowe**. The other two were grown—**Razor and Chop**. Razor flipped a knife like a toy. Chop paced like he wanted a reason.

"How much do you think your life is worth?" Razor asked with a grin.

Bay looked up through one half-swollen eye. **"Tell me the price... my folks'll pay."**

"Half a million," Razor said, crouching close.

"Let me call. They'll bring it."

"Beg," Razor demanded.

Bay swallowed hard. **"Please... let me call."**

Razor pulled out a burner phone.

"Number?"

"404... 730... 6630."

Razor dialed. It rang.

SPLIT SCREEN – EXT. SUGAR'S HOUSE – NIGHT

Sugar answered, voice sharp with suspicion.

"Hello?"

"Bae... listen..." Bay managed.

Razor grabbed the phone. **"You got 'til sunrise. Half a mill. No cops."**

Click.

Bay exhaled.

PARKING LOT – NIGHT

T-Money paced like a storm about to hit. Ash leaned on the hood of a sedan, arms folded.

"Been a ghost all day," T-Money said. **"It doesn't feel right."**

"Hope the alphabet hasn't boys picked him up," Ash muttered.

"That'd be better than finding him cold."

T-Money lit a blunt, mind racing.

"You going to Sammy's later?"

"You and old man Sammy?" Ash asked. **"What is he on now?"**

"He stay on the next level shit hell he was the one who inspired The Fist. He has come a long way. Got a big house, nice cars now—said he wanna talk."

T-Money's phone rang. *Sugar.*

He answered. **"Hey, Sugar. Everything good?"**

Her voice hit like a siren. **"No. Bay got kidnapped."**

T-Money froze. Ash straightened up.

"What are they saying? What do they want?"

"Half a mil."

A slow nod passed between them.

"We'll come up with it. How long have we got?"

"Till six AM."

"We will be at your house soon."

Ash flicked his blunt away. The street just got real again.

INT. ABANDONED SCHOOL – LATER

Razor turned to Chop and Rowe. **"We have to go take care of some things. Y'all hold it down."**

Chop leaned in, grabbed Slime and Chubby by the mouth. "**Don't fuck this up. Or you next.**"

They nodded.

As soon as the others were gone, Bay whispered, "**They are not splitting that money. They gon' kill y'all too.**"

"**Shut up,**" Chubby snapped.

"**If you do, you're dead for sure.**"

Slime paused. "**He right.**"

"**Right about what?**" Chubby said.

"**Everything.**"

Bay sat up. "**Free me—I'll give y'all twenty bands each.**"

"**How do we know you won't play us?**"

Bay shook his head. "**I told y'all at the gas station—y'all remind me of me. I ain't tryna use y'all. I'm tryna help.**"

They stepped back, talked low. Then came back.

"**We want twenty. Each. And if you cross us—everything gettin' smoked.**"

Bay nodded. "**My word. Give me the phone.**"

They dialed. Bay gave a number.

INTERCUT – PHONE CONVERSATION

"**Yo,**" T-Money answered.

"**It's me.**"

"**You good?! We are on the way to Sugar's.**"

"**Change of plans. Meet me at Old National. Liquor store. Bring forty grand. I worked something out.**"

"**Forty cool. We are on the way.**"

Chubby looked tense. "**Hope your boys don't try us.**"

Bay gave a weak smile. **"I'll make sure they don't. You saving my life."**

In the streets, loyalty is loud until tested. The ones you trust the least might save your life. And the ones you trust the most? Might be the first to disappear when the bullets fly.

Bay always moved smoothly. Calculated. Untouchable.

But tonight, his life sat in the hands of two kids who couldn't even buy a beer.

The Fist was about to be tested.

And this time—it wasn't chess.

It was a war.

Chapter 5

The Game Behind The Game

LIQUOR STORE – NIGHT

The air was tense. Still. Like the street itself was holding its breath.

Bay pulled up first, sitting in his own car. Slime and Chubby in the back seat, heads low, watching everything.

Then came the cavalry—**four black SUVs**—quiet, controlled, but deep. The Fist had arrived. The sound of tires cracking gravel was the only thing louder than the pounding in Bay's chest.

Eddie B stepped out first, clean but cautious. His eyes locked on the two teens before shifting to Bay.

"Where the money?" Slime asked, eyes twitching.

Eddie scanned the scene. **"Y'all outnumbered out here. You in a parking lot full of wolves."**

Chubby didn't blink. **"Then we all die together. Our boys here too— trained to go. Watching every move with nothing to lose."**

Bay leaned forward, still sore, still bruised—but clear.

"No, Eddie. Pay them. They kept their word. I'm keepin' mine. The others? They were gonna kill me for sure."

Eddie studied him, nodded once. Then motioned behind.

Tom Tom, Dee, and D-Bo stepped forward. Dee carried a heavy black duffel.

Bay took it from him, unzipped it briefly—then handed it straight to Chubby and Slime.

"Give them the money," he said flatly.

Chubby popped his headlights twice. Within seconds, **two more sedans pulled up**.

The boys hopped out of Bay's ride and into the new ones, vanishing into the night.

D-Bo watched them go, jaw clenched.

"Did we just get handled by some young niggas?"

Bay winced, holding his side. **"Yeah... but trust me, it all comes full circle."**

Buck stepped up with T-Money.

"You good?"

Bay gave him a look. **"Hell naw. Razor burnt my nuts."**

T-Money's eyes widened. **"We gotta get bro to the hospital fast."**

Eddie B chuckled. **"Razor gon' has to be dealt with."**

OLD SCHOOL – NIGHT

The air was thick with confusion and rage.

Razor, Chop, Body Count, Coco, and Rowe stood frozen, staring at the **empty spot** where Bay once sat, zip-tied and bleeding.

"No way Bay got away," Razor growled.

"Them young niggas double-crossed us," Chop muttered.

"I told you not to trust them," Rowe added.

"They all gotta die," Body Count said coldly.

"We need to be careful," Coco warned. **"They deep... and they move like roaches."**

Razor nodded, face tight. **"I got a plan. We take out the traitors first—then circle back. Wipe out The Fist. Every last one."**

BASEMENT – NIGHT

Down in a dark, hazy basement lit by red bulbs and bad decisions, the **Young Nigga Gang** threw a party like they didn't just flip the hood on its head.

Chubby, Slime, and three others huddled in the corner while music bumped and smoke danced in the air.

"Y'all sure you made the right move crossing Razor?" asked Blackie, one of the few females who could hang with them.

Chubby didn't flinch. **"It's done. Time to let the streets know—new kings are in town. Dope boys either pay up... or deal with us."**

Slime nodded. **"They were already tryin' to check us. Look around—all these heads? Every one of 'em ready to ride."**

Chubby smirked. **"And more wanna join. School kids. We hittin' the schools next week. We recruitin'."**

Blackie licked her lips. **"And the money was on point."**

The power was shifting. Fast.

HOSPITAL WAITING ROOM – NIGHT

The Fist filled the room, but nobody spoke.

Plastic chairs. Fluorescent lights. Beeping monitors in the background. That cold hospital smell that reminded you of life could change in a blink.

Then the door creaked open.

Sugar walked in, her face tired, her spirit rattled but standing.

Silence.

"He's stable," she said. **"He's gonna be okay... but it'll take a few weeks."**

A pause.

"And we won't be making any new babies anytime soon."

The silence cracked. Nervous laughter rippled through the room.

Eddie B leaned forward. **"That's what your mouth sayin'."**

T-Money grinned. **"Right? I see baby number three already."**

Laughter filled the space. For a minute, it felt like the old days.

SAMMY'S HOUSE – NIGHT

It was quiet, low-lit, the walls warm with age and knowledge. A group of young men—Buck, Tom Tom, Dee, Eddie B, Ash, and Kareem—sat in a semicircle, watching **Sammy and T-Money** locked in a chess match.

Sammy moved a pawn with surgical precision.

"Checkmate."

T-Money groaned. **"You beat me every time with them pawns."**

Sammy smirked. **"To me, they are the most powerful piece on the board."**

Buck chuckled. **"They are bad."**

Sammy leaned forward, serious now. **"Glad I got most of y'all here. I wanna put something on your mind."**

He held up a piece of paper.

On it—two words: **Asset** and **Liability**.

"Y'all know what these mean?"

Kareem shrugged. **"Not really. Break it down."**

"Before I do—let's test something. I'mma ask questions. If it's no, mark 'Liability.' If it's yes—'Asset.'"

He passed out pens and paper.

Eddie B groaned. **"Damn, Sammy—this a quiz night?"**

They all laughed.

"School should've taught y'all this. But it's never too late."

SAMMY ask them

"Do you own or are buying a house?"

"Got a business or LLC?"

"Got a savings or investment account?"

"Got life insurance?"

Each question chipped away at the jokes. Pens slowed. Heads dropped.

Buck shook his head. **"Man, I put no on everything."**

T-Money sighed. **"Me too."**

Sammy nodded. **"Now here's the breakdown. Assets make you money. Liabilities take it."**

He broke it down like a professor from the block. Money in the bank. Real estate. Stocks. Business. Intellectual property.

Liabilities? Credit cards. Rent. Loans. Car payments.

"To grow wealth, increase assets, drop liabilities."

Silence. Heavy.

"How do we even start?" T-Money asked. **"Nobody ever taught us this."**

Ash spoke low. **"First time I ever heard any of this."**

Sammy saw the hunger in their eyes.

HOUSE – LATER THAT NIGHT

Blunts sparked. Smoke floated. Liquor bottles clicked.

Dee leaned back. **"No disrespect, but I need air. This is deep."**

Sammy nodded. **"Go ahead. I puff too—but joints only. Weed straight from the earth."**

Kareem passed him a nug. Sammy rolled with surgical skill.

"Look—owning a house gives you equity. So if y'all ever in need of money? You can pull from it."

Buck leaned in. "**I'm with it. I ain't tryna end up broke like them old hustlers.**"

Sammy grinned. "**First step? Open a car lot. Y'all love whips. Put up 25K each. Make it $250K. Set up an LLC and Trust.**"

T-Money blinked. "**Where do we put the money?**"

Sammy tapped his joint. "**Give it to me. I'll gift y'all checks. Paper trail legit.**"

Buck nodded. "**I like the plan.**"

Tom Tom jumped in. "**Might as well get tow trucks too.**"

Sammy smirked. "**Now y'all thinkin'. Life's chess, not checkers. It's what you keep.**"

Eddie B squinted. "**Why are you helping? What's in it for you?**"

Sammy leaned forward. "**I've been where y'all at. I made it out. Now I want in on the legacy. Twenty percent of the legal money I help set up. CPA game. That's it.**"

Tom Tom raised a brow. "**So basically, you are taxing us?**"

Sammy laughed. "**I work for every cent. I'm filing paperwork, building foundations, walking y'all through it. Look at the plaques. I will do this.**"

T-Money looked at his boys.

"**What y'all think?**"

Buck shrugged. "**We risk our lives every day. I'm down.**"

One by one, heads nodded.

Eddie B grinned slowly. "**Sammy slick... but I'm in.**"

Sammy leaned back. "**Cool. Come up with a name. I'll file the LLC and Trust.**"

He hit his joint again.

"**Damn... I'm baked.**"

The whole room cracked up.

Kareem shook his head. **"That Cali got you high out of your mind. You used to mid-grade."**

Sometimes the hood teaches you how to survive—but never how to build.

And for years, The Fist had mastered survival—fast money, tight loyalty, and code over chaos.

But what Sammy brought into the room that night wasn't just knowledge—it was direction. And direction changes everything.

Because in a world where power shifts like shadows...
The smartest move ain't the loudest—it's the most **calculated**.

And The Fist just leveled up.

Chapter 6

Fire In The Roots

T-MONEY'S HOUSE – NIGHT

The living room breathed a low, mellow energy—smoke curling into the corners, soft R&B humming from the speaker like a heartbeat trying to forget. T-Money and Zuri sat close on the couch, a slow drag from the blunt passing between them. Glasses clinked on the coffee table. Outside, the city moved like a restless giant.

Zuri exhaled, concerned in her eyes.

"Bay... is he gonna be okay?"

T-Money nodded, taking a pull, eyes low but clear.

"Yeah, he's good. I stopped by Sammy's tonight. He put us on some real game... made me realize we been playin' with our freedom like it's just another dice roll."

Zuri leaned in, curiosity rising.

"What do you mean?"

T-Money glanced at her, then down at his drink.

"Look at us... all rentin'. No savings. No investments. No life insurance. If something happens to me tomorrow, you and the kids will be lookin' broke and crazy."

Zuri paused, his words hitting harder than the weed.

"**You right... I've been thinkin' about that too. But what can I do to help?**"

T-Money turned to face her fully.

"**We've been building our future on quicksand, baby. It's time we laid a foundation. That starts with you thinkin' beyond Macy's. What do *you* wanna build?**"

Zuri's eyes welled slightly. A smile tugged her lips.

"**Okay, baby.**"

He leaned in. Their kiss wasn't rushed. It was a vow sealed in silence.

TOM TOM'S HOUSE – NIGHT

Streetlight shadows danced across Tom Tom's face as he stared through the window. The night outside was still, but his mind raced like a runaway train.

Tamika, curled on the couch behind him, watched.

"**You good?**"

He didn't turn, just nodded slowly.

"**Yeah... just thinkin' about life. My next moves gotta be my best ones. Ain't no more room for slip-ups.**"

Tammika stood, wrapping her arms around him from behind.

"**Whatever move you make, I'm ridin'. All the way.**"

Tom Tom finally turned. Their eyes met—two warriors in love. No fear, no doubt. Just fire and loyalty.

They kissed like tomorrow wasn't promised.

SAMMY'S BEDROOM – NIGHT

Sammy lay stretched beside his wife, Linda, her head resting gently on his chest. Her fingers traced soft, wordless comfort on his skin. The room was dim, calm, the quiet kind of peace that came after storms.

"**You sure this won't get you in trouble?**" Linda asked, eyes searching for him.

Sammy chuckled low. "**Ain't doin' nothin' illegal, baby. I'm just leading them to the water.**"

"**I just don't want no problems, Sammy.**"

He wrapped his arm around her.

"**We good. Those young men... they *listen*. Somebody gotta reach back. Somebody who *gets* it.**"

Linda studied him. "**You lived it. You speak their language.**"

Sammy nodded, eyes distant but passionate.

"**If we keep saying' 'I got mine' and leavin' the hood behind, we are killing' our future. Gotta feed minds, not just mouths.**"

Linda slowly smiled. "**You sound like a preacher.**"

He smirked. "**Nah. Just a man who figured out how to turn pain into plans.**"

He kissed her. She kissed him back.

No more questions. Just belief.

YNG HANGOUT – NIGHT

The room pulsed with wild energy. **Teenagers danced, drank, smoked**, their joy teetering on chaos. Graffiti crawled up the cracked walls. Music pounded through busted speakers. Weed smoke blurred the lights into halos.

Then—

GUNSHOTS.

Screams sliced through the beat. Glass exploded. Bullets turned celebration into war.

A girl in a white dress dropped—**her gown turning crimson**.

Bodies fell like dominoes.

Some dropped to the floor. Others drew weapons—**firing blind into the shadows**.

OUTSIDE YNG HANGOUT – NIGHT

Under the flicker of faulty streetlights, **Body Count, Razor, Chop, and Rowe** stood like executioners.

They emptied their clips.

Glass shattered. Screams echoed.

Then, with ghost-like precision, they jumped into a blacked-out car and vanished into the smoke.

YNG HANGOUT – NIGHT

Blood soaked the floor.

Blackie dropped to her knees, cradling a small, broken body—**her little brother**. His eyes fluttered. Breath shallow. His white tee soaked red.

"My lil' brother... somebody call for help!"

No one moved.

This was the code: **No cops. No snitching. No sound.**

Slime, gun in hand, wiped his brow.

"We can't have the law showin' up here. We gotta move."

Blackie's hands trembled, covered in blood. Her eyes locked on her brother's fading light.

Slime 's voice sharpened.

"We take 'em. Drop 'em at the ER. Pull the van around. Now."

Blackie froze—torn between loyalty and love.

HOSPITAL – NIGHT

The van skidded to a stop in the ER loading zone.

Doors flew open. **Three bleeding bodies** were dumped onto the pavement like trash bags. One moaned. Another didn't move.

Blackie stepped out last, trembling, her brother's blood staining her jeans.

Sirens in the distance.

Slime looked at her, eyes hard.

"Let's go, Blackie. Now."

She didn't move.

Her brother coughed—wet and gurgling.

"I can't leave him..." she whispered.

Slime clenched his jaw. **"Then figure it out. We gone."**

Tires screeched. The van disappeared.

Blackie stood there alone. Breathing heavy.
Her brother's blood on her hands.

There are moments in the streets where the rules you were raised by get tested by the life you love.

And when bullets fly, the world shows you who's real—and who's just *playing real.*

Blackie watched her baby brother bleed out in her arms... and realized the code didn't care who you loved, who you lost, or what you stood for.

It just demanded silence.

But that silence?

It was starting to crack.

Chapter 7

The Foundation And The Fire

HOSPITAL ROOM – NIGHT

Machines hummed steady like a heartbeat refusing to quit. The lights were low, casting shadows against the walls where pain still clung. **Bay** walked slowly across the room in a hospital gown, the IV trailing beside him like a leash. His steps were stiff, but his eyes burned with unfinished business.

Across the room, **Suga** stood beside **Run-Run**, their voices low and deliberate.

"I moved ten whole ones," Run-Run said, his tone clipped. **"We got five out in the streets working."**

Bay nodded, slow and tight. **"Good. Get the money to Suga. What's the word in the streets?"**

Run-Run looked down, then back up. **"YNG clubhouse got hit. One dead."**

Bay froze for a beat, jaw grinding. **"Bet Razor had something to do with that."**

Run-Run didn't have to answer. The truth was already in the air.

Bay's voice dropped. **"The Fist pulling up later. After we talk, I'll let you know how to move. Watch your back. Streets smell like war."**

THE OFFICE – DAY

The trap house looked more like a war room now. **Buck** sat at the head of the table. **Eddie B** leaned against the wall, arms folded like a coiled plan. Around them—**White Boy, Dee, Ash, Tom Tom,** and **T-Money** counted stacks while **D-Bo** kept one eye glued to the window.

"We gotta get Razor and his crew," Eddie B said. **"Can't let this pass. Gotta do something nasty. Something that makes people scared to even *think* about crossing us."**

D-Bo cracked his knuckles, the sound loud. **"Call Skinny. Let him eat. You heard about that Young Nigga Gang?"**

Eddie B nodded. **"They still part of the fallout. Bay didn't get hit alone."**

"Clubhouse got lit up," D-Bo added. **"One down."**

White Boy smirked. **"Razor and them wildin' out, huh?"**

"They outta control," Dee said. **"Time to put that leash on 'em."**

"Or maybe," Buck said calmly, **"they just takin' care of each other."**

The room went quiet.

Then Tom Tom broke it. **"Enough about the bodies—let's talk numbers."**

Buck leaned forward. **"Cuz a couple hours out from Houston. Az said he sending us an extra 250 on top of the 200 we already bought."**

"What's the number?" T-Money asked. **"We need better margins."**

"The ones we buyin'? MJ. The ones he frontin'? Kobe."

Ash nodded. **"We can work with that."**

"I'm thinkin' we call the car lot *Cars R Us*," T-Money added.

D-Bo laughed. **"I like that. Got a ring to it."**

"Hard. Like Toys R Us with grown man problems," Kareem agreed.

Eddie B's face hardened. **"Y'all really trust Sammy with this whole operation?"**

Dee shrugged. "**He knows better than to cross us.**"

"**We only puttin' in 25K each,**" T-Money said. "**We blow that on strip clubs and chains without blinking. Time we put it on something that multiplies.**"

"Facts," Buck said. "**Juju coming through later to cook up. I'm sending that batch straight to Bama.**"

T-Money stood up. "**Cool. I'll be at the hospital around three. We'll run all this by Bay.**"

POLICE DEPARTMENT – INTERROGATION ROOM – NIGHT

The room was steel cold, lit by one flickering light that buzzed like it hated its job.

Blackie sat at the metal table, arms crossed, hoodie soaked in dried blood. Her jaw was tight. Her eyes, unreadable.

Two detectives stood over her, trying to read her silence.

"**So you're telling' us,**" Detective Johnson started, "**that you and your crew were just walkin' down Washington when a car pulled up, sprayed the block, and some *random* Samaritan scooped y'all and dropped you at the ER?**"

"**Yes, sir.**"

The detective scoffed. "**We got a dead body, two with holes in 'em, and you wanna play quiet?**"

Blackie didn't flinch. Just stared at the wall.

Detective Reid narrowed his eyes, spotting the **YNG** tattoo inked on her forearm.

"**YNG, huh? That's rare for a female.**"

Blackie blinked slowly. Still nothing.

She knew the rules. She also knew what Razor did. But the street code was carved in blood.

BAR – NIGHT

A thick haze of smoke floated in the dark bar. Neon beer signs flickered, casting light over worn leather booths.

Eddie B and **D-Bo** sat at the corner table.

Across from them, **Skinny**—thin, twitchy, glasses slightly crooked, like a mix of preacher and executioner.

"I need you to track down Razor and his crew," Eddie B said flatly. **"Handle them. They torched my dawg's nuts."**

Skinny grinned, one side of his mouth only.

"Say less. They won't see next week. I'll be in touch."

He downed his drink like holy water, set the glass down gently, and left like a shadow.

D-Bo shivered. **"Man, I get chills every time I'm around him."**

Eddie B cracked a smile. **"Yeah... that's exactly why I called him."**

He waved down the waitress.

"Two more shots."

HOSPITAL ROOM – NIGHT

The room was warmer now. Not by temperature—by energy.

T-Money, Bay, and **Buck** sat around the bed. A bag of snacks sat untouched on the table. The remote blinks but no one watches TV. Business was the only show on.

"We are about to open a car lot," T-Money said. **"Get some tow trucks rolling, too."**

Bay leaned up slightly. **"What's the setback?"**

"Twenty-five apiece. By the time we are done, we'll have 250K legit in the bank."

Bay smiled, eyes bright. **"Now that's what I like to hear. What else?"**

"**Cuz made it to Houston. Truck loading up in a day or two. AZ dropped the number down—MJ. Plus he fronted us 250 at Kobe.**"

Bay grinned wider. "**Now you speaking my language.**"

"**Eddie out meeting with Skinny. Razor and them? Done deal.**" Ash said, stepping in.

Bay blinked. "**Skinny? Y'all went *there*?**"

Buck stared.

"**We went there.**"

Bay exhaled. "**I come home tomorrow. Run-Run gave Sugar 300K. I'll pay y'all back for everything y'all put up for me. Real talk.**"

T-Money waved him off. "**C'mon, Bay. You know how The Fist moves. This ain't just street money no more. We about to make real plays. Houses next. Life insurance too.**"

Bay raised a brow. "**Life insurance?**"

T-Money grinned. "**Yeah. And the policies we getting? We can borrow from 'em. Tax-free. Sammy has been lacing us with knowledge.**"

Bay laughed, light but impressed. "**Now *that's* a play**
There comes a time when the street mentality either evolves—or eats itself.

The Fist had always been tight. But what was forming now? It wasn't just a crew—it was a blueprint.

They weren't just chasing money anymore.

They were building **power**.

And when power gets focused, organized, and protected?

It stops being a hustle...

And starts becoming **a legacy**.

Chapter 8

Bloodlines & Blueprints

The house was quiet, the kind of quiet that sits on your chest. Shadows stretched long across the walls. A single lamp flickered in the corner, its light barely reaching the couch where Lou sat clutching a framed photo of her daughter. Her fingers trembled against the glass as tears ran silently down her cheeks. The girl in the picture smiled wide—innocent, glowing. That version of her was gone now.

Across the room, San stood stiff, arms folded, eyes burning with fury. Every second that passed without justice made her angrier. Behind her, two uniformed officers hovered by the doorway, trying to navigate grief with clipboards and caution.

Uncle Willie paced like a caged bull, wide-shouldered and tense. His fists clenched and unclenched by his sides, each breath deeper than the last.

"I know this is difficult, Mrs. Carter," one of the officers began.

"Difficult?" Lou's voice cracked through her pain. "My baby is dead. Seventeen. And all y'all got are questions."

"We're doing everything we can—"

"That's a lie," San cut in. "Y'all say that every time. And then nothing. Cold files and empty promises. We know how this goes."

"We're following leads."

Willie stopped pacing.

"Leads don't mean shit when another Black girl's gone and y'all movin' like it's a parking ticket," he snapped, slamming his fist into the wall. The photo frames shook. Lou flinched.

"Sir, I need you to calm down."

"You don't get to tell us to calm down," San hissed. "Her daughter is gone. You think these suits and soft voices are gonna fix that?"

Lou looked up slowly, her voice small but sharp. "Do you even care?"

The officers didn't answer. They didn't have to.

Willie's voice dropped. "If y'all don't handle this, I will."

Lou grabbed his arm. "Please… not like this."

"We don't want that," one officer said, his voice a whisper. "Let us do our job."

"Then prove you can," San snapped.

The room fell silent again. The officers nodded, but the weight of doubt stayed behind even after they left.

The stash house had a different kind of tension. Run-Run leaned over the table, a half-sealed bag of work and a gas station sack of cash in front of him. The scent of loud clung to the walls.

"You going love this,?" he said, grinning at Kemp. "Jumpin' back in like you never left."

Kemp chuckled, 'dapped' him up. "Had to. My girl cleaned me out for her birthday."

They exchanged a few quiet words as Kemp walked out. Down the block, a dark car idles with tinted windows. Inside, Razor sat in the passenger seat, eyes fixed on the house. Body Count sat behind him, cold and quiet. Snake leaned forward in the driver's seat, his voice low.

"That's Run-Run. He handles Bay's whole backend."

"Set up a buy," Razor said. "We come in behind it. Clean the whole spot out."

"Don't fuck this up," Snake warned. "If my name gets dirty out here, it's over for me."

Body Count cracked his knuckles. "This time I'm in the room. Every step."

As Kemp's car disappeared into the night, Razor's crew slowly rolled past the house. Inside, Run-Run shut the door and locked it behind him.

Back at the YNG hangout, the aftermath still stained the floor. Blood had dried into the hardwood. Slime and Chubby scrubbed silently, the sound of glass being swept the only noise.

"Tay gone," Chubby muttered. "That's on us."

Slime nodded, eyes red. "I keep seeing that white dress… soaked in it."

"We can't let that go. We need Cold Heart, Shade Tree—somebody who can pull real intel on Razor."

"10-4."

This wasn't about hustle anymore. This was personal now. The kind that kept you up at night.

The gym was alive with iron. Clanking plates, deep grunts, and the occasional burst of laughter bounced off concrete walls. T-Money was spotting Kareem while Tom Tom checked his phone nearby.

"This city is different now," T-Money said, wiping sweat from his forehead. "These young cats don't even hustle for a check anymore."

"Nah," Tom Tom said. "They want fast fame. Robbin', crashin' out—no plan, no code."

"Back in our day," Kareem added, exhaling between sets, "you repped your block, stacked your paper, and kept it clean. Now they gangbangin' for status they can't cash in."

Ash chuckled from the incline bench. "We used to hustle for cars, clothes, and women. Now? They hustle for IG comments."

T-Money shook his head. "And the gang leaders got no vision. Just drama and death. Folks dyin' for hashtags."

Tom Tom looked at his phone. "Load should be here any minute."

Kareem cracked his knuckles. "Let's get it. Then slide to Sugar's later—Bay touching' down today. She's cooking."

T-Money grinned. "We need that. Been too much darkness lately."

In the back office, chess pieces clicked while smoke floated above the game. Buck leaned forward, eyes on the board. JuJu worked in the kitchen shirtless, flipping a fresh batch with steady hands.

"Damn, she's pretty," JuJu said, admiring the solidified slab. "Chef JuJu. 125 back to 200. Hard as bricks."

Buck smirked. "That's what I like to hear. Check."

White Boy moved. "Out of check."

"Checkmate."

Buck stood, stretched, and walked into the kitchen. The scent of baking soda and diesel filled the air.

"Still can't believe folks out here buying' hard like it's the '90s," Buck said.

"Keepin' me paid," JuJu said with a grin, flipping the tray. "That's all I care about."

They shared a laugh as the weight cooked down to profit.

The nail shop was a different world—buzzing with drills, the smell of acetone, quiet gossip floating through the air. T-Money sat next to his mother, Joyce, both of them relaxed in side-by-side massage chairs.

"You gotta make my favorite this Sunday," T-Money said.

"You know I got you," Joyce smiled. "How many people?"

"Probably all of us once they hear you cookin'—Zuri too."

Joyce laughed. "I gotta save energy. My class reunion is next week. You still comin'?"

"I wouldn't miss that for nothin watching y'all old folk moving and groveling '."

"Boy, please. We know how to party. That rhythm you got? Came from me."

T-Money shook his head. "Mom, you have *no* rhythm."

They laughed together, easy and unbothered.

"Your sister is in love again," she added.

"She stays in love," T-Money jokes. "But we movin' forward. Me and the crew—opening a car lot."

Joyce nodded. "I like that. You know how proud I am of you?"

"Every day. And I'm proud of you too."

He paused.

"I'm going to see my dad at the end of the month."

Joyce looked over, her expression softening. "That's good, baby."

Amid the hustle, the pain, and the planning—there were still rooms with warmth. Still conversations that didn't revolve around guns, drops, or revenge. The nail shop, the family dinner, the chess table… they reminded The Fist what they were really fighting for.

Because when the world burned outside, it was the quiet moments that saved them.

And if you can't protect what brings you peace…

Then what's the point of having power at all?

Chapter 9

The Weight Of The Game

The house was quiet except for the faint hum of cartoons in the background. A dim lamp flickered beside the couch where Bay sat, shirtless, in pain. A bandage wrapped around his side, stained from earlier. Sugar kneeled in front of him, carefully peeling back the gauze. Her touch was tender, but the cloth turned red with each press.

The kids ran in circles behind them—laughing, wild, unaware of how close they came to losing their father.

"Bay," Sugar said, her voice low, "do we have an end game?"

Bay winced. "End game?"

"You know… getting out the dope game."

He didn't answer at first. Just stared at the floor.

"Never really thought about it," he said finally. "I know I can't do this forever. Maybe the car lot is a good idea."

Sugar finished wrapping the wound, her eyes filled with worry. She looked up at him, voice trembling.

"When you got kidnapped… so much ran through my mind. It made me realize how vulnerable me and the kids are if something happens to you."

Bay's face tightened.

"The Fist'll take care of y'all. That's our law. You saw how we held T-T down. When Eddie B came home, everybody gave him fifteen racks each."

Sugar nodded but her expression didn't change.

"I know y'all got each other's backs. I love that. But I still wanna feel secure. We don't wanna lose you, Bay."

Bay looked away. The silence that followed wasn't dismissal—it was the weight of a truth too heavy to argue with.

The bar was alive, neon bouncing off walls, hookah smoke twirling between laughter and flirtation. Kareem sat at a booth with Stacy and Tisha, sipping his drink with confidence and charm.

"I put this trip together for us," he said with a grin.

Stacy raised an eyebrow. "We like that... but don't be selling us no dreams, Kareem."

He leaned in. "Relax. In two weeks. We outta here"

Tisha giggled. "I can't wait to wear my two-piece on somebody's beach!"

They clinked glasses and downed their shots. Kareem tossed a few bills on the table, nodded for them to follow.

They stood, laughing, ready to end the night upstairs.

Down the street, a dark-colored car sat idling by the curb, its windows tinted, its engine humming softly. Inside, Skinny sat in the driver's seat, eyes fixed on a house across the street.

Two other men sat with him, silent, watching.

"We sit tight," Skinny said. "Just watch."

Tension filled the car like smoke—thick and waiting.

The YNG hangout was dim and cluttered, the aftermath of pain still lingering in the air. Blood stains had been scrubbed, but the scent of gunpowder hadn't faded.

Blackie sat at the table with Slime and Chubby. Her hands trembled as she lit a cigarette.

"They took me down to the station," she said. "Interrogated me hard."

Slime narrowed his eyes. "What you tell 'em?"

"Nothing. Just said some random car sprayed Washington Road."

Chubby nodded. "Good. No police in our business."

"We hitting that pawnshop tonight," Slim added.

Blackie shook her head. "We gotta get Razor. My brother's gonna be okay—caught one in the arm. But Tay…" Her voice broke. "Tay died in my arms. I saw her soul leave."

Chubby stayed calm, but his voice had an edge.

"Shade Tree and Cold Heart out hunting. Razor ain't safe."

Blackie stared into space.

"I don't want help. I wanna do Razor *myself.*"

Up in the hotel room, Kareem leaned back in the recliner, shirt off, joint burning between his fingers. A bottle of D'USSÉ rested on the side table. Across the room, Stacy and Tisha laughed, playing around in lingerie, brushing each other's hair, taking turns pouring shots.

Kareem smiled, exhaled a cloud of smoke, eyes flickering with amusement and desire.

The office was quiet but charged with motion. Papers shuffled. Keys clicked. The hum of progress filled the space. Sammy sat behind his desk, serious but calm. T-Money, Buck, Tom Tom, and Dee sat across from him.

T-Money handed Sammy the gym bag .

"here the Two hundred and and -fifty."

Sammy opened it, thumbed through the money.

"When the business name comes back clear, I'll write the check so y'all can deposit it."

Buck frowned. "How long does that take?"

"Seven to thirty business days," Sammy replied. "Gotta make sure no one else is using it. I already ran 'Cars R Us.' That name's clean."

T-Money nodded. "Cool. We lookin' for a lot. You got any leads?"

"There's a spot," Sammy said. "Three and a half acres off 138."

"Can we put that under the same LLC?" T-Money asked.

Sammy shook his head. "Nah. Y'all need a separate one. A real estate LLC."

Dee raised an eyebrow. "Why all the different names?"

"Protection," Sammy said, leaning forward. "Say somebody tries to sue 'Cars R Us.' They can't touch you personally. They can only go after the business. And if that business is owned by another business, inside a trust?"

He smirked.

"They can't touch nothin'."

Buck grinned. "So, keep everything separate?"

"Exactly. That's what white folks do. But we're gonna take it further. Ain't just about protecting assets. It's about protecting our legacy."

They exchanged glances. Something was shifting. Something real.

The gambling house glowed in grime. Neon lights pulsed over stained carpet and smoky air. At the center—chaos. A poker table, surrounded by bodies and bills.

Eddie B sat on tilt. Sweating. Losing bad.

Big Tony sat across from him, smug and stacked with chips. JC hovered on his last legs, one chip and a prayer. Dollar Boy sat calm, sipping brown liquor, waiting for the perfect storm.

Mimi, drunk, swayed hard on the pole behind them. One wrong move and she'd collapse.

Big Tony grinned like the devil.

"Y'all don't gotta rush. I got all night… and all your money."

Eddie B glared. "Man, shut the hell up."

Tony chuckled. "I would, but I think I just won your rent money."

The crowd roared.

"Damn, Eddie, you might have to start an OnlyFans," someone shouted.

Eddie's jaw locked.

JC looked like he was about to cry.

Dollar Boy folded. Took a sip.

Then—final hand.

"Put up the car title," Tony said. "Let's get real."

Eddie sat up. "Now you talkin' my language."

"Loser walk home," someone in the crowd yelled.

"Ooooh," the crowd echoed.

Eddie pushed in the last of his chips. "Run it."

Big Sha, the dealer, flipped the cards.

Eddie had a strong hand. He leaned back, tried to play it cool.

Tony flipped his.

Better hand. Silence. Then chaos.

"Boy just lost his car *and* his pride!"

Eddie didn't move. Just stared. His hand trembled on the felt. His jaw ticked.

Then—

When the hustle gets too loud and the room starts spinning, the game has a way of reminding you—*you ain't in control.*

Bay's trying to heal. Sugar's trying to save him. Sammy's building empires. Eddie's losing bets. Razor's plotting murder. Blackie's seeing ghosts.

And through it all?

The streets don't stop.

They don't slow down.

They don't forgive.

Only question left:
Can you outrun the weight before it buries you?

Chapter 10

Kingdoms, Chaos & Consequence

The poker room exploded like a powder keg. Eddie B shoved his chair back and flipped the table—chips, cards, drinks, and egos flew in every direction.

"Yo!" someone shouted.

Glasses crashed. Whiskey spilled. Two men ducked. A waitress screamed. Mimi—the drunk stripper who'd been wobbling on the pole like she was hanging on for dear life—finally lost her grip.

"Shiiit—!"

She tumbled straight into another waitress carrying drinks. Glass burst. Ice flew. A dude trying to dodge the mess slipped and face planted into the slick floor, sliding into the bar like a drunk bowling pin.

Big Sha, the poker dealer, stood up slowly—stone-faced, built like a refrigerator.

He grabbed Eddie B by the collar.

"You done?"

The room froze. All eyes locked on Eddie. Big Tony leaned back in his chair, sipping whiskey like it was just another Friday. White Boy stood in the corner, ready. Mimi was on the floor cackling.

Eddie looked around. Big Sha stared through him. After a long pause, Eddie nodded.

Big Sha let go.

Eddie picked up his last drink, tossed it back, and stormed out through the parted crowd.

"Yo Eddie," Tony called after him, smirking. "Good game!"

Laughter followed Eddie to the door. He flipped Tony off without looking back.

Big Sha reset the table.

"Game's over," he said. "Everybody out."

RUN-RUN'S HOUSE – NIGHT

A streetlight buzzed above like a nervous witness. Razor sat in a black SUV down the block, watching. Lil Rowe cleaned his pistol while Body Count checked his phone.

Another car pulled up—a beat-down muscle car with mismatched doors.

"That's Snake," Rowe muttered. "He always looks like he is expecting death to tap him on the shoulder."

Razor didn't laugh. He just stepped out of the SUV and pulled his hoodie over his face.

"Snake is only loyal to what fits in his pocket. Let's go."

BAY'S HOUSE – NIGHT

Bay's house was another universe. Music thumped, smoke floated, and good vibes wrapped around everyone like velvet.

Bay sat in a lazy boy, drink in hand, eyes low and satisfied. Sugar stood behind the bar, mixing margaritas like a pro. Her gold bracelets clinked with every shake. Zuri, Meke, Savannah, and T-T sipped drinks and laughed in a tight circle, heels kicked off, eyes glowing under soft light.

In the corner, T-Money, Buck, Dee, D-Bo, Ash, and Tom Tom stood in a circle talking loud—big moves, bold jokes, even bigger laughter.

"We so glad you are home," T-Money said, clinking glasses. "The Fist strikes again."

Bay raised his cup.

"Who you tellin'? God is good."

Zuri handed him another drink.

"We toasting' to that!"

Savannah snapped a selfie with Bay and the crew—Bay flashed a peace sign, grill gleaming.

Buck grinned. "We need to run Monopoly tonight. Five thousand buy-in. Kareem, White Boy, and Eddie on the way."

"I'm taking home *all* the money," D-Bo announced.

Sugar slid onto Bay's lap and fed him a lime wedge. The room erupted in whistles and cheers.

Bay grinned, arms wrapped around her waist.

"Y'all know what it is. Good vibes, big business. Ain't nobody stressin' in here tonight. I'm back."

WHITE BOY'S CAR – MOVING – NIGHT

Streetlights zipped by in gold streaks. White Boy gripped the wheel tighter than usual. Eddie B slouched in the passenger seat, jaw clenched, tapping against the window.

"You gotta quit with this gambling shit," White Boy muttered. "We stand' on business, not throwing' it away."

"That car was dead anyway," Eddie said. "T-T ran it with no oil while I was locked up. Motor was already on the way out."

White Boy glanced at him. "All our moves gotta be calculated. Chess, not checkers. One of us off? We are all off."

Eddie rolled his eyes. "Man, just drive to Bay's. I already get lectures from T-T. I don't need one from you and the Fist."

White Boy didn't answer. Just pushed the gas harder.

MOTEL ROOM – NIGHT

The lights were low, the air thick. Two women lay tangled in sheets, nude and laughing. Kareem stood at the dresser, fixing his chain in the mirror. His shirt hung open. A thick wad of cash bulged from his pocket.

He tossed the stack on the nightstand.

"That's for y'all," he said, voice cool. "Be easy."

One of the women blew him a kiss. Kareem smirked and walked out, the door clicking softly behind him.

RUN-RUN'S HOUSE – NIGHT

Stacks of cash and uncut product sat on the table between Run-Run and Snake.

"I'm tellin' you," Snake whispered, "we need to move fast."

Run-Run counted bills calmly. "You're always in a rush. Patience my nigga."

BOOM! The front door exploded inward.

Run-Run leapt back. Snake reached for his waistband.

BANG! BANG!

Razor. Lil Rowe. Body Count. All masked. All armed.

Doug tried to run. Body Count tackled him, gun pressed against his temple.

"Yo, what the fuck?!" Snake yelled, ducking.

Snake scrambled to shove cash and work into a duffel. From the stairwell—movement. A shadow with a Glock.

BANG! BANG! BANG!

Lil Rowe spun back, hit in the shoulder. He howled but kept his grip on the trigger.

Razor and Body Count returned fire. The shooter collapsed on the steps, groaning.

"We're out!" Razor yelled.

He dragged Rowe out the front, blood dripping in streaks.

CITY STREETS – NIGHT

A black SUV swerved down the road. Razor drove, wild-eyed. Rowe gritted his teeth, pressing a bloody cloth to his shoulder.

"You good?" Body Count asked.

"I ain't dead," Rowe muttered.

Razor grinned. "Then we still winnin'."

City lights blurred in the windshield. The war had begun—and the night was far from over.

BAY'S HOUSE – NIGHT

The music was still bouncing, but the energy shifted when White Boy and Eddie walked in. All eyes turned. T-T read Eddie's face instantly.

"What the hell has Eddie B done?" she said, standing up. "I see it all over him."

White Boy walked straight to the bar. "I need a drink and a smoke. I'm stayin' outta this."

The room grew quiet. Even the playlist faded into background noise.

Eddie looked around. "What is this, confession time? I ain't Usher."

T-T crossed her arms. "Don't play with me, Eddie."

Just then, the front door swung open. Kareem stepped in, fresh shirt, wrist iced out.

"Look what the wind blew in," Savannah teased.

"What'd I miss?" Kareem asked.

T-T pointed at Eddie B. "He was just about to confess."

Eddie exhaled. The room stared at him.

"I lost a few dollars gambling…" he muttered. "And my car."

A wave of murmurs swept the room.

"Your *car?*" Buck said. "Man, that doesn't look good for the Fist."

T-T nodded. "Knew it. I saw it in his face."

"Big Tony's poker game," Eddie said.

Everyone paused. That name carried weight.

D-Bo clapped his hands. "Yo, how 'bout we switch it up? Drinks, Monopoly, let the ladies do karaoke or somethin'."

"Let's change the energy," T-Money agreed.

Laughter returned slowly. The night pressed on.

RAZOR'S SPOT – NIGHT

Stacks of cash, six bricks of coke, and loaded guns filled the table. Smoke rolled across the room like a fog of war. Razor weighed product. Body Count checked clips. Snake counted green. Rowe rolled up with one hand, shoulder bandaged, eyes bloodshot.

"Tonight looks like a good night," Razor grinned. "How much, Snake?"

"Sixty-three grand. Still countin'."

"And the bricks?"

"Twenty-six, maybe thirty apiece."

"Good product moves itself," Body Count said.

Rowe turned up the TV. Everyone paused.

ON TV

News cameras lit up a pawnshop crime scene. Shattered glass. Flashing lights. Police tape.

A news anchor spoke over footage of a sedan crashing through the storefront, followed by armed figures stealing crates of guns.

"Suspects remain unidentified," a cop said. "We will be releasing video footage—these weapons need to be off the street."

Razor watches the images on the tv.

Bay's voice echoed in another house.

"I swear, two of them look like Slime and Chubby."

"Who?" Sugar asked.

"The ones who kidnapped me," Bay said. "But let me go."

T-Money sat forward. "They got *all* them guns now. The streets are about to get bloody."

Back in Razor's trap, he grinned.

"So YNG wanna play?" he said, leaning forward. "Things just got interesting."

"We're gonna need more firepower," Body Count added.

Then—darkness.

Lights out. Pitch black.

"Yo—what?" Snake said. "You ain't pay the bill?"

Before anyone could blink, **three masked figures** stepped from the shadows. Headlamps clicked on.

Silenced weapons. Precision kills.

Bodies dropped.

The room turned red.

And the war—
had officially begun.

The city was a chessboard, and every move had consequences. Pieces were in motion—some desperate, some deliberate, all dangerous.

Eddie B was reckless. Snake was double-dealing. Razor was bleeding. Bay was rebuilding.

But the streets?

The streets never sleep.

And when the lights go out…

Only the predators know how to see in the dark.

Chapter 11

Storms, Shots & Sacred Codes

The music had long faded, replaced by low conversation and tense glances. Inside Bay's home, the leather couches were occupied by kings and soldiers—men who'd bled and built together. Outside, the night breathed heavily.

Bay's phone buzzed on the table. He picked it up, eyes narrowing as he listened. He didn't say much. Just nodded. Then he hung up.

"Run-Run and Doug are gone," Bay said, his voice low, almost a growl. "G-Ray's in the hospital—shot, cuffed to the bed."

Buck sat forward, eyes wide. "What the hell happened?"

"Snake," Bay said. "Set 'em up with Razor. Took the money. Took the dope."

Eddie B stood, pacing, shaking his head. "Man... Skinny slippin'. We losing ground."

Before anyone could speak, Eddie's phone rang.

He answered, listened.

Skinny's voice buzzed through the speaker. "Come see me. I have your package."

Eddie hung up and scanned the room. His face tightened.

"Ladies, give us a moment."

Sugar, Zuri, and T-T exchanged glances but respected the command. They stepped out of the living room.

The crew rose without a word. The Fist moved together, slipping outside beneath the weight of war.

YNG HANGOUT – NIGHT

The warehouse was filthy, loud, and alive with madness. Liquor poured like rivers. Pills got crushed and shared like Skittles. The youngest was fifteen. The oldest? Maybe twenty-three. They danced like devils, tongues locked, souls lost in basslines.

Smoke curled into the rafters as if the building itself was sweating.

But in the center of the storm stood three figures.

Chubby. Slime. Blackie.

No smiles. No games. Just weapons on the floor and power in their eyes.

Chubby scanned the room like a general surveying his kingdom.

"A storm's coming," he said. "And we *are* the storm. Either you rockin' with YNG—or you gettin' buried under us."

The crowd exploded. Cheers. Fists. Screams. Like a church on fire.

Blackie stepped forward, feeding off the electricity.

"From now on, we don't just run blocks—we run *cities*. Southside. Westside. Eastside. Dealers pay us *taxes*. And we boostin' whips like GTA on steroids."

They roared again. Some slammed bottles. Some slammed fists. One kid even cried tears of rage.

Slime grinned like a monster in the dark.

"We are on demon time. Razor? His whole crew? *Dead men.*"

Cheers turned to chaos. Gun clicks echoed. Bottles shattered. And then—

BOOM! BOOM! BOOM!

Gunshots fired into the ceiling.

No one flinched.

BAY'S HOUSE – NIGHT

The black SUV purred like a beast on pause. The neighborhood was quiet, but inside that silence, something stirred. Outside, under the amber glow of streetlights, the core crew of The Fist huddled tight.

Eddie checked his phone, smirking. "Skinny got Razor."

Bay didn't flinch. "Good. I want my money. My dope."

"I'll know more when I get there."

Buck lit a blunt, the flame dancing off his gold ring. "Real talk, though—when you getting a new ride?"

Eddie grinned. "Soon, just. Y'all gon' be sick when you see it. Plus I just bought T-T a new one"

T-Money stepped forward, voice steady, cutting through the laughter.

"Before we get too caught up in shoot-'em-up... we got news."

The others nodded. They followed him inside.

BAY'S HOUSE – NIGHT

The energy shifted. The music was back on, but softer—controlled. Sugar and Zuri moved like queens behind the bar, pouring shots. T-T leaned against the counter, sipping and watching everything.

T-Money raised his glass.

"First... Bay. Welcome home."

The room erupted—claps, cheers, even a couple of gun taps on the glass table.

T-Money let it settle. Then he raised his voice again.

"Second—we movin' different. The Fist ain't just Street hustlers. We opened a car lot and a tow truck empire. Legit money. Real legacy, a lot more to come!."

Louder now. Fists to chests. Heads nodding. The energy in the room felt like history being born.

"To wealth, health, and prosperity!" someone called.

Glasses clinked. Liquor burned throats. And Bay? He leaned back like a man on a throne, Sugar on his lap, the crew in his corner.

"Now," he said, voice smooth, eyes sharp. "we making chess moves"

POLICE STATION – NIGHT

Flickering lights. Papers scattered. Coffee cups half-full and going cold.

"We need to get these guns off the street," officer Reid barked, slamming a file on the desk.

Officer Buffet leaned in. "Three tips. Same name. Same gang. YNG."

Officer Johnson joined in. "Remember that girl with the tattoo? The one dresses like a boy? Her brother was in that shooting."

"The one we just found dead?" officer Reid asked.

"the other one with the dead girl," officer Johnson said. "the dots... they're starting to connect."

"Where's that girl living?"

"I got her address."

"Good. Let's ride by. Time to shut this circus down."

SKINNY'S BASEMENT – NIGHT

It smelled like blood and gun oil.

Four men sat zip-tied in chairs, heads slumped, dried crimson staining their clothes. They weren't screaming. They'd passed that point hours ago.

Across the room, a flat-screen TV blared a Dave Chappelle special. Skinny and his crew laughed like they didn't have a care in the world.

Then—

The doorbell.

The room went still.

Moments later, Eddie B and D-Bo stepped down the stairs. They stopped at the bottom, eyes on the tied-up men.

Eddie clapped slowly.

"Damn," he said. "How the tables turn."

D-Bo cracked his knuckles. "Laugh now, cry later."

Eddie turned to Skinny.

"Did you recover anything? The drugs? The money?"

Skinny shrugged. "Nah. Just the people."

"Two of ours are dead," Eddie said, eyes darkening. "And we still missing something."

Skinny leaned back. "That must've been that house off Main. We followed 'em a few times. Didn't know it was our business."

Eddie stared at him.

"I wanted 'em dead," he said. "But I got outvoted. Now The Fist questioning their manhood over this."

Skinny's crew broke into dark laughter. Skinny grinned wide.

"Say less," he said. "I got the perfect plan."

A pause.

"You boys," Skinny added, "are gonna *love* this."

Some crews fight for territory. Others for profit. But The Fist? They were starting to understand they were fighting for something bigger—**survival with purpose**.

Because the streets weren't just taking bodies anymore.

They were taking **souls**.

And the war?
Was just getting personal.

Chapter 12

Checks, Trauma & Vows

ABANDONED CLUBHOUSE – DAY (FLASHBACK)

The wind sliced through the yard, carrying whispers of pain and promise. A torn-up couch sat outside the boarded-up clubhouse like a throne for the broken. Young T-Money sat slouched deep in it, fists clenched, jaw tight, eyes burning with everything he didn't have words for.

His shirt had holes. His sneakers leaned. But his spirit? Untouched.

Tom Tom, Ash, and Bay approached quietly, like soldiers returning to base.

Tom Tom locked eyes first, voice sharp with pride.
 "Homie, you ain't gotta be embarrassed. We ran them fools off. Made 'em eat their own laughs. Kicked a few of them dead in the ass."

T-Money shook his head, his voice low but trembling with thunder.
"I ain't embarrassed... I'm mad. Mad I can't do nothin' for my people. Since Pops went in, it's been hell. Mama, lil' sis—we just got put out. Ain't got no place to sleep tonight."

His eyes glossed, but he blinked the tears back like a warrior on the edge.

Ash crouched beside him. "Your fam needs you, bro. I know it feels like the world is closing in, but we gon' make it."
T-Money stood. Eyes locked. Spine straight.

"Nah. I ain't letting this happen again. I swear on *everything*—we gon' eat. I'm about to hustle—BIG TIME. Ain't nobody ever gonna' put us out again."

Bay grinned, dapped him. "That's what I'm talkin' about. All or nothin'. No in-between."

T-Money looked each of them dead in the eye.

"We all we got. Ain't no turnin' back."

They dap hands. One fire. Four fists. The wind howled through the trees like it knew something had just been born.

PARKING LOT – PRESENT DAY

The lot was fenced in, cracked concrete stretching around uneven lines of parked cars. T-Money walked up to find Sammy, Buck, Ash, and Tom Tom in deep conversation.

Sammy pointed around like a general showing off land.

"All y'all need is two double-wide trailers, a few cars, and a couple tow trucks," he said.

"How much we talkin'?" T-Money asked.

"Originally three hundred and -thirty thousand. Talked him down to two-eighty. You drop eighty cash, he'll owner-finance the rest. interest Ten years to pay off."

T-Money nodded slowly, soaking in the blueprint of legitimacy.

OFFICE – NIGHT

Stacks of cash. Vacuum sealers humming. Boxes piled shoulder-high. Bay, D-Bo, Eddie B, Kareem, White Boy, and Dee moved with precision—packaging the street into something that looked like a Wall Street deal.

Eddie B leaned back, looking satisfied but dark.

"Bay... your justice has been served," he said. "Skinny had somebody with HIV hit them boys in the ass. Said they begged for death instead."

Kareem blinked, stunned. "You were there?"

Eddie shook his head. "Nah. Skinny sent me the video. Y'all wanna see it? It's wild but…"

Everyone shook their heads. No one needed to see hell with sound.

Dee spoke up, more focused. "Each box got a mil. Cuz on his way to scoop."

White Boy looked up from taping a box. "Man, them YNG boys out here wildin'. Pullin' up in traps, demanding' tax or blood some State Property type shit."

"All the streets been talkin about," Kareem muttered.

"We gon' have to handle them soon," Eddie said. "Before they come to *our* door."

Bay's eyes narrowed. "They have no leader. Just a gang of blind fools swingin' in the dark."

D-Bo changed the subject. "Y'all seen the car lot spot?"

"Nah," Kareem replied. "That's where they are at now."

Eddie chuckled. "Sammy got us spending' more money than a first baby mama."

White Boy smirked. "You know the game—you gotta spend money to make money."

YOGA STUDIO – EVENING

The sun dipped low, gold light spilling over relaxed smiles. Zuri, Savannah, Sugar, Tamika, Renae, and Summer stepped out of the yoga studio glowing, stretched out and light.

Sugar inhaled deeply. "Girl, I had my doubts... but this class hit different. My mind feels clear. My body is loose."

Zuri smiled. "Two years strong. Told you, peace is a muscle—you gotta train it."

Renae checked her phone. "Where we eatin'?"

"Milk & Honey," Summer offered.

"Mr. Everything sounds right too," Tamika added.

"I need a drink," Zuri grinned.

They all laughed, walking toward their cars like a crew of queens off the clock.

PARKING LOT – NIGHT

A white man in a suit looks at the eighty thousand cash smiling knowing he is not going to pay no taxes on the money the Fist just gave him.

Sammy. T-Money. Buck.

They leaned against the hood of his car, relaxed but ready. T-Money held a paper. Their eyes locked with his.

Sammy spread his arms. "How does it feel? Owning' y'all first piece of land."

T-Money smirked. "Man thought we were playing'."

Tom Tom chuckled. "Did you see his face when we pulled out the money?"

Laughter burst out of them.

"He ain't paying' taxes on that eighty," Sammy added. "And he got more land. Solid plug to know."

Buck's tone turned serious. "So what's next?"

Sammy walked to a blacked-out sedan, popped the trunk, and returned with a check. Slapped it against Buck's chest.

"Two-fifty. Take it to the bank. They waitin'."

Ash stared at the paper, shaking his head. "Legit cash. Legit business. My mom said book sense and street sense together... that's unbeatable."

Sammy leaned in. "This? Just a sip from the water tank."

BODY COUNT'S HOUSE – NIGHT

The room was heavy with shadows. Razor, Body Count, Snake, and Rowe sat around a splintered table. Each held a piece of paper—each marked with a silent sentence.

"My life ain't never gon' be the same," Body Count said, voice flat. "I hate the Fist."

Snake shook his head, rubbing his temples. "Checkmate. They broke us. My head won't stop spinning."

"We all got HIV," Razor said quietly. "I feel... useless. Numb."

Rowe trembled. "I ain't slept. When I close my eyes... I hear it. That laugh. That scream."

Razor stood and opened a black bag—drugs inside. He passed them out like communion wafers.

"This'll numb the pain," he whispered. "When we wake... we burn 'em all."

They each took a dose. One by one, their bodies slumped. Froth on lips. Fingers twitching. Breath gone.

Razor, the only one untouched, walked to each man and closed their eyes. Razor Exchange wallet with one of them

A prayer escaped his lips.

Then he walked out into the night.

Some wounds don't bleed.
They echo.

In the streets, revenge ain't just served cold—it's laced with shame, trauma, and destruction.

The Fist had struck again. But as their enemies fell, new storms began to brew.

And the war was no longer about turf.

It was about **legacies.**
And **which ones would survive the fire.**

Chapter 13

Checks, Raids & Cold Oaths

OUTSIDE A BANK – DAY

The glass doors swung open, and sunlight spilled across four sharply dressed men walking with purpose. Sammy, T-Money, Buck, Tom Tom, and Ash stepped out into the light, their confidence damn near blinding. The air felt like victory.

T-Money took a deep breath, soaking it all in.
"That felt good."

Tom Tom clapped his back, laughing. "Damn right. We are making real moves now!"

Sammy checked his watch, then scanned his phone. "Proud moment, fellas. I got some errands to handle, but I'll hit y'all later. Best is still ahead."

They exchanged nods like brothers-in-arms. Ash's eyes scanned the lot—always watching.

Buck lowered his voice. "Cuz movin' close to H-Town. Nephew says everything in motion."

Tom Tom grinned. "Good. We need a new *check*."

Ash nodded. "I got some things to check on myself. I'll hit y'all later."

"And don't forget," Buck added, "birthday dinner tomorrow."

T-Money smirked. "The big 28. Yeah—we got a lot to celebrate."

"Hell yeah, we do," Buck said, smiling wide.

DEA FIELD OFFICE – HOUSTON – DAY

The tension in the office was thick as Kevlar. Phones rang. Papers shuffled. Maps were taped to every wall—red pins stabbing across states.

At the center, DEA AGENT Jobs paced in front of a whiteboard covered in mugshots and sticky notes.

He turned to the others.
"The shipment's confirmed. Warrant's on the judge's desk. Once it hits— the warehouse gets blitzed."

Agent Robbins nodded. "Eyes on it round the clock. No slip-ups."

Agent White leaned against a table, smirking. "AZ and his crew supply twenty percent of the whole damn East Coast. This bust? We are making history."

The room quieted. Everyone knew what was at stake.

SUBURBAN SILENCE

The quiet cul-de-sac in College Park was anything but peaceful that night. Red and blue lights pulsed against the siding of modest brick homes, casting eerie reflections on rain-speckled windows. Police cruisers lined the street. Yellow tape fluttered in the wind like a flag of surrender. It was the kind of night that makes a neighborhood hold its breath.

Detective Reece Carter stepped over the threshold of the small suburban house, his face unreadable, eyes scanning the chaos inside. Three bodies. No signs of struggle. Paraphernalia everywhere.

"Looks like another triple," he muttered, crouching beside the nearest body.

Officer Jamal Denton stood nearby, his gloves already on. "All DOA," he said grimly. "We found residue on the counter, empty vials. Probably heroin mixed with fentanyl."

Reece didn't answer. He was staring at a photo on the wall—three smiling faces, alive and untouched by whatever hell had unfolded here.

Outside, Channel 5 News was already live on the scene. Across Atlanta, living rooms flickered to life with the sound of the anchor's voice.

"We're live from a quiet street in College Park tonight," reporter Jenna Holloway announced, her voice clear but tight. "A neighborhood now shaken by a scene straight out of a nightmare."

The feed cut to a wide-eyed neighbor, flamboyant and breathless. He wore slippers and a silk robe and looked like he'd just stepped off a reality show set.

"Child—listen," the neighbor gasped, waving his hand for emphasis. "I just came over to borrow some bread and butter. Knocked on the door… and it creaked open. I stepped in and—Lord have mercy! Bodies everywhere!"

He clutched his chest dramatically, eyes wide with remembered fear.

"I ran out, baby. I ain't waiting around to be the next one!"

Inside the house, medics moved with precision. The camera caught a glimpse of them loading a body bag onto a stretcher. A hush fell over the growing crowd outside. Flashbulbs popped from phones as neighbors recorded a tragedy in real time.

Back on the air, Jenna Holloway's voice turned solemn.

"Police are investigating what appears to be a triple overdose. The names of the victims have not yet been released."

The camera panned across the lawn. A child's toy tricycle sat tipped in the yard, one handle broken. A porch light blinked in slow rhythm above the door, casting long shadows on the walkway.

Reece Carter stepped back into the night air, jaw tight, mind spinning. Something about the scene didn't sit right. Too clean. Too quiet. No needles. No cookers. No sign of a fight—but three lives gone, just the same.

Atlanta had seen its share of blood and secrets. But tonight, College Park had something else.

A message.

And the city had better listen

WAREHOUSE – NIGHT

Dust hung in the air like fog. The warehouse buzzed with quiet purpose—cash stacked, kilos packaged, and the hum of power unspoken.

AZ sat at a steel desk, writing in a tattered notebook. Hardened. Calculated. Dangerous.

Behind him, Ruben, Rodriguez, and his nephew worked methodically—packaging brick after brick.

AZ glanced up.
"You got ATL Buck down for 150?"

"Yeah," Nephew nodded. "He buying' 200 more."

AZ didn't smile—he just calculated. "I'm throwin' in another 200. When's the truck getting here?"

"Few hours out."

"Park him overnight. Load everything by five A.M. sharp."

AZ turned to Ruben. "Your people pay?"

"They sent it. No extra though."

AZ shook his head. "That's why I rock with Buck. Steady money. Real operation."

Nephew smirked. "Unk, they move like a machine. They call themselves *The Fist.*"

OUTSIDE WAREHOUSE – NIGHT

A surveillance van crouched in the shadows across the street. Inside, two DEA agents sipped burnt coffee and scanned the warehouse through binoculars.

"What's taking' so long' with that warrant?" one muttered. "We're losing ground."

"Got two cars leaving' already," the other said. "One had Chicago plates. Other was D.C."

They clicked photos silently—watching, recording, waiting.

RAINBOW'S APARTMENT – NIGHT

The air was a cocktail of coke dust and paranoia. Razor stood in the shower, hands pressed to the tile, steam curling off his skin like smoke off a barrel. He muttered to himself—eyes wild, body twitching.

Rainbow sat on the couch topless, her hair dyed in five colors and her vibe somewhere between chaos and collapse. She snorted a line, eyes glassy.

Razor stepped out, dripping. Walked to the table. Snorted. Shot. No hesitation.

Rainbow barely looked up. "You good?"

He exhaled like a demon letting go.

"Had to release it," he said. "Now I'm ready."

"Was that... was that your people on the news?" she asked. "The house in College Park?"

"What'd the news say?"

"Overdose," she mumbled.

He nodded. "Yeah. That was them."

She tilted her head. "What happened?"

"I don't wanna talk about it."

Razor continued "You know Buck? Eddie B?"

"The Fist?"

"Yeah. Girls in the club talk about them like celebrities."

Razor's eyes narrowed. "Who in the club mess with them for real?"

"Tan," she said, not missing a beat. "She locked in with Buck. That's her world."

Razor grinned slowly. A grin that didn't reach his eyes.

"Good to know."

In the underworld, revenge comes wrapped in silence.
And grief?
It wears different faces—some weeping… some plotting.

The Fist was rising. The game was shifting. But for every play they made…

There was always someone watching from the dark—
Waiting to make the next one deadly.

Chapter 14

Game Time

T-MONEY'S HOME – DAY

A calm, picture-perfect suburban street. The sun shines down on trimmed lawns. Children laugh in the distance. A warm breeze carries the scent of fresh-cut grass.

T-Money stood in the yard with a plastic tee-ball set, coaching his young son, Emon, who gripped a bat with focus in his tiny hands.

"Good job!" T-Money shouted as Emon smacked the ball. "You might be the next Jackie Robinson!"

Zuri, standing on the porch, recorded with her phone, smiling wide. "Alright, last one," she called. "Time for Mommy to run that bath."

Emon groaned dramatically, begging for one more swing. After a few more playful attempts, Zuri finally scooped him up with a kiss on the cheek and carried him inside.

T-Money smiled to himself, scooped up the plastic ball, then sank into the patio chair with *Rich Dad Poor Dad* in hand. A breeze flipped the page before he could read it.

Zuri reappeared in the doorway, drying her hands on a towel.

"Been hearing that's a good book," she said, eyeing the cover. "That's why I bought it—for us."

T-Money nodded. "I've heard about it too. Thinking differently already."

She stepped closer, her tone shifting. "I've been thinking… I am ready to take classes on event planning. You know I already do it—might as well make it official."

T-Money looked at her like he was seeing her for the first time all over again. "You'd be great at that, bae."

Their kiss started soft but deepened, slow and magnetic. He stood, pulled her close, leading her toward the bedroom as the sun dipped behind the trees.

MRS. MILLS' HOUSE – NIGHT

Kareem and Savannah entered a cozy home filled with warmth, the smell of jerk chicken and shrimp hugging the walls.

"Hey, bra! Hey Savannah!" Kim, Kareem's younger sister, greeted them at the door, all smiles. "You looking' stunning as always."

"Thanks, Kim," Savannah replied. "Sure smells amazing in here."

"Mom cooked your favorite," Kim added, "and Sonny in the living room watching the game."

They made their way through the home, greeted by Mrs. Mills with a tight hug.

"Boy, you need to eat more!" she said to Kareem. "Savannah, you're not cooking for my son?"

"He eats," Savannah laughed. "Plenty."

"Where's Pop?" Kareem asked.

"In the back. You know your daddy—watching Judge Judy like she is paying his bills. And when am I getting a grandbaby?"

"Don't worry, Mom," Kareem said with a smirk. "He or she is coming soon."

They laughed. Kareem stepped into the den, where Sonny sat with his two young boys, eyes glued to the NBA playoffs.

"What up, Kareem?" Sonny greeted.

"Cooling," he replied, dapping his brother. "What's up with the store?"

"All good. Flooring going in now. Are you sure you don't want in?"

"Nah," Kareem said. "I'm into car lots and tow trucks now."

"Solid," Sonny nodded. "Just don't sell any lemons."

They all gathered around the table, plates full, drinks clinking. Laughter flowed louder than the TV.

HOUSTON, TX – NIGHT

Cuz backed the 18-wheeler into a fenced industrial lot. His nephew signaled him from the side, clipboard in hand.

"We have it loaded. 5 a.m. sharp," Nephew said.

"I'm crashing in the back," Cuz replied, hopping down. "As soon as I'm loaded, I'm rolling. You gettin' money now?"

Nephew nodded. "Money behind false walls. We got the routine down."

A camera shutter clicked in the shadows. Someone was watching. Taking photos. The silence hid a lot more than trucks.

HOTEL ROOM – NIGHT

A luxury suite glowed under dim lights. Buck reclined on a velvet headboard, sipping brown liquor from a crystal glass. The door creaked open.

Renay walked in wearing heels and a smirk—with two women in long trench coats flanking her.

Buck sat up. "Well damn... what's all this?"

Renay sauntered over. "Birthday vibes. I got a surprise for you."

The women dropped their coats. G-strings. Nothing else. Buck grinned like a kid in a candy store.

Low music rolled in—slow, seductive bass. The women moved like liquid, sensual and precise. Renay threw a stack of ones in the air. Buck leaned back, eyes wide.

"Happy birthday," she whispered.

THE OFFICE HOUSE – NIGHT

The air was thick with kush and quiet tension. A basketball game played in the background. Red cups sat sweating on tables. Eddie B, White Boy, Tom Tom, and D-Bo were deep in the cut, the room lit only by lamp glow.

Eddie B stared at his phone. "They say Razor and them committed suicide."

Tom Tom frowned. "Who's they?"

"The news," Eddie answered. "TV. Streets. Three bodies near Main, close to the station. Skinny confirmed the count."

Tom Tom shook his head. "Damn. Skinny broke them."

Eddie held up his phone. "Wanna see it?"

"No," D-Bo said, disturbed. "Delete that shit."

White Boy agreed. "We told you."

Tom Tom changed the subject. "Eddie, when you getting a new car?"

"Already did," Eddie said. "Dropped a new motor in. Ready in a few days."

White Boy nodded. " Them Y.N. still pressing folks."

"They bleed like we do," Eddie snapped. "Ain't nothin' special."

White Boy leaned forward, forearms on his knees.

"Yeah, but they're deep," he said. "And they got middle school and high school kids following them."

Eddie B shook his head slowly, voice laced with frustration. "These young niggas actin' like grown men... so we gotta treat them like grown men. They messing up your money."

White Boy nodded grimly. "One of my traps—I had to double staff it. But who really wanna go to war with kids? It's a lose-lose situation no matter how it plays out."

Tom Tom rubbed his face with both hands, leaning back into the couch. "Yeah, that's not good. We gotta figure something out."

A tense silence crept into the room like fog.

Then D-Bo spoke—voice low and cold. "Smoke their ass. That's all they understand. We'd be doin' the public a favor."

No one responded, but the silence said enough.

HOUSTON, TX – WAREHOUSE – NIGHT

The warehouse sat cloaked in shadows, a fortress of secrets. Inside, workers moved fast, loading crates of furniture hiding bricks of narcotics deep in the walls.

Cuz stood by his rig, clipboard in hand. His breath fogged in the air as he pulled out his phone.

CUZ (TEXT): Game time. About to head back.
BUCK (TEXT): Good news to wake up to.
CUZ: Will hit you when I'm close.
BUCK: Bet. 10/4.

OUTSIDE WAREHOUSE – PARKED VAN – NIGHT

Inside the black DEA van, red lights flickered on a control panel. Agents scanned monitors, faces hard with anticipation.

"Can't believe we still don't have a warrant," Jobs muttered.

"Judge is en route," Robbins replied. "We'll move in under an hour. Operation Doomsday is a go."

"Call in extra bodies. We'll need at least a hundred."

"Already did. Setting up checkpoints now."

The van went silent again. The trap was tightening.

DEE'S HOUSE – MORNING

Sunlight filtered through blinds into a clean kitchen. Dee sat across from

Lil Dee and Destiny, his hand wrapped around a coffee mug. Summer stood at the counter making toast.

"Summer," he asked, "what time is the meeting with Lil Dee teacher?"

"Nine. Are you still going?"

"Yeah. I need to hear what really happened."

Lil Dee stared down at his plate, jaw tight. "Dad, I'm telling the truth. She always picks on me."

"We gon' find out," Dee promised.

Destiny handed her brother a napkin. "Maybe she just doesn't like smart boys."

Everyone chuckled except Lil Dee, but even he cracked a half-smile.

BUCK'S BEDROOM – MORNING

The room was a battlefield of pleasure—clothes, condoms, empty bottles, dollar bills. Buck stirred, then reached for his phone, eyes squinting at the screen.

BUCK (GROUP TEXT): Cuz on his way back.

Replies flooded in—fire, thumbs-up, and money bag emojis.

Buck grinned, rolled over and kissed Renay on the shoulder. "Babe, last night was something else."

Renay stretched, half asleep. "Don't expect an encore every week."

Buck laughed. "I'm about to shower. You comin'?"

"Mmm," she groaned. "Five more minutes."

He slipped out of bed and padded into the bathroom.

HOUSTON, TX – WAREHOUSE – NIGHT

Red and blue lights flashed in all directions. DEA agents swarmed like wasps—guns drawn, trucks surrounded, men yanked from rigs and slammed to the concrete.

Fifteen suspects, face down. No resistance left.

BLACK SUV – MOVING

AZ sat shotgun, eyes fixed ahead. His nephew drove with quiet focus. The city blurred past in silence.

"We got the tip just in time," AZ said. "Still took a major loss. But better this than twenty years."

"Mexico, here we come."

"I got some trucks off—some cash, some product," Nephew added. "The money truck's already headed west."

AZ nodded slowly. "Good. Send the money trucks to Cali. Split the routes. Keep the eyes off us."

Nephew typed encrypted texts, his thumbs moving fast.

OFFICE – NIGHT

Low music played under the hum of conversation. The room glowed red from LED lights. Tom Tom and Eddie B sat over a chessboard. Kareem, Dee, and T-Money talked near the fridge. Buck leaned against the counter, glued to his phone.

"What time's your thing tonight?" Kareem asked.

"Nine," Buck said. "Cuz should be back by then."

T-Money glanced at Buck. "He matched us?"

Buck nodded. "Five hundred."

"That's what I like to hear," T-Money said. "Let's make the donuts."

Buzz. Buck's face darkened. He read the message. A moment passed.

D-Bo noticed. "You good?"

Buck didn't answer right away. "Nephew said... the warehouse got raided. Cuz already left, but... might be followed. Or pulled over."

Everyone straightened.

Tom Tom kept it level. "Call him. Act normal."

Buck pulled the burner from his pocket. Dialed.

CUZ (V.O.): "What's up?"

BUCK (playing it cool): "Just checking'. You still on time?"

CUZ: "Yeah, man. Traffic's a breeze."

BUCK: "Cool. See you later."

Click.

Silence followed.

"He sounds good," T-Money said.

"Yeah... he did," Dee added, unsure.

T-Money looked around. "Still—send some eyes. We walked him in. Anything off, we disappear."

Kareem nodded, hand on chin. "Even if he makes it back safe... we gotta ask—how long have they been watchin'? How deep?"

Ash stood in the corner, arms folded. "Feds play the long game. Could be years."

Buck exhaled. "Damn... This was supposed to be a celebration."

T-Money took a long sip of brown liquor. "A minute ago, I was feelin' good. Now? Now the whole room just turned black."

Chapter 15

Pressure Points

DEA OFFICE – HOUSTON, TX – NIGHT

Dim light flickered off stainless steel and brown case files. The room buzzed with urgency. Five tables stood cluttered with cocaine bricks, weapons, and wrapped bundles of cash—seized war trophies from a cartel supply chain. A dozen agents surrounded the evidence.

DEA AGENT JOBS flipped through a ragged ledger, voice tight.

"We're holding a press conference in the morning. Arrest warrants for AZ go out at sunrise. Somehow, he slipped through... but odds are, he's already back in Mexico."

DEA AGENT REID pointed to a specific line.

"Here—ATL Buck. Five hundred kilos. Every two weeks. That's our next move."

GAS STATION – NIGHT

A black SUV sat still beneath dead pumps, headlights off. Across the lot, Cuz's truck rolled through. The SUV waited, silent. Then peeled out, slow and steady.

Inside, the DRIVER thumbed out a message: ON SCREEN TEXT: Behind target. Everything looks clean.

DEA OFFICE – CONTINUOUS

Over a map riddled with red pins, DEA AGENT WHITE spoke with urgency.

"Coordinate with Atlanta. Everything we have on Buck goes their way."

DEA AGENT JOBS added, "Three trucks slipped past us tonight. Two had Georgia plates. I bet one of them's his."

He turned to a junior agent. "Run every plate, and freeze every property AZ holds in the States. We raid before sunup."

RANCH-STYLE HOUSE – NIGHT

Moonlight painted silver lines across the driveway. Three U-Haul vans and an 18-wheeler lined the front like soldiers. A flurry of movement as crates were offloaded—fast, precise, military-style.

MELBO barked out orders.

"First van—Long Road! Second—Dirt Road! Third—through the park! Move!"

AG lit a cigarette, watching like a hawk. "I'll make sure they all got tails."

MELBO checked his watch. "Ain't nobody slowing down my night. Buck's birthday at The Plug. We move, we meet, we toast."

Engines ignited. One by one, the U-Hauls tore into the night, each shadowed by a blacked-out sedan.

CLUB PLUG – NIGHT

Neon, bass, velvet ropes. The city's elite poured liquor and lust into the night. VIP lit up like royalty. But tension choked the room.

BUCK sat at the head of the table, king for the night but wary. RENAY leaned into him.

"It's your birthday. Smile for me."

BUCK scanned the crowd, then whispered, "Too much poppin' off to relax, baby."

Across the table, T-MONEY, TOM TOM, EDDIE B, WHITE BOY, DEE, BAY, KAREEM—all checked their phones or the exits.

A waitress dropped a bottle. No one touched it.

HOTEL BAR – NIGHT

Low ceilings. High anxiety. AZ nursed his whiskey while NEPHEW leaned in.

"Where'd the heat come from?"

"Two trucks. Got popped over a year ago. That's when eyes got on us."

"Which state?"

AZ shook his head. "Couldn't say. But they stalled the judge as long as they could. The second they knew it was me, they moved."

"What now?"

AZ snarled. "My business accounts are frozen. Spots raided. Fifteen mil? Gone."

"Did the trucks make it?"

"Yeah. But that ain't the problem."

"Then what?"

"We got snitches. Maybe one. Maybe more."

Silence.

"We find 'em," Nephew said, dead calm. "And we burn 'em."

CLUB PLUG – LATER

The crowd was lit now. Bottles exploded in sparks. Fireworks danced on LED screens. DJ dropped 2 Chainz.

Buck lifted a glass.

"To another year of making' money and dodgin' trouble!"

TOASTS. CHEERS. LAUGHTER.

Then the new arrivals entered—MELBO, AG, SNOW, CHE CHE, MARC, and CUZ.

T-MONEY greeted Melbo with a nod. "Everything good?"

MELBO grinned. "All locked away."

ASH asked, "Y'all double check?"

SNOW laughed. "We blocked a road, caused a jam. Three minutes. Nobody tailed us."

BUCK spit out his drink, laughing. "Y'all stupid as hell. That's my kind of security."

DJ's voice thundered.

"Everybody get a drink! Time to sing Happy Birthday to the man himself—BUCK!"

Crowd roared. Champagne sprayed. Dancers closed in. Buck raised his glass.

"To The Fist. To my family. To staying free."

The whole room echoed: "TO BUCK!"

Behind the smoke, behind the smiles... the storm brewed.The music was loud, but the tension was louder. Behind the champagne bottles and flashing lights, behind the birthday toasts and grinning faces, there were quiet wars being mapped in real time. Every laugh was shadowed by suspicion. Every drink masked a plan. The Fist moved like brothers, but they knew the walls had ears and the streets had eyes.

Out in Houston, the DEA tightened their grip. In Club Plug, Buck celebrated another year alive—knowing the next one wasn't promised. Trucks were still rolling. Secrets were still leaking. And somewhere, somebody was snitching.

The game was changing.

And not everybody would survive the shift.

Chapter 16

The night around the YNG clubhouse was thick with noise, neon, and reckless abandon. The building itself, tucked off a backstreet in the heart of a forgotten part of town, pulsed with heavy bass and the scent of smoke, sweat, and synthetic highs. Inside, chaos reigned: music blasted from massive speakers, pill bottles rattled across tabletops, and coke-dusted hands passed liquor bottles like war trophies.

A long table stretched across the back wall, cluttered with the spoils of the day: handguns, jewelry, designer bags, and stacks of rubber-banded cash. Like some twisted altar to fast life and fast death.

Outside, the air was cooler, but just as alive. Four guards stood on alert, hoodies up, eyes locked on every shadow that moved. These weren't boys playing gangster—they were foot soldiers, waiting for war.

Blackie stood inside, counting bills with precision, the dull club lights reflecting off the gold chain resting on her collarbone.

"They did good today," she said, nodding. "Hit over fifty cars. Got all kinds of shit."

Slim leaned against the wall beside her, smirking. "Messed the Tower parking deck up real bad."

Blackie gestured with her chin toward the dance floor. "Look at Smurf—dude high as hell."

Sure enough, Smuf spun lazily in circles, his pupils swimming in his head, a grin stretched across his face like he'd won the lottery.

Chubby shook his head, laughing. "Man, we got the whole city shook. Time to press more. As soon as they hear 'here come them YN,' everybody panics."

Blackie tilted her head, interested. "What do you have in mind?"

Chubby stepped in close, dropping his voice to a near whisper. "One thing I learned from Razor—he went after the big fish. And Bay? He handed us that forty ball easy. Bet we could've got more."

Slime face grew serious. "Yeah, but we gotta do our homework. They move different. Plus... heard they're the ones behind Razor's death."

For a moment, Blackie said nothing. Her eyes swept the room—kids barely old enough to vote, partying like cartel dons, living like every night might be their last. Some were already nodding out. Others danced like their hearts were bulletproof.

"Look around," she murmured. "You see what I see?"

Slime and Chubby followed her gaze. There it was. Hunger. Loyalty. Desperation. Fire.

"I see them," Slime said quietly.

Blackie grinned, dark and deliberate. "We don't have to lift a finger. These YN? They'll take a life for us, no hesitation. All we gotta do is snap our fingers and point."

Down the block, a black car eased past the clubhouse like a ghost gliding through the fog. Inside, Razor sat in silence, the orange glow of his cigarette casting flickering shadows across his face.

No music. No words. Just the steady hum of the engine and the storm brewing behind his eyes.

He watched the guards, his fingers tapping against the steering wheel. The cigarette flared again. Then he pulled off into the night—his destination unclear, but his mind set on revenge.

Inside the clubhouse, the energy turned up another notch. Blackie was now grinding against Trice, the two of them swallowed by the rhythm. In the far corner, Chubby and Slim kept talking.

"We need to keep our eyes on Blu," Chubby said. "Dude just copped a new Demon. He got it."

SLIME nodded. "Say less. We'll track him tomorrow."

Behind them, the party throbbed. Young soldiers sipped out of red cups, passed around straps like mixtapes. They weren't afraid. They were ready.

Across state lines in Texas, in a DEA surveillance van parked under the sodium glow of a busted streetlamp, two agents watched grainy footage on a screen.

"Took too long to get the warrant," one of them muttered.

"AZ was tipped off," the other said. "Left everything behind but still got out. Somebody inside leaked."

"Who the hell is ATL Buck?"

That name lingered in the air.

At Club Plug, Buck and The Fist circled up like a tribe in wartime. The women waited in the SUVS. The streetlight made their faces look carved from stone.

"This changes everything," Buck muttered.

"Maybe we need a reset," T-Money offered. "Somewhere quiet."

"We lose this load, we got no re-up," Kareem warned.

"Then let's regroup," Buck ordered. "Office. Noon. No excuses."

They nodded. No argument. Just understanding.

At a private airstrip, a jet engine screamed into the night sky. Inside, AZ and his nephew sat in silence.

"Built a solid team," AZ whispered. "And just like that..."

He snapped his fingers.

"...it's all gone."

His nephew leaned in, hungry. "I got this."

"Trust is the problem," AZ replied. "We collect what we can. Then we move."

"Where to now?" the nephew asked.

AZ closed his eyes. "Out the country. Far from this mess."

The plane disappeared into the clouds.

It was all unraveling. Not in silence, but to the rhythm of basslines and gunshots. YNG danced in the flames of their own rise, too high to feel the heat. Razor was a shadow with a grudge, and The Fist—powerful but not invincible—was learning the cost of moving weight with no parachute.

Somewhere in the chaos, loyalty was thinning, ambition was thickening, and survival meant more than street clout.

The war hadn't begun.

But the pieces were on the board.

And the streets were watching.

Chapter 17

The Memory Burned Like A Brand.

Outside a grimy apartment complex lit by a flickering streetlight, a police car idled. Inside the back seat, a scrappy, furious teenager known back then as Young Eddie B sat in handcuffs. His eyes, even then, were full of rebellion—not fear. He didn't blink as he studied the scene around him, already searching for a crack in the system.

Just 25 feet away, two cops leaned against the hood of their patrol car, chuckling to themselves, unaware that they were seconds away from being outmaneuvered.

The crowd had gathered. Eyes whispered what mouths wouldn't say. And standing right in front—T-T. Younger, thinner, her nerves buzzing through her fingertips.

Eddie B met her eyes. He mouthed the words.

Open the door.

T-T froze.

Then, she moved.

A beat later—click.

The door swung open and Eddie B exploded from the car like a shot, his cuffed wrists swinging wildly as he dashed through the lot.

"Hey! Stop!"

They never had a chance.

Trash cans. Fences. Porches. Apartment doors.

By the time the cops caught their breath, Eddie was gone. Gone into the night, gone into legend.

STEAM ROLLED OUT OF THE BATHROOM LIKE MEMORY.

Present day. Eddie B emerged from the mist, water trailing his tattooed chest, a towel slung low around his hips. T-T lay across the bed, wrapped in silk sheets and his past.

"Girl, I love you to death," he said, his voice gritty but soft. "I'd kill somebody over you."

T-T smirked, biting her lip. "Then come show me."

The towel hit the floor.

A tangle of heat and need followed, fast but deep. A quickie—but one that left echoes.

After, Eddie stood, slipping on jeans and stacking cash from the nightstand into his pocket.

"What are you got going on today?" he asked.

"Me and Red gon' shop around, grab something to eat," she said.

He tossed her a few bills. She caught them like second nature.

"Everything good with y'all?" she asked. "The vibe has been off since Buck's birthday."

Eddie paused. The light dimmed behind his eyes.

"We don't know yet," he admitted. "Plug got raided, but Cuz was already gone."

T-T sat up, the silk sliding off her shoulders. "Y'all be careful."

He kissed her. Deep. Then gone.

DOWNTOWN ATLANTA. MAGNOLIA APARTMENTS. NIGHT.

Chaos spilled from the parking garage like a busted dam.

Red-and-blue lights painted broken glass. Residents cursed, raged, pointed fingers. A child's teddy bear lay beside a shattered tail light.

"Breaking news from Midtown Atlanta," came the voice of a local news reporter. "More than fifty cars were broken into overnight. Residents are furious. Police are scrambling."

The reporter stood before the camera with all the poise she could muster, through her eyes sparkled at the drama.

Behind her: three residents, all pure ATL.

Jared. Mid-20s. Gay. Dramatic. Karen. White. 40s. High blood pressure and low tolerance. Tasha. Black. Slick with the shade.

"How do I feel?" Jared gasped. "Girl, my Gucci sunglasses are GONE. Emergency lip gloss? GONE. Beyoncé Renaissance tickets? GONE. Atlanta is NOT safe!"

Karen snapped. "I BEEN told management! Get cameras! Now everybody is mad but me? Nooo—CRIMINALS out here like DoorDash with crowbars!"

Tasha kept it cool. "You know what I lost? My whole damn car. They ain't even break in. They took the whole thing. I walked out late for work—turns out I ain't got work OR a ride."

In the background, a man held up a single car key like it was sacred. Another kicked a busted taillight, yelling at it like it owed him money.

A detective sighed against a patrol car.

"Used to be, they just stole radios," he muttered. "Now they're taking' the whole ride."

He straightened when he noticed the camera.

"No witnesses. No cameras. We're pursuing leads," he told the reporter.

Jared scoffed. "They saw my sunglasses, didn't they?"

The camera panned across the lot, finally settling on a cracked sign: WE PROTECT OUR COMMUNITY.

It lay face down in the grass.

And Atlanta stayed hot.

Trust doesn't come easy in the dirty South. Not when cars vanish like smoke, the plug's gone ghost, and old memories sprint faster than bullets.

But if there's one thing the streets of Atlanta know—it ain't about who started the fire. It's about who keeps feeding it.

And tonight? Everybody's throwing gasoline.

The noon sun poured over the skyline, bathing the glass towers of Atlanta in golden heat. Inside a high-rise news station, tension buzzed like static.

A news anchor sat behind a sleek desk, posture crisp, eyes locked on the teleprompter. Behind him, the city glowed like a beacon. A red banner flashed across the screen: BREAKING NEWS.

"We interrupt your program with a developing story out of Houston, Texas," the anchor began, voice smooth but urgent. "A massive federal operation is unfolding as we speak."

Houston. Night. Flashing red and blue lights danced across the exterior of a cavernous, abandoned warehouse. Inside, a long table stretched beneath buzzing lights—its surface loaded with stacks of cash, bricks of cocaine, AR-15s, and glinting handguns. Federal agents moved with precision, barking commands.

Three masked suspects knelt with hands bound behind their backs. Cameras clicked. The media swarmed outside the barricade.

"Over twenty million dollars in drugs and cash seized," a Houston field reporter relayed from the scene. Her eyes were wide, adrenaline sharp in her voice. "Fifteen suspects are in custody, and federal agents say more arrests are imminent."

A makeshift federal command center. A massive map of the United States hung on the wall, riddled with red dots. Atlanta. D.C. Chicago. Phones rang nonstop. Agents scribbled notes, flipped folders.

One lead agent stood still among the frenzy—his presence cold, commanding.

"We just dismantled a major drug distribution ring," he said directly to the camera. "They were pumping twenty percent of the East Coast and Midwest with poison."

His voice lowered, tone a warning.

"More arrests are coming. Atlanta. D.C. Chicago. If you think we don't know who you are..."

He leaned closer.

"...we're coming."

Back in Atlanta, in the plush silence of a luxury home, five men sat frozen around a widescreen TV.

Buck. T-Money. Bay. Dee. Tom Tom.

The news played out in real-time, each word hitting harder than the last.

"Authorities confirm a year-long investigation has led to multiple arrests," the anchor said. "With more expected in cities including Atlanta, D.C., and Chicago."

A thick silence hung in the room.

"That was our people," Buck said at last, voice low. "I know that warehouse. I have been there three times."

T-Money nodded grimly. "They said they have been watchin' over a year."

Bay dropped his head into his hands. "Man... I feel sick."

A hard knock shook the front door. Tom Tom rose slowly and cracked it.

Eddie B stepped inside, a duffel slung over his shoulder. "What I miss?"

"AZ bust made world news," Dee told him. "Over year long investigation"

Eddie's eyes darkened.

"More arrests are coming," T-Money added. "Atlanta's on the list. We need to move smart. New rentals. Burners. One for the family. One for us. One for the lieutenant."

D-Bo nodded. "We gotta stay low. Quiet."

"But when we movin' the work?" White Boy asked from the kitchen entry.

T-Money looked around. "I say wait two weeks. Let it cool down."

"I'm cool with that," Buck agreed.

"Same," Dee said.

Kareem shook his head. "Nah, we move now. AZ gonna want his money."

Buck rubbed his jaw. "Damn. Ain't even thought about that."

"I'm with moving now," White Boy said.

"Now," Bay echoed.

"Now," Eddie B agreed.

"Wait," D-Bo countered.

"Wait," Tom Tom added.

All eyes turned to Ash—the calm strategist. The tie-breaker.

Ash looked up slowly.

"We wait," he said, voice steady. "We need to cross our T's and dot our I's."

Nobody argued. The decision was made.

The television still flickered in the background, but no one looked. All that remained was silence... and the sound of time closing in.

ATLANTA FEDERAL DETENTION CENTER – INTERROGATION ROOM – NIGHT

A dimly lit room with a single metal table. A video camera records the conversation. KEITH, a scruffy-looking inmate, devours Popeyes chicken, washing it down with a can of Coke. Across from him sit TWO DEA AGENTS.

"Keith, have you ever heard of a Buck that can move hundreds of kilos?" one agent asks.

Keith doesn't stop eating. He takes a long sip of Coke, then finally looks up.

"There's two. Westside Buck and Southside Buck," he says, licking his fingers. "Southside Buck run with The Fist. They real strong."

"So you're saying both got that kind of motion?"

Keith shrugs. "Hell yeah they both have been having a good run under the radar. And they are both solid only dealing with their circle."

The agents press further. "Can you help us identify them?"

"How the hell am I supposed to help from here?"

"You know their real names?"

"Nope."

"You got someone on the outside who can help? We could cut your time—Rule 35."

Keith hesitates. He knows the weight behind those words. He wipes his mouth, leans back in his chair.

"My baby mama. She dances. She knows 'em. Sees 'em all the time."

The DEA agents exchange a look. A slow, knowing smile creeps across their faces.

I BAR AND GRILL – EVENING

The place is alive—music playing, glasses clinking, people laughing. At the bar, T-T and RED sit with drinks in hand, chatting.

"Girl, you shoulda been out last night! We had a good time!" Red giggles, sipping her drink. "Yayya got up for karaoke, didn't know a damn word, then BOOM! Straight to the floor."

T-T laughs. "You know Eddie doesn't like me out too much. Plus, Eva wasn't feelin' good."

"Aww, my little pumpkin okay? I miss hangin' with you. But you can't let Eddie dictate your life."

"She's good. She was running a fever. At my momma house now. And for the record, Eddie don't run nothin'."

Just then, the entrance swings open. BIG TONY, BUCK, and BIG RICH strut in like they own the place. Red locks eyes with Big Rich. He flashes a cocky smirk and strolls over.

"Damn, Red. You lookin' good," he grins.

"Thanks, Big Rich. This is my bestie, T-T."

"What's up, T-T?" He sizes her up. "Red, y'all need to come sip with us."

"I'm good, about time for me to head out," T-T replies.

Big Rich leans on the bar. "Damn, shawty, we don't bite. All we do is get money and take trips."

"She's good, Rich," Red says.

"See, you keep saying that, Red, but I'm startin' to think you just like keepin' me on ice."

"Nah, you just think you are colder than ice. But ice melts, baby."

Big Rich laughs, throwing up his hands, then swaggers off.

DEA OFFICE – CONFERENCE ROOM – NIGHT

A large screen flickers on. A group of agents sit around the table. On screen, a TEXAS DEA AGENT joins via video call.

"Any updates?"

"Well," the Atlanta agent replies, "there's two Bucks in this city capable of moving that kinda weight. Girl dances at a club, knows 'em both. Says she can ID 'em."

"Good. We're still looking for AZ too. I got two guys flying out that way."

"Alright. If anything shifts, I'll let you know."

The screen flickers off. Silence hangs heavy. Something big is coming.

THE OFFICE – NIGHT

Smoke lingers in the air. ASH and DEE are locked in an intense chess game. WHITE BOY and KAREEM go head-to-head in Madden. TOM TOM scrolls his phone.

"Man, my phone's been blowing up like it's a drought," he says.

"If a drought hits, we start back working," T-MONEY says. "Be the only ones working. To the fucking moon we go!"

"That's the mindset," Buck adds. "Speak it into existence. Turn lemons into lemonade."

"Check," Dee calls.

"Boy, outta check!" Ash laughs.

"Touchdown! Ayyy!" White Boy jumps.

"Car lot tomorrow will be set up," T-Money says. "Ross gon' have whips in a few days. I'm getting my dealership license."

"I think we all should," Bay nods.

"Yeah," D-BO agrees. "Can't depend on no one all the time. Plus, I'm picking up the two tow trucks too."

"Look at my bros sounding like businessmen!" Tom Tom jokes.

"We gotta get through this situation first. But after that? Bigger things," T-Money says.

INT. POOL HALL – NIGHT

CHUBBY, BLACKIE, SLIME, and a group of YN crew members shoot pool. Blu is at the far end, with a woman by his side.

"That's Blu," Chubby points. "One of his regular spots."

"We snatch him up strong-arm or finessin'?" Blackie asks.

"Definitely strong-arm," Slime replies.

"We calling hands now or wait? Looks like it's just him and that bitch."

Just then, EDDIE B and D-BO walk in. They greet Blu.

"Tell me something good. I'm dry dry," Blu says.

"Give it a few days," D-BO responds. "Double tequila, double Henny. Blu, you want something?"

"I'm good."

Chubby tenses. "That's the nigga who brought the money for Bay ransom. Tonight ain't the night."

"Yeah… the cocky one," Slime agrees.

Eddie B notices them. "That was them Y.N shit not safe" he says.

"Where?"

"Slipping out. Blu, I don't know if it's coincidence or they're plotting on you. Be careful."

Blu sips, eyes locked on the door.

PARKING LOT – NIGHT

A black SUV is parked under a flickering streetlight. Inside, T-MONEY, ASH, and KAREEM are deep in conversation.

"We gotta talk to Eddie B," Kareem says. "Folks complaining—say he's cutting the work."

"My man hit me too," Ash says.

"And he is always late," T-Money adds. "Next time, we will check that."

"For real. If he runnin' them off, I'll get mine back," Ash replies. "What y'all on tonight?"

"Just takin' it in," T-Money says. "Feels like I'm waiting for them to bust through the door."

"Yeah, I stress too," Kareem says. "And when I stress, I gotta release. About to link up with my two… fun fun."

"I feel you. I gotta make a stop," Ash says.

They dap up. Ash and Kareem exit, leaving T-Money in the shadows.

Chapter 18

The night outside the club cracked with tension. Cigarette smoke curled out from a beat-up Honda parked along the curb, the street lights flickering above it. Inside, Razor leaned back in the driver seat, his eyes fixed on the entrance. Rainbow sat beside him, twirling her fingers through her hair, eyes locked on the foot traffic.

"That's her right there," Rainbow said, nodding toward a woman in heels and a bright pink handbag.

Razor didn't blink. "See you at two."

Rainbow grabbed her purse and slipped out the car, merging into the crowd. Razor tracked her until she and the girl disappeared inside the club.

The hotel room was soaked in dim amber light. A near-empty bottle of Don Julio leaned against a pile of crumpled clothes on the floor. Blunts burn slow on the ashtray, their smoke hanging in the air like secrets.

On the bed, White Boy and Lucky lay tangled, both half-dressed, sharing a slow drag.

"You tryna make me settle down?" White Boy smirked, eyes low. "Pussy so good..."

"What are you waiting for?" Lucky shot back playfully. "One day, I won't answer. Might have me a lil' boo by then."

White Boy laughed, but his tone dipped seriously. "Nah, I'd hunt y'all down with a flashlight in the daytime. You good with me. I treat you right."

Lucky turned toward him. "You do. But I still get lonely. My best years passin' me by, waitin' on you to get serious."

He stared at the ceiling. "I don't wanna get serious till I'm out these streets."

"Your boys have families. They making' it work. I'm down, whatever comes with it."

White Boy sighed. "When it doesn't go right? That stress hit me differently."

"Don't wait too long."

He pulled her closer, voice thick with desire. "Climb on top... let me remind you what got you hooked."

Kandi's house was small but alive. Toys scattered on the floor. Her two kids chased each other through the hallway, giggling. She paced by the window, phone pressed to her ear.

"Look, bae," Keith's voice said over the line. "That opportunity we talked about? It came up. Are you still down?"

"Yeah," Kandi replied. "We need you home."

"You know both Bucks? They are still ballin' in them clubs?"

"Yeah. Westside Buck got a party comin' up. He's been trying to get some of this pussy."

"Don't do that," Keith chuckled. "Just ID him. The folks gon' call you tomorrow."

"How much time do you think they'll cut?"

"If they move like I think? Might get me straight out."

Kandi smiled, biting her lip. "Damn... just thinking about your home got me wet. Us over them, any day."

"Love you, girl."

She hung up and stared at her kids. Her eyes burned with hope and something colder—resolve.

T-Money stepped away from Thumbs Up Diner with Zuri and the kids. His son begged to ride with him, but he waved them toward Zuri's car.

"Gotta make a quick stop. See y'all at the park."

Inside the Atlanta precinct, the captain paced in front of a dozen officers.

"Election season. The mayor's breathing down my neck. I need results."

"No suspects yet, sir," one officer said. "But the reward got folks talkin'."

"Think it's tied to the pawnshop hits?"

"Could be. Footage lines up."

An undercover agent chimed in. "I got two CIs workin' Zone 3. We're on it."

The park smelled of fresh grass and sunscreen. Kids cracked baseballs into the sky. Zuri stood with the other moms, sipping water and trading glances.

"Something's off with the Fist," Sugar whispered.

"Ash has been tense," Skyy said. "Told him to pray."

"Something happened out West," Zuri added. "They tryin' to keep it quiet."

On the bench nearby, Ash and the crew posted up, eyes roaming, energy off. T-Money arrived with a camera and Tom Tom beside him. They exchanged nods. But no one was really watching the game.

Back at Kandi's, her phone lit up.

"Can we meet today?" the voice asked.

"Yeah. Obie's BBQ. Six."

"We'll be there."

She set the phone down and stared out at the neighborhood. She wasn't nervous.

She was ready.

A beat-up warehouse bumping music. Inside, Blackie, Chubby, Slime, and Trice surrounded two new faces: Tank and Man Man.

"These are my cousins," Trice said. "They wanna buy."

"How much y'all spending?" Chubby asked.

"Ten grand. We need Dracos. FNs."

They opened a back room. Flickering lights lit up a small arsenal.

"Man... y'all ready for World War III," Tank said, eyes wide.

Slime grinned. "Stay ready."

As the cash came out, the street war stocked up.

And across the city, the clock kept ticking.

Chapter 19

The Park Was Electric.

A crisp afternoon sun glowed overhead, casting long shadows across the baseball field where dreams collided with dust and determination. Bleachers buzzed with chatter and cheers. Kids in oversized uniforms sprinted across the diamond while parents clutched foam fingers and cell phones, capturing every moment like it was the World Series.

On third base, Eman wiped sweat from his brow. His jersey clung to his back, streaked with dirt from his earlier slide. The bat cracked. A clean shot. The crowd's roar was instant.

"Run!" someone shouted.

Eman took off, cleats pounding the grass, arms pumping like pistons. Outfielders scrambled, chasing the ball into no man's land. At home plate, the catcher squatted, glove raised.

T-Money stood up in the crowd, locked in.

"Hen! Did you get everything?!"

Hen, unfazed, leaned against the fence with a camera.

"Why do you always ask me that? You know I did!"

Eman dove—cloud of dust.

SAFE.

The crowd exploded. Cheers, laughter, claps, and high fives all around.

T-Money met Eman at the fence.

"How'd I do, Dad?"

T-Money beamed. "Great."

Moments later, the diamond reset. Next game loading.

On the sidelines, Lil Dee warmed up, swinging his bat like it owed him something. Aaron, his teammate, adjusted his helmet with a grin.

"Lil Dee, stay sharp," Dee warned, hands folded.

"I'm knockin' it out the park, Dad."

Ash leaned in from the other side. "Aaron! Stay focused. Run hard!"

The kids nodded.

Parents yelled. Uncles barked. Aunties recorded.

"You got this, nephew!"

Aaron winked. "I'm stealing two bases."

Tension rose as the umpire signaled.

The game was on.

Lil Dee took his stance. He looked like a boy, but moved like a man. The pitcher stared him down, twisted up, and—strike.

The other side went wild.

"He can't hit!" they chanted.

Lil Dee ignored it.

Strike two.

Noise. Pressure. Grit.

The pitcher was wounded again. Time froze. The world narrowed to one moment—bat and ball.

Contact.

The ball launched like it caught a ride with NASA.

Crowd: gone mad.

Aaron bolted. Third base cleared.

A dust storm brewed at home plate. The catcher waited. Aaron dove—

SAFE.

The team swarmed the field. Chaos. Joy. Celebration.

And then came the whisper.

A smug parent scoffed, "That boy can hit."

Wrong move.

Summer and Skyy turned like scene stealers in a Tarantino flick.

"What. Did. You. Say?" Summer demanded.

Skyy leaned forward. "Say it louder."

The parents didn't get a chance. Summer shoved. The crowd gasped.

The parents stumbled, clutching their lips.

The field froze.

Dee, Ash, T-Money, and Bay rushed over. So did everyone else.

"It's getting' real now," a dad muttered.

Coach, already on his phone: "Yeah... I'm gonna need security."

Cut to pizza.

Team devouring slices, laughter erupting like nothing happened. Lil Dee, calm as ever, licked his cone with a grin.

"So... we doin' this again next weekend?"

Chapter 20

A warm breeze drifted through the night, brushing against the side of the parked sedan across from the restaurant. The street was dimly lit, the distant hum of city life bleeding into the shadows. Inside the car sat Blackie, Slime, Chubby, and Shade Tree. All eyes were on the front door of the restaurant, where their target sat unbothered.

"He is in there with that same female from the pool hall," Blackie muttered, squinting. "What's the play?"

Chubby grinned. "Got an idea. Let the air out his tire. When he steps out to fix it—we run up, make it do what it do."

"I like that," Slime smirked.

"Shade Tree," Blackie nodded toward the door. "Back left tire. I'm 'bout to head inside."

Without a word, Shade Tree slipped out the car and moved low like a shadow, crouching beside the rear wheel. A faint hiss escaped into the night.

The restaurant pulsed with a late-night buzz. Inside, Blu and April perched at the bar, drinks in hand, laughing harder than they probably should have.

"Girl," Blu grinned, slightly buzzed, "you gonna make me go crazy on you later."

April leaned in, teasing, "I'm tryin' to mess up a happy home."

"Damn," Blu exhaled. "You gotta be so blunt?"

"You're always talking about how unhappy you are... but she's still getting all the benefits."

"You know why I'm still there."

"The kids," April smirked, raising her glass. "That's all y'all excuse. Ready for another round? She's getting really wet."

"Miss," Blu flagged the bartender. "Two double shots. Imma teach your ass tonight."

"The night is young," April laughed.

They clinked glasses, downed the shots, and began their unsteady walk to the door. Across the room, Blackie watched. Her phone buzzed. A single word: Ready.

Blu and April stepped into the night. As they neared his car, Blu frowned.

"Damn, bae—my tire looks flat."

He knelt down, running a hand across the rubber. April bent beside him.

Then chaos.

Shade Tree, Chubby, and Slime erupted from the shadows, weapons drawn. Guns flashed. Blu tried to jump up, fists swinging.

"What the fu—!"

April froze as Blackie emerged, her pistol inches from April's cheek.

"Move and you die."

Across the street, someone lifted their phone, recording.

Blackie spotted it.

"Oh, you wanna be determined, dedicated, dependable? Fox 5 News?"

She FIRED.

The shot rang out, sending bystanders scrambling. The phone clattered to the sidewalk.

Blu fought hard. A second gunshot tore through the air. He collapsed.

April screamed.

Slim cursed. "Shit!"

Blackie didn't blink. She turned the gun, aimed at April, and pulled the trigger. April fell.

Chubby yanked chains from Blu's neck, dug through his pockets.

"Can't waste no mission."

From the apartment windows above, shadows moved. Witnesses.

Chubby FIRED one last round into Blu.

Then the crew vanished into the night.

Bystanders rushed to the bloody scene, frantic, yelling. Lights turned on. Sirens far off.

The van tore through the backstreets, a blur under the orange glow of street lamps.

"Damn," Slime said . "He bucked on us."

Blackie stared at her lap, reloading. "I had to bust at them—they were recording."

"We're gonna have to lay low," Chubby said, eyes lit as he examined the stolen jewelry.

"We'll get some stacks for sure," Slim nodded.

The van disappeared into the dark.

At the car lot, The Fist huddled beneath strung-up lights and hoodless cars. Red cups in hand, bottles open.

T-Money raised his cup. "Let's toast."

Cups lifted high.

"Out of many, we become one. Nothing comes before us. Wealth, health, and loyalty—a lifestyle. To more business, more life!"

Laughter broke out.

"Man, our ladies are a handful," Bay joked. "Dee, you better watch Summer. She hit that lady in the lip so fast!"

Dee nodded. "Yeah, her and Skyy were like pit bulls."

"I thought we were gonna have to pull straps," T-Money chuckled.

"I wish me and T-T were there," Eddie B said.

"No, we don't," Buck replied. "Woulda been ten times worse."

Tom Tom turned serious. "Eddie, you gotta quit cutting your work. Folks complaining. We only re-rock when it's a drought."

"Man, I'm trying to get all the way back," Eddie B sighed.

"No excuses," White Boy cut in. "We looked out for you. Now do right. Quit gambling."

Eddie nodded.

"When Ross said the cars be here?" Buck asked.

"Tuesday," T-Money replied.

D-Bo's phone rang. He answered.

"Hello?"

"Blu been shot," Mook B's voice came through, tight with fear. "He might not make it."

D-Bo froze.

"Which hospital?"

"Grady."

D-Bo hung up.

"Blu been shot," he told the group, voice low. "They say he might not make it."

The air turned heavy. Silent.

"Damn," Eddie B muttered. "I just told him to be careful. Bet it was them Y.N. "

"Why do you say that?" Kareem asked.

"Me and D-Bo pulled up on him the other day at the pool hall. Saw them there. They crept out as soon as they saw us."

The crew exchanged looks.

The game had changed.

The night moved like smoke—thick, choking, and impossible to contain. Blood on pavement. Fear in the air. A life gunned down over territory, ego, and silence. And just like that, Blu became another name etched into the growing list of street martyrs.

But this wasn't just a hit. It was a message. A shift.

In the shadows, alliances would be tested. The Fist was tightening, and the city would feel its grip.

Everybody watching just realized... the war wasn't coming.

It was already here.

Chapter 21

A dim hallway swallowed the silence, save for the faint, irregular beep of a dying fire alarm battery. The sound bounced off peeling walls and warped floorboards like a pulse waiting to flatline.

A shadow moved.

Silent. Deliberate. Lethal.

The figure stepped into the bedroom—Chubby, deep in slumber, flanked by two women tangled in red satin sheets. Sweat glistened on their bodies, unaware of the storm standing over them.

A bucket tilted.

Water crashed.

Chubby bolted upright, sputtering. The women screamed. All three blinked against the blur of wet lashes.

And then they saw him.

Razor.

Alive. Lean. Face gaunt like a resurrected ghost with no mercy left to give. In his hand—a gun pointed like judgment day.

"Razor?" Chubby gasped, wiping water from his face. "I thought you were dead."

Razor didn't answer right away. He let silence do the talking, a smirk ghosting across his lips.

"Yeah," he finally said. "That would've been a nice ending. But we have unfinished business."

Chubby's eyes darted toward the nightstand. Inches away—a pistol. A last hope.

"Look," Chubby said, voice cracking. "We were wrong. I admit that. But I can fix it. I got money, I got soldiers—anything you want, Razor. I submit."

Razor's chuckle was low, grim.

"Chubby," he said, taking a slow step forward. "If you didn't stay high all night, you mighta heard me walk in. Oh, and say hello to Rowe, Snake, and Body Count... in hell."

Chubby dove.

Too slow.

BANG. BANG.

The shots ripped through the room. Blood sprayed across the sheets. Chubby's body slumped, mouth still open mid-plea.

The women screamed.

Razor turned. Expression blank. Eyes cold.

"Please... please, don't—"

BANG. BANG. BANG. BANG.

Silence.

Bodies limp. Sheets soaked.

Razor walked out, calm as wind through graveyard gates, humming softly.

"Ain't No Love in the City."

THE OFFICE – DAY

Twenty men around a long table. The atmosphere—focused and hungry.

T-Money leaned forward, tone even but electric.

"Today's the day we get back to work."

Tom Tom nodded. "Price just went up. Thirty a pop. Each lieutenant gets a grand off the top."

Ash scrolled through texts. "Stash houses prepped. Burners distributed."

Buck tossed keys on the table. "No flashy rides. Buckets and rentals only."

Bay added, "No clubs. No jerseys. Just hustle."

"No fronts," Dee said. "Cash on delivery."

Kareem's gaze swept the room. "If something feels off—speak up."

D-Bo flipped through rubber-banded stacks. "Every 150K goes straight to the drop. No errors."

White Boy lit a smoke. "Clean phones. No pillow talk."

Eddie B cracked a grin. "We about to make a real check."

Fireball flicked ash. "Streets dry. Time to feast."

Che-Che rubbed his hands like sandpaper. "Let's cook."

FADE TO:

DEA OFFICE – NIGHT

Agents gathered under stale light, eyes bleary but sharp.

"Kevin Jones," Agent Harington said. "Picked up with a key and a Glock. Cascade Road."

Agent Parker raised an eyebrow. "Tied to Westside Buck?"

"Could be. No priors. Forty-two years old. Folded like laundry."

They grinned.

The trap had already been set.

YNG HANGOUT – EVENING

A haze of smoke. Grand Theft Auto chaos blasts on a TV. Guns laid out like jewelry.

Blackie paced, heat in her chest.

"I been calling Chubby all day. Nothing."

Slime shrugged. "Probably laid up."

Blackie paused. Eyes narrowed.

"He know what today is."

Slime stood. "Another hour. If he doesn't check in—we go see what's what."

MAYOR'S OFFICE – NIGHT

Rain tapped glass like ticking clocks. Inside, the air was heavier than politics.

"Atlanta's a mess," Mayor Smith growled. "Buckhead ready to break off. Lenox a warzone. It's election season—I need wins."

Chief Brown folded his arms. "Then fund us. My officers ain't paid to bury friends."

Smith scoffed. "You think I got magic money?"

"No," Brown said, stepping in. "But I think you forgot what it feels like to fight."

Tempers flared. Two men once shoulder-to-shoulder, now toe-to-toe.

Captain Woods finally broke in. "This ain't who we are."

They stepped back.

"How's your boy?" Brown asked, quieter now.

Smith rubbed his temples. "He doesn't talk to me. Thinks I sold out."

"Maybe he's wrong."

"Maybe not. Your daughter?"

"Law school," Brown replied. "Like her mama."

A pause.

Not peace—but memory.

The war outside would wait another hour.

Chapter 22

No Days Off

The game never sleeps—and neither do the players. In a city pulsing with ambition and betrayal, every breath could be your last if you're not paying attention.

NIKKI'S HOUSE – BEDROOM – NIGHT

The walls of the small bedroom pulse with dim red light from a nearby alarm clock. BUCK sits on the edge of the bed, shirtless, in jeans and socks, muscles tense like he's already halfway out the door. TAN, fully naked, is sliding on her tight jeans, her curves catching the glow.

"Buck, I need your help getting my own spot," she says, not looking at him.

"How much do you need?" Buck's voice is calm, like he already knew it was coming.

"I wanna go high-rise. Midtown. About five grand." She zips up her pants and pulls on a crop top.

"Cool," he nods. "But I need it low-key. Can't have no dudes coming in and out."

TAN laughs softly, slipping her feet into heels. "Hell naw. You all I need. I don't mind being a side piece—you do right by me."

Buck pulls out a thick stack, peels off the money like it's nothing, and hands it to her.

Tan smirks, kisses him on the cheek, and walks out like she owns the room.

A beat later, NIKKI—Buck's sister—steps into the doorway with arms folded, face twisted in disapproval.

"Buck, that ain't cool. Bringing your side piece over here? You know me and Renay are cool."

Buck shrugs. "I'm your brother. That rule over sisterhood."

"That ain't the point. I don't like giggling in her face, acting all cool and shit. Makes me feel fake. What you do is on you—but don't put me in the middle."

"I can respect that," he says.

Nikki gives him a last look, shakes her head, and walks out. The silence in the room grows loud.

CAR LOT – NIGHT

Streetlights buzz overhead, casting long shadows across rows of used vehicles. DEE, ASH, and D-BO huddle near a parked car, tension rippling through the air.

"Man, it ain't looking good for Blu," D-BO mutters. "He ain't never gonna be the same. And his side piece? She died. Baby mama pissed."

"Damn," DEE breathes.

"Said she begged him to come to her mom's house," D-BO continued, "but he lied. Said he had work. Out trickin'."

ASH shakes his head. "Hope his money's in the right hands. Y.N. gang? They need to be dealt with."

The low rumble of a subwoofer rolls into earshot. The men turn their heads. A long, black HEARSE creeps onto the lot, tinted windows, chrome rims catching the streetlight.

"What in the hell?" Dee mumbles.

The door creaks open. EDDIE B steps out, dressed sharp—black slacks, crisp shirt, dark shades on his face despite the night.

"Call me the grave digger," he says with a straight face.

Ash busts out laughing. "Boy, you a fool."

Dee shakes his head. "Never a dull moment with you."

Eddie B smirks. "Y'all said ride low-key."

The tension breaks slightly, but the air is still heavy with unfinished business.

T-MONEY'S HOME – DAY

Sunlight filters in through gauzy curtains. The living room smells of coffee and ambition. ZURI sits cross-legged on the couch, a clipboard in her lap, flipping through pages of colorful event plans.

"I got everything set for your grand opening," she says. "Big cookout, free hot dogs, hamburgers, chips, drinks. Gift bags too. Live DJ."

T-MONEY, standing by the window, nods. "What's the hit?"

"Five grand, including the live remote." She grins.

"I see you doin' your thing," he says, admiration in his voice.

"I have another event next week too. My Auntie's 60th. Hustle doesn't stop."

T-Money leans over and kisses her. "Keep that same energy."

He grabs his keys and heads to the door. "I'm about to slide by Sammy's, then hit the lot."

"Don't forget snacks for the kids," she calls.

"Got it," he replies, and he's gone.

MONTAGE – TRANSACTIONS IN MOTION – DAY INTO NIGHT

INSIDE A HOUSE – MEBO flips bills rapidly under a humming ceiling fan. The air is thick with cash, resin, and paranoia.

INSIDE A CAR – AG deals like clockwork. One man out, another in. His eyes never leave the rearview.

CAR WASH – SNOW leans against his hood, rolling up with one hand, stacking cash with the other.

FAST FOOD PARKING LOT – FIREBALL moves like a machine. Bag in. Cash out. A dirty napkin used to wipe sweat from his neck.

INSIDE A HOUSE – TWIN and another DEALER measure out grams with surgeon precision. A duffel bag waits, gaping open like a hungry mouth.

MUSIC STUDIO BACKROOM – CHE CHE counts hundreds with one hand, puffing smoke with the other. A beat vibrates the floor.

APARTMENT WINDOW – WEEZY peeks through the blinds like a prisoner of war. Behind him, money and product flow like blood.

BATHROOM COUNTER – WADE moves a pack under fluorescent light, nodding once before the client disappears.

STREET – NIGHT – CJ steps out of a matte black SUV, duffel in hand. He walks with silence, menace, and purpose.

INSIDE A HOUSE – COUP cracks open the bag. It's full of money. The other men in the room—MEBO, AG, SNOW, FIREBALL, TWIN, CHE CHE, WEEZY, WADE, and CJ—light up with victory.

A money counter whirs.

A Hennessy bottle empties.

Smoke rises like prayers to the hustle gods.

The streets didn't rest, so neither did the ones who owned them. While bodies dropped and feelings twisted, the engine of the empire roared louder. Loyalty wasn't a tattoo—it was a currency. And every play made now, whether out of love, greed, or vengeance, would ripple through the blocks like thunder after lightning.

Chapter 23

Crimson Roots, Golden Streets

CHUBBIE'S HOME – NIGHT

Darkness blanketed the house, but evil had already left its prints. The blood on the walls wasn't just spilled—it was a message, a siren blaring through silence. Blackie's hand trembled on the doorknob as her eyes locked onto the carnage. Her breathing, shallow. Her heart? About to beat out of her chest.

The laughter that echoed moments earlier now twisted into a breathless panic. SLIME, still in disbelief, just stood there, frozen—his mind replaying every memory with Chubbie like a broken tape.

CHUBBIE hadn't just been their homeboy. He was family.

As SHADE TREE stepped deeper into the room, his eyes hardened into something darker. Something final.

They didn't scream. They didn't cry.

They ran.

CASH HOUSE – NIGHT

Two SUVs slid into place like chess pieces, engines humming low and hungry. The doors creaked open—silent wolves stepping into the den.

Inside the cash house, the vibe was all money and muscle.

AG posted at the door like a sentinel. No smiles. No small talk.

Gym bags lined the countertop like trophies. One by one, they were claimed—tossed to the city's most dangerous men like bonuses at the end of a bloody fiscal year.

T-MONEY juggled his bag, felt the weight, nodded.

"The streets are dry-dry. Might be time to go up more."

KAREEM smirked. "Must say... autopilot and repeat."

BAY shook his head, grinning. "Sounds about right."

FIREBALL blew smoke from his nose. "Ain't that the damn truth?"

WHITE BOY cracked up. "Best drought we ever had."

BUCK smiled low. "Love how T-Money spoke it into existence."

The hum of the money counter clicked like a metronome, counting not just bills, but power. If blood was spilled, the city bled gold.

KEVIN JONES' HOUSE – NIGHT

The room was dim. The tension? Blinding.

KEVIN sat slouched, sweat collecting under his chin. Across from him, two DEA agents leaned forward—not aggressive, just assured. They didn't need to bark. Their confidence was the threat.

"We're coming as friends," said Agent 1.

But friends didn't come with mandatory minimums.

They laid out the terms. Kevin didn't argue. He folded—fast.

"Westside Buck... Big Tony..."

The names came easy. And like that, the strings to the next act were pulled.

Magic City. Saturday. A trap dressed in temptation.

YNG HANGOUT – NIGHT

It wasn't a hangout tonight—it was a war room.

Smoke twisted in the air like bad intentions. Blackie's face was lit only by the low glow of a nearby lamp, her jaw clenched, her voice even sharper.

"This wasn't no accident. This was retaliation."

SLIME slammed his fist against the table. "It had to be The Fist."

"But Blu wasn't even with them," someone mumbled.

SLIME turned, wild-eyed. "He was something to them. That pool hall? That wasn't just a run-in."

Silence.

Then **SHADE TREE**, calm as ever, delivered the final line.

"We TTG. Train to go. This city's about to be bloody red."

The streets were boiling now. Chubbie's blood soaked more than bedsheets—it soaked loyalty, memory, and revenge. As the money flowed, so did rage. Feds tightened their circle. The Fist sharpened their focus. And YNG?

YNG wanted war.

And in Atlanta, when the sky turned red… no one was innocent.

Next move determines who lives... and who's just another story whispered through the bricks.

Chapter 24

Int. The Office – Night

The smoke curled upward like secrets whispered in a closed room. The walls, lined with surveillance monitors and faded city maps, bore silent witness to countless conversations—some brilliant, others bloody. Tonight, The Fist gathered again, seated around a long oak table cluttered with notepads, cash counters, and half-drunk bottles of brown liquor.

TOM TOM leaned forward, eyes low and voice steady. "We need a new connect—fast. The Lieutenant is running through the work too quick."

T-MONEY scoffed, flipping a rubber band from a stack of bills. "Yeah, our hands are about to be tied behind our backs."

ASH pulled out his phone. "I'll reach out to Puerto Rico Johnny, see what his numbers look like."

"I'll pull up on Hecker," BAY said, tapping his watch. "See what he's talking about."

TOM TOM nodded. "I'm waiting for Carlos to hit me back."

Suddenly, the TV buzzed on with an emergency alert. The room hushed.

TV NEWS REPORT

The anchorman's voice was calm but sharp. "Breaking news: A triple homicide—one male, two females—has occurred in College Park."

The Fist stared at the screen.

"Details are still coming in, but police have ruled it as foul play. Authorities are asking anyone with information to contact the tip hotline."

T-MONEY shook his head. "We're living in the wild, wild west."

TOM TOM leaned back, jaw tight. "Those YN fools keep messing up the game. I'm about to agree with Eddie B—we need to take them out."

"What makes you think it's them?" BAY asked.

Tom Tom didn't blink. "Every fucked-up thing going on in our city—somehow, they're involved."

T-MONEY exhaled, quiet. "Our city's a ticking time bomb."

POLICE DEPARTMENT – NIGHT

The precinct was buzzing. Fluorescent lights cast a pale glow over cluttered desks and weary faces. Officer Benjamin burst into the captain's office, waving a file.

"Cap, thought you should know—two of the guns found at the crime scene were traced back to the pawnshop heist."

Captain Woods looked up slowly, eyes narrowing. "Alright. Let's run everything. Find out who Mr. Claybone rolls with, who he's been seen with."

He stood and crossed the room. "Go back over the crime scene. Dig up pictures. Track down his mother, sister—any next of kin."

He turned, voice stern. "Move. If we solve this, we will solve a whole lot of murders."

TRUCK STOP – NIGHT

The air smelled like exhaust and distance. The dull roar of eighteen-wheelers echoed in the darkness. CUZ, tall and broad-shouldered, approached his rig, boots crunching against gravel.

Two men stepped from the shadows—dark suits, hard eyes.

"Mr. Hill, may we have a minute?" Agent 1's voice was smooth but clipped.

Cuz sized them up. "What can I do for y'all?"

"When was the last time you were in Houston, Texas?"

Cuz didn't blink. "I go there often—maybe two, four weeks ago."

"Where'd you go?"

"Look, I got a load to drop. Don't have time for back and forth."

Agent 2 pulled out a tablet. On it: a still image—Cuz in his truck at a Houston dock.

"That's your truck, right?"

Cuz nodded slowly. "Yep. Got my log sheets to prove it."

Agent 2 smirked. "Funny... we raided that dock an hour later. Found large quantities of drugs and cash."

Cuz shrugged. "I haul frozen meats."

The agents chuckled.

"Well, let's hope so. 'Cause someone's saying you left with 500 kilos."

Cuz's heart pounded. He didn't show it.

Agent 1 handed him a card. "Think of it like a pizza. Every deal takes a slice. When it's gone—so are the deals."

They walked away.

Cuz leaned against his truck, chest tightening. He grabbed his inhaler. Breathed. Then grabbed his phone.

TEXT TO BUCK: We need to talk. ASAP.

REPLY: Meet at Wing Spot.

THE OFFICE – NIGHT

The Fist counted money with jokes and smoke. Then Buck stood up, face dark.

"Cuz just hit me up. Something's up."

The room went still.

"Where?" T-Money asked.

"Wing Spot. I'm on my way."

They knew. Trouble was circling.

BAR – NIGHT

The room buzzed with laughter and energy. On stage, a female comedian had the crowd in tears.

"Fellas, ever text 'good night' just to see if she says it back, and she doesn't? Now you are wide awake, paranoid, like a security guard with no flashlight!"

At a corner booth, T-T, RED, YAYA, and LOU laughed over cocktails.

Then the swagger walked in—Big Rich, Big Tony, and Westside Buck.

"Damn," Rich grinned. "God must be trying to tell us something."

"It's my girl's birthday!" Red said.

"Ours too!" Tony shot back. "We are throwing a party tomorrow—Magic City."

Then Eddie B and White Boy rolled up. Tension shifted the air.

"They are good players," Eddie B said.

The men stared. Long. Quiet.

On stage, the male comedian kept the laughter alive.

"Ever see a dude buy drinks like he rich, then at the ATM sweating like he ran a marathon?"

Back at the booth, Westside Buck broke the silence.

"What's good, Eddie B? No harm, no foul."

"Cool," Eddie said.

But Tony wasn't done. "You owe me for that lemon car! Broke down after I won it from you!"

Eddie's face tightened. T-T caught it.

"Walk with me to the bar," she said.

He followed. She always knew when to step in.

In a city stitched together with secrets, it only takes one thread pulled too hard to unravel everything.

The Fist felt it. YNG felt it. Law enforcement smelled blood, and the block buzzed like it knew something was about to snap.

The game was shifting. And nobody wanted to blink first.

Chapter 25

Wing Spot – Night

The Wing Spot buzzed with low conversation and clinking glasses, the air thick with fry grease, hot sauce, and tension. A dimly lit booth in the back corner played host to five men—BUCK, T-MONEY, ASH, DEE, and CUZ. Their voices were low, their eyes sharp.

BUCK leaned in, his tone clipped. "You sure you weren't followed?"

CUZ nodded, wiping sweat from his brow with a napkin. "Yeah. Took the back roads. Ran a couple red lights just to be safe."

Their gazes scanned the room. Every table. Every shadow.

"Two agents rolled up on me," CUZ continued. "Showed me pictures— me, my truck. Claimed I left a warehouse in Houston just before a raid. Said it was 500 keys."

ASH muttered under his breath. DEE froze with a wing halfway to his mouth.

"Somebody's talking," DEE said, the words dragging the temperature of the booth down to freezing.

T-MONEY rubbed his temples. "They ask for names?"

"Nah. Just slid me a card and walked off like it was nothing."

CUZ tossed the card onto the table. The men stared at it like it might explode.

"Lawyer. Tomorrow," BUCK said.

DEE shoved his plate away. "I was hungry. I'm getting my wings to go."

DARK SEDAN – CITY STREETS – NIGHT

A black sedan glided through Atlanta's arteries, its tinted windows reflecting neon lights and flashing signs. Inside, two DEA agents sat, cold and calculating.

"You lost him," Agent 1 snapped. "He was gonna lead us straight to Buck."

Agent 2 smirked, unfazed. "We get a warrant in the morning. Slap a tracker on the truck and the sedan."

"They're too clean. No heat. No slips. Loyal customers, big volume..." Agent 1's voice trailed off.

"Yeah," Agent 2 replied, eyes narrowing. "But that kind of clean? Means they're seasoned. Means they've been through war."

YNG HANGOUT – NIGHT

The basement reeked of sweat, smoke, and old secrets. A busted couch, a flickering TV, and a sagging ceiling gave the place its charm.

COLD HEART stood in the center. "We need to hit their traps."

SLIME scoffed. "They don't run traps. They move weight. Straight wholesale."

"Then we wait," SHADE TREE said, voice like a blade. "And when the door cracks, we kick it in."

POLICE BRIEFING ROOM – NIGHT

The mayor, police chief, DA, and Captain Woods surrounded a long table. Tension thickened the air.

"YNG," Woods said. "Young Nigga Gang. They're flooding the system with middle school foot soldiers."

DA Willis flipped open a file. "One of their lieutenants got smoked. His phone gave us everything—photos, texts, socials. This ain't small-time."

"RICO," the mayor whispered, smiling with cold calculation. "This is just what I need."

"For justice or reelection?" Willis asked.

"Both."

MAGIC CITY Monday – NIGHT

A stretch of Lambos, Benzes, and Bentleys wrapped the lot. Trap anthems poured from cars. Velvet ropes stretched wide, cameras flashing. The glow of the iconic neon sign painted the sidewalk with temptation.

A black hearse pulled up.

Gasps. Phones rose.

EDDIE B slid out, tailored in jet-black silk. Behind him, KAREEM and WHITE BOY COOL stepped from a rented Charger, grinning.

"Park it up front, partner," Eddie told the valet. "And don't scratch the coffin."

They stepped inside.

The moment the doors swung open, it hit—bass shook the foundation, bodies moved like liquid temptation, and dollar bills flew like feathers in a storm.

A stripper with legs like pistons danced upside down. Champagne bottles cracked open like gunshots. Smoke drifted from hookahs and blunts. The scent of cash and perfume blanketed everything.

DJ VOICE (O.S.): "Happy birthday to the money man—BUCK! Magic City is up tonight!"

VIP was a warzone of money. BIG RICH, WESTSIDE BUCK, and BIG TONY held court. Their table looked like a rap video set—models, money machines, and more ice than a hockey rink.

KAREEM, EDDIE B, and WHITE BOY slid to the bar. The tension was thick, but the night was young.

Across the floor, KANDI—heels sharp, dress tighter than a secret— knocked back shots. Her eyes locked on BUCK. One. Two. Three.

From a booth, two UNDERCOVER DEA AGENTS watched. One sipped water. The others took photos: Buck, Big Tony, Kandi. All of it.

Then KEVIN walked in, all white everything. He dapped up Big Tony, then Buck.

Click. Camera flash.

KANDI approached BUCK with beads. New Orleans style.

"Happy birthday, baby," she purred.

She dropped it low, spinning into his lap. Money rained. The crowd howled.

BUCK (grinning, drunk) "Girl, stop playing. You know what I want."

KANDI (whispering) "I might just let you have it. Tonight feels... dangerous."

EDDIE B, watching from across the club, locked eyes with Big Tony.

"Tony," he said, strolling over. "Let's switch bitches tonight?"

Big Tony stared, unamused.

"Damn, Eddie," he said. "You off your meds again or using your own supply?"

"Nah," Eddie said, nose twitching. "Two things I have never seen: A UFO and a bitch I can't have!."

And then—

FLASH OF SILVER.

A knife. Deep into Big Tony's gut.

Music played on. But chaos bloomed. Screams. Blood. Big Tony dropped.

EDDIE B stood over him, breathing hard.

Strippers scattered. Drinks crashed. Security scrambled. The club was a war zone now.

He walked over to KAREEM and WHITE BOY.

"Y'all ready? Party's over."

They stared at him like he was a ghost.

"What just happened?" KAREEM whispered.

"I just gutted Big Tony like a Turkey for Thanksgiving," Eddie said, then smiled.

And just like that, they disappeared into the crowd as chaos swallowed the night.

Chapter 26

The woods were quiet that night, the air thick with humidity and secrets. Ten young men, barely out of high school, stood in a tight circle under the broken canopy of trees. Shadows danced across their faces, the moon slicing through the branches in long, jagged streaks. Each boy wore the same hardened look, a look shaped by loyalty, struggle, and survival. They called themselves **The Fist**.

T-Money raised his hand, fingers spread apart under the silver light. His voice was low, deliberate.

"Look at my hand," he said, turning slowly so each brother could see. "Yeah, I can slap you—it might hurt. But if I make a fist..." He curled his fingers inward, making a tight ball. "I can knock you out."

The circle nodded, eyes gleaming with understanding. No one spoke, but the energy among them crackled like static.

Tom Tom stepped forward next, his voice even sharper. "We stand together on everything. Move as a fist."

Ash followed, his tone steady. "One of us represents all of us. We hold each other accountable."

Bay crossed his arms, nodding. "If nine of us got a hundred dollars, each of us give the one with nothing ten. Everybody eats."

Kareem leaned in, adding, "When one hurts, we all hurt. When one wins, we all win."

White Boy smirked. "We gotta be different from the rest. Learn from their mistakes."

Dee stepped into the faint light, his voice calm but serious. "Trust each other. Never snitch. We take care of our own."

D-Bo's voice was a quiet growl. "No females come between us. United front. No looking at another brother's lady."

Eddie B, rough around the edges but loyal to the core, spoke next. "Fear no man. We are our brothers' keepers."

Finally, Buck, the quiet one, the thinker, finished it. "No gambling among us. If there's a problem, we put it on the floor. Majority vote settles it."

They all nodded. The pact was real.

T-Money pulled out a knife, the blade catching the moonlight. One by one, they sliced their palms, blood dripping onto the dirt. Together, they pressed their fists into one solid mass—blood and brotherhood sealed in a sacred bond.

In unison, they yelled, "THE FIST!"

The night swallowed the sound. But the oath, the power, would follow them forever.

The present day felt colder.

DEA HEADQUARTERS – LATE NIGHT

A cramped room overflowed with open files and crime scene photos pinned to a corkboard. Red string crisscrossed like veins, connecting names, faces, addresses. Tension hung heavier than the smoke from stale coffee.

Agent Palmer flipped through a folder, his voice cutting through the room.

"We made good progress last night. We can finally put a face to the name Westside Buck."

Another agent, Ramirez, leaned forward. "Any word on the stabbing?"

Palmer shook his head. "Nothing solid yet. Still waiting on intel from Kandi and Kevin."

"Looks like Westside Buck could be our guy," Ramirez said, closing his file with a snap.

The agents exchanged hard glances. They knew they were close—too close to let up now.

ATTORNEY LATHAM'S OFFICE – DOWNTOWN ATLANTA

In a sleek, upscale law office lined with towering bookshelves, Buck, Ash, Cuz, and D-Bo sat in stiff leather chairs. Anxiety clung to the room like humidity.

Attorney Latham, a sharp man in his fifties, laced his fingers together on his desk.

"From what I've heard," he said, "people in Houston were under an unsealed investigation. There's a good chance someone was talking."

Cuz leaned forward, voice tight. "They got anything on me?"

The lawyer gave a slow shrug. "Depends. The feds play by their own rules. Conspiracy covers a wide range of possibilities. It gets tricky."

He leaned back, steepling his fingers.

"Good news—they made arrests, but they didn't have warrants for y'all. Bad news? They could start a new investigation if they get new information."

Buck frowned. "So we're just sitting ducks. Waiting for them to show their hand?"

"Pretty much," Latham said. "Move light. Assume they're watching. Assume everything."

Silence hung heavy over the room. No one dared breathe too loud.

T-T'S APARTMENT – THAT SAME NIGHT

Inside a cozy but cluttered living room, T-T and Yaya sat on the couch, half-drunk but dead sober from the weight of reality.

Yaya sipped from her glass, her voice low. "Girl, we were having a good time in VIP with Big Rich and them... then your man came in, shook the whole party up. Stabbed that poor boy up like it was nothing."

T-T wiped her face, her hands trembling. "His ass ain't been home. I knew Eddie was gonna get him. Where's Red?"

Yaya shrugged. "Who knows? Probably with Big Rich."

T-T stood up suddenly, grabbing her purse. Her heart pounded against her ribs.
"I gotta find Eddie before this gets outta control."

She slammed the door behind her, the night swallowing her up.

THE CAR LOT – DAY

The air smelled like burnt rubber and gasoline. Kareem, White Boy, T-Money, Dee, and Tom Tom leaned against a row of dusty cars, talking low and serious.

Kareem shook his head. "Man, I think Eddie B is back messing with that stuff. Ain't no way he'd do that in his right mind."

T-Money crossed his arms, his face grim. "This ain't good. Last thing we need is a war with Westside Buck."

They all paused, the weight of the possibility sinking in.

Dee sighed. "Buck and them should be back from the lawyer's office soon."

White Boy kicked a loose rock across the pavement. "Man, can't lie... Big Tony been asking for it. Been poking the bear for too long."

"Yeah," T-Money muttered. "Just bad timing."

"Anybody heard from Eddie B?" Kareem asked.

"Nope," Bay said from behind them. "Calls go straight to voicemail. I wonder if he even went home."

T-Money exhaled. "We're gonna have to sit him down. Last time he spiraled out of control, he caught five years."

Nobody argued.

HOSPITAL WAITING ROOM – NIGHT

The fluorescent lights buzzed overhead, casting a sickly pale light over the small crowd gathered. Buck, Big Rich, Dee Dee, and a handful of family members sat stiff and silent.

Big Rich paced back and forth, anger pouring off him like heat from an engine.

"I'ma get that nigga," he muttered under his breath. "So damn disrespectful, walking into our space like that. We were vibin', having a good time... now our man is fighting for his life."

Westside Buck, sitting with arms folded tight across his chest, nodded grimly.
"I agree. We gotta handle this. But you know what comes with it."

Big Rich didn't hesitate.
"Yeah... war with the whole Fist. But hey, we got guns, bodies, and cash. We ain't scared."

Buck nodded slowly. "I'll get the crew together later. We plan."

Big Rich's eyes gleamed with something darker than rage. "I think I know a way."

Just then, two uniformed officers approached, their faces unreadable. The entire room stiffened.

"May we ask a few questions?" the lead officer asked.

Big Rich barely glanced at him.
"Look, don't waste your time. Nobody knows nothing."

The younger officer shifted, uneasy. "Sir, we just—"

Big Rich cut him off, his voice like a blade.
"I said what I said."

The officers exchanged a look, then turned and walked away without another word.

As they disappeared through the double doors, Buck leaned forward, speaking in a voice only the inner circle could hear.

"Clock's ticking," he said. "And Atlanta 'bout to feel it."

The war had already begun.

There was no more peace left in the streets. Just silent deals, whispered threats, and the kind of loyalty that demanded blood in return for blood. In the end, it wasn't about who started the war—it was about who finished it.

And The Fist? They were just getting warmed up.

Chapter 27

The sun had long disappeared behind the dusty hills of Sonora, and the sprawling estate was alive with soft music and laughter. Beyond the marble terrace, where two women massaged his shoulders, AZ lounged on a custom-built massage table. His silk robe barely clung to his shoulders, and a half-empty bottle of top-shelf tequila sweated on the table beside him.

His nephew, sharp in a pressed white shirt and jeans, stood nearby, tapping away on his phone.

"Look," AZ said, his voice low and relaxed, "make contact with everyone who owes. Set up times to collect."

His nephew nodded without looking up. "Will do."

AZ cracked a lazy smile. His mind was already three moves ahead. "I've been thinking..." he said, motioning lazily with his hand. "Maybe you can run the business in the States. This time, we set up shop in Atlanta. Let's go into the tire business. Tires are cash, boy."

The nephew pocketed his phone, nodding seriously now. "Alright. I'll call our lawyer. Get the LLC set up. I'll also get our real estate agent looking for a spot."

"Good," AZ said, closing his eyes as the masseuse dug into his shoulder. "Keep me posted."

As the desert wind stirred the palm trees outside the estate, a new empire quietly took root.

EDDIE B'S HIDEOUT – NIGHT

The city pulsed outside the window—neon lights flickering against the blinds of the dimly lit house. Inside, the air was thick with smoke, sin, and danger.

Eddie B lounged shirtless on a plush leather couch, a half-crazed smile on his face. Two topless women draped themselves over him, laughter bubbling from their lips like champagne. On the TV screen, a muted *Scarface* movie played—the iconic "The World is Yours" scene bathing the room in an eerie glow.

A nightstand held two Glocks and a pile of burner phones. Nearby, lines of cocaine stretched across a mirrored tray like little white highways to destruction.

Eddie leaned forward and snorted a thick line off the arch of a woman's back. He leaned back, wiping his nose, exhaling like a king surveying his crumbling empire.

"I crave him like a pumpkin on Halloween," Eddie murmured, eyes wild.

Across the room, Tab paced anxiously, sweat glistening on her forehead. Her voice cut the tension.

"The streets are talking, Eddie."

Eddie chuckled darkly, reaching for another line. On a torn-up chair, Chissy—barefoot and high—took a lazy drag from a blunt, blowing smoke into the low-hanging ceiling fan.

"Big Tony's fighting for his life," Chissy added, as casual as discussing the weather.

Eddie B laughed—a sound that didn't belong to any sane man—then took another greedy snort. The women followed, giggling as they wiped their noses and chased the powder with shots of cheap whiskey.

Eddie leaned back again, his grin dripping madness. "Then let's give 'em something to talk about," he said, staring at the ceiling. "I run this city."

And in his mind, he did.

THE CAR LOT – NEXT DAY

Under the hazy noon sun, the car lot buzzed with activity. Engines hummed, deals were whispered, and The Fist huddled in a tight circle near the back.

Kareem and Dee played a slow game of chess on a fold-out table, but nobody was paying real attention. The focus was on business—and survival.

Buck leaned forward, his voice steady but hard. "Basically, the lawyer says it's 50/50. No way of knowing until they show their hand. But we gotta act like we're being watched or investigated. No mistakes."

Ash nodded, flipping a pawn between his fingers. "We keep things moving through our LTs. If it ain't broke, don't fix it."

"I agree," T-Money added, his voice rough.

Buck shifted his stance. "Meanwhile, we gotta get AZ's money together. Nephew said he'll be in town soon."

"Think we can trust him?" D-Bo asked, rubbing his chin.

"He called and gave us a heads-up from the start," Buck replied.

Bay raised an eyebrow. "Just be careful. You know the saying—Mexican snitching on Blacks ain't snitching."

Buck didn't smile. He looked across the lot, eyes narrowing. "Now, the other elephant in the room... where's Eddie B?"

Nobody answered.

Dee moved his rook. "Nobody's seen or heard from him."

"Check," Kareem added softly, snapping Dee back to the chessboard.

"We need to find him," Buck said. "A war's about to break out—us against them. We gotta get in touch with Skinny and his people."

Tom Tom looked grim. "Maybe we should talk with Westside Buck first."

T-Money shook his head. "Ain't no talking. Word is Big Tony's fighting for his life—Eddie hit a main vein."

On a lighter note, Dee cracked a rare smile. "On a good note, all the cars we bought were green-lit—good motors, strong transmissions."

T-Money smirked. "Grand opening a few weeks out. Zuri's putting something nice together."

They nodded, but the tension never left.

DEA OFFICE – DAY

Inside a sterile, fluorescent-lit room, Kevin sat across from two stern-faced DEA agents. The walls were lined with case files, maps, and mugshots. The atmosphere was electric—something big was about to break.

Kevin leaned back, arms crossed, eyes darting.

"Man," he began, his voice trembling slightly, "the other night was crazy. You know the guy that stabbed Big Tony? He's part of The Fist. Eddie B."

The agents exchanged quick glances, trying to hide their excitement.

"Wait a minute," Agent Parker said, leaning forward. "You're telling us the guy who cut Big Tony is connected with Southside Buck?"

Kevin nodded. "Yep. They boys-boys. Real close."

Agent Harrington scribbled furiously. "The Fist? What is that—a gang?"

Kevin shook his head. "Nah. I wouldn't call it that. They don't recruit. Nothing you can do to join. Just a small group of dudes that grew up together. College Park, East Point."

Agent Parker flipped open a file. "Eddie B... Show me some pictures. We need confirmation."

Kevin leaned forward. "Yeah, that's him."

"And the contact info for Westside Buck's crew?"

Kevin smirked. "Big Rich. I got it."

Agent Harrington nodded. "Set up a buy. Let's start with five. Keep it clean."

Kevin nodded slowly. The weight of what he was doing settled on his shoulders.

POLICE DEPARTMENT – DAY

Inside the precinct, the hum of busy officers filled the air. Phones rang, printers whirred, and somewhere in the distance, a radio crackled with a pursuit.

Officer Shaw slid a thick manila folder across Captain Woods' desk.

"From Terence's social media page," Shaw said, "we've identified over fifteen members associated with YNG. All linked to the stolen guns from the pawnshop heist."

Captain Woods leaned back in his chair, steepling his fingers. "You got names?"

Shaw hesitated. "You remember the girl in the white dress? The one who got killed?"

Woods nodded slowly. "Yeah. I remember."

Shaw's voice dropped. "That was our crew. Her brother and sister are deep in this."

Woods exhaled sharply. "Enough to bring them in?"

Shaw smiled grimly. "Exactly. We start with them. The whole operation crumbles like dominoes."

Captain Woods nodded, already seeing the headlines. "Run it by the DA first. No mistakes. We can't afford mistakes."

Shaw turned on his heel and disappeared into the maze of desks, leaving Woods staring at the case files.

War was coming. And the city wasn't ready.

In the shadows of loyalty and betrayal, the line between survival and downfall blurred. The Fist had been born in blood—and it looked like they were destined to end in it, too.

Chapter 28

Street Corner – Night

The city pulsed under a low-hanging haze. Street Lights flickered over broken sidewalks. In a beat-up, parked sedan across from the action, Eddie B, Tab, and Chrissy sat like lions ready to pounce.

In the distance, a group of YNG boys worked the corner—moving bags, exchanging money in quick, greasy handshakes. Young. Reckless. Loud.

Inside the car, the tension was thick enough to taste.

Tab leaned forward, whispering, her voice hoarse with urgency. "I'm tellin' you, YNG be rollin' through here all the time, shaking my brother down like they own the block."

Eddie B smirked, reclining back, hand resting lazily on the butt of his pistol. "Let's give it a few," he said, voice slow and dangerous. "See what happens. I owe them one... and they out here thinkin' they Deebo."

Chrissy shot him a sharp look from the back seat. "Eddie, what you thinkin'?"

He chuckled low, a dark rumble in his chest. "What do you think I'm thinkin'?"

Chrissy scoffed, sensing the blood in the water. "You 'bout to start some shit."

Eddie grinned wider, eyes glinting under the streetlight. "I ain't startin' nothin'. Just making' sure they remember who they playin' with."

Outside, laughter echoed off the walls. Inside the car, it was a loaded silence—tight, waiting to explode.

BAR – NIGHT

The dive bar smelled like old beer and broken promises. Red and Big Rich sat tucked into a corner booth, swirling whiskey in their glasses.

The world around them buzzed with life—drunken laughter, clinking bottles—but at their table, the mood was sharp, surgical.

Big Rich leaned in, lowering his voice. "I got twenty grand. Ten now, ten when the job's done."

Red lifted her glass slowly, studying him over the rim. "And what exactly do you need from me?"

Big Rich smiled, the kind of smile that promised trouble. "Just tell me where Eddie B is."

Red smirked, shaking her head. "Ain't nobody knows where Eddie is right now."

Big Rich chuckled, pulling out a fat envelope. "Oh, he gon' show up at some point. The question is—do you want this money or not?"

Red's fingers tapped the rim of her glass, thinking. She knew the streets too well to pretend loyalty meant survival.

Big Rich's phone buzzed. He snatched it up.

"What's up, Kev?" he said, glancing around.

On the other end, Kevin's voice crackled. "Was just checking'—the store open?"

Big Rich chuckled. "Not right now. Got some business to handle."

"Bet," Kevin replied.

Big Rich hung up, pulled out a wad of cash, and slid ten grand into Red's pocketbook.

Red looked down at the money, fingers brushing the leather. Choices, she thought. Always choices.

"I'll let you know soon as I hear something," she said. "But, Rich, this better not come back on me. You lucky I don't care for Eddie like that."

Big Rich grinned. "Don't worry. I gotcha."

Red sipped her whiskey, but the bitter taste wasn't from the drink.

DEA OFFICE – DAY

Fluorescent lights buzzed overhead. A cluster of DEA agents leaned over a war table littered with photos, maps, and warrants.

The Head Agent slapped a document down hard.

"We have the green light," he announced. "Pole cams, trackers, phone taps—on Larry Durr. Westside Buck."

Murmurs filled the room. Heads nodded.

"Boss," Agent 2 said, sliding a folder across the table, "you won't believe who stabbed one of Westside Buck's top men."

The room froze, hanging on the moment.

"I'm dying to know," the Head Agent said, voice cool.

"Eddie B," Agent 2 revealed, flipping open the file. "Just got out of state prison. Happens to be part of the Fist."

The Head Agent leaned back, a slow grin forming. "What a gift."

Agent 1 chimed in. "No warrants. No victim testimony. It's tight."

"Maybe we can change that," the Head Agent mused. "But keep our CI clean."

Agent 2 added, "The Fist isn't a gang—not technically. They grew up together. College Park. East Point."

"Good," the Head Agent said. "More leverage. Set up the buy through Big Rich. Let's bring it all down."

CAR LOT – NIGHT

Moonlight bounced off hoods and windshields. The lot was mostly dark except for the glow of a few cigarettes and the occasional flash of a burner phone screen.

The Fist gathered in tight.

T-Money broke the news first. "Just got word—Chubbie got killed. Remember that triple homicide on the news? That was him."

The group went still.

Kareem shook his head, voice low. "Damn... somebody got some street justice. Just hope it wasn't Eddie B."

Bay leaned back against a car, grinning wistfully. "Man, I miss moving work in the streets. That rush... that money stacking up fast."

Dee shot him a look. "Chill, man. You are still making money. Stay focused. Idle hands, devil's workshop."

Tom Tom cracked a small smile. "I'm hitting up a music showcase tonight. My lil' cousin's rapping."

T-Money nodded. "I'm rolling with you. Been thinking about investing in that, too."

Bay stretched. "Y'all have fun. But if anything, we should open a bar or something."

Dee chuckled. "People drink and eat like crazy in this city. Money's there."

T-Money smirked, tossing his keys in the air. "I can't wait till we open for business."

Around them, the cars sat silent—shiny coffins waiting for the next war.

PEARL MOSLEY'S APARTMENT – EVENING

The air was heavy with grief. Pearl Mosley's small living room overflowed with mourners—neighbors, cousins, old friends from the block.

The photo of Terance "Chubby" Mosley sat on the cluttered table, surrounded by flickering candles and wilting flowers.

Pearl stood tall in the center of it all—aged beyond her years, but unbowed.

A woman gripped her hand tightly. "You did everything you could, Pearl. Ain't nobody blames you."

Pearl nodded, silent. Grief tightened around her throat like a vice.

The door creaked open. Heads turned.

Blackie, Cold Heart, Spike, and a few others from YNG filed in. Their presence brought an uneasy hush over the room.

Blackie approached Pearl and pressed a thick envelope into her hands.

"For the funeral," he said, voice low.

Pearl hesitated. She opened the envelope—$10,000 stared back at her. She closed it, holding it against her heart.

"Thank you," she whispered.

The room softened. Heads nodded in approval. Some even smiled, broken smiles.

Then—

BAM!

The front door BURST open.

Two uniformed officers stormed inside, hands hovering near their belts.

"Everyone stay where you are!" one barked.

Chaos.

The YNG boys scattered instantly, knocking over chairs and plates as they sprinted toward the back.

Pearl screamed, spinning around, hands raised.

"Why y'all busting' up my house? We are burying my son!"

Officer shoved past her. "Step back, ma'am!"

Out the back door—

BACK ALLEY – CONTINUOUS

The night exploded with sirens. Red and blue lights bathed the alley in violent color.

Spike and two others sprinted across the cracked pavement—but they didn't make it far.

Cops tackled them hard, bodies slamming into the ground. Spike thrashed, cursing.

"Get the fuck off me, man!" he shouted.

Neighbors poured into the yard, shouting and recording on phones. Pearl stood in her doorway, the framed photo of Chubby clutched against her chest, her screams lost in the chaos.

The streets weren't grieving tonight.

They were preparing for war.

Chapter 29

Rainbow's Apartment – Night

A heavy neon haze swallowed the room in soft pinks and electric blues. The city's heartbeat seeped through thin curtains, car horns wailing like distant ghosts.

The sharp *click, click* of heels echoed against the hardwood.

Rainbow—striking, dominant, unapologetic—stepped into view. Nothing but high heels, a strap-on harness gleaming under the light, and a leather whip dangling from her hand like a threat.

On the bed, Razor sat—muscular, breathing hard, stripped down to nothing but his boxers. Sweat gleamed on his chest. His eyes flicked up at her—eager, guilty, already defeated.

Rainbow smirked. Her voice cut through the thick air.
"I heard somebody's been a bad boy."

Razor swallowed hard, his eyes lowering immediately. "I'm sorry," he mumbled, voice breaking.

Rainbow twirled the whip once in her hand, the leather snapping like a live wire. "You know what to do."

Obedient, Razor turned, dropping to all fours. His breath hitched in his throat.

SNAP!
The whip cracked the air, slicing down across his back. A gasp tore from Razor's lips.

SNAP!
Another strike—sharp, intimate, deliberate.

Tossing the whip aside, Rainbow grabbed the KY jelly from the nightstand. Her grin widened, slow and predatory, as she stepped closer.

The soft squeak of leather. The smell of sweat and submission.

A new night was just beginning.

SUGAR'S HOUSE – NIGHT

The living room flickered under the lazy swirl of hookah smoke. Plates of half-eaten wings, scattered chip bags, and red Solo cups littered the low table. The air buzzed with bass-heavy music vibrating from a cheap Bluetooth speaker.

SUGAR, T-T, SUMMER, SKYY, Tamika, ZURI, and SAVANNAH lounged on sagging couches, drinks in hand, tired but still standing.

T-T exhaled deeply, smoke curling from her nostrils, shaking her head in frustration.
"I'm just tired of Eddie's foolishness. I ain't heard from him in three damn days."

Summer shrugged, eyes half-closed from the buzz.
"Eddie's gonna be Eddie," she said flatly. "I wish I had something better to tell you."

Sugar tapped her nails on her cup.
"He'll come around. You know he was mad after Big Tony embarrassed him in front of you."

T-T's voice cracked, a raw edge showing.
 "Yeah, I know... but not coming home? Not answering my calls? That only means two things—he's back on drugs or laid up with some dopehead bitches."

Zuri sipped slowly, studying her friend.
"T-T," she said quietly, "you gotta focus on the kids. Eddie gets off track, but he loves y'all—dirty draws and all."

T-T smiled faintly but the sadness was heavy in her bones.
"I know that... I'm just tired of the unexpected. Feels like I'm always holding my breath."

Without warning, Zuri sprang up and cranked the speaker volume.
"Lean Wit It, Rock Wit It" by Dem Franchize Boyz erupted from the speakers, thumping through the walls.

Cheers broke out. Cups slammed down. The women jumped up in a messy blur, instinct pulling them into the rhythm.

They danced—laughing, swaying, rocking—pushing their worries into the smoke-choked night.

WESTSIDE BUCK'S SPOT – NIGHT

Low lights. Stale cigar smoke. Fat stacks of cash lined the battered coffee table.

Big Rich leaned back in a cracked leather chair, grinning wide.
"We good on Eddie B," he said. "Got inside info. Bitch Red on payroll."

Westside Buck tapped ash off his cigar, skeptical.
"You sure we can trust her?"

Big Rich laughed without humor.
"If she crosses us," he said coldly, "her whole family will die. She knows better than to play games."

Westside Buck nodded, eyes glinting.
"Big Tony is doing a lot better. Time we get back to business."

Big Rich sat up straighter, energy surging.
"Plug said his people will be in town any day now."

"Good," Buck said. "Time for a new check. This drought has been hell."

They slapped hands, rubbing them together like wolves.

"Streets still payin' thirty-two or better," Buck said. "Might be time to bring the rerock machine out."

Opportunity was back on the menu.

THE OFFICE – NIGHT

The office smelled of money, sweat, and faint desperation.

Members of The Fist gathered tight. Bags of cash sat heavy on the tables. A muted TV flashed crime scene reports in the background.

Melbo was the first to speak, pacing in small circles.
 "We're getting low," he muttered. "This drought ain't lettin' up."

White Boy leaned forward, nodding grimly.
"Yeah. Streets hurtin'. Folks getting flexed left and right."

Ag shook his head, frustration boiling under his calm tone.
"CB got robbed. I heard over half a mil—gone."

T-Money exhaled hard.
"Shit gettin' real ugly out there."

Wade slammed his fist into his open palm.
"That Eddie money—still no word. His phone is dead."

Kareem smirked, tapping a cigarette against the table.
"He gon' show up..."

T-Money chuckled dryly.
 "Yeah. Like nothing's ever happened."

The tension in the room crackled.

YNG HANGOUT – NIGHT

A crumbling apartment hidden in the maze of the West End. Peeling paint. Cigarette butts in the carpet. Traps lined the counters—guns, scales, money.

Blackie paced back and forth, her voice sharp with fear.
"They just showed up. My brother, Nut, and KK got locked up. One of the officers who questioned me was there..."

Slime slouched on the couch, tapping ash into a beer can.
"Wonderin' for what?"

Shade Tree grabbed his jacket from the chair. Cold Heart adjusted his hoodie.

"We 'bout to shake down a few traps," Shade Tree said coolly. "Be back later."

Blackie looked ready to crack.
"My mama gon' trip," she whispered. "I don't want her to find out."

Slime stood, pressing a hand to her shoulder.
"Just chill. They gon' call. I'll get my cousin to sign their bonds."

Trice, grinning like a devil, slid behind her and started massaging her shoulders.
"Yeah, baby. Relax. Here, take this."

She pressed two little white pills into her palm.

She hesitated—then swallowed them dry.

Slime grinned.
"Seems like The Fist disappeared from the earth..."

The room filled with uneasy laughter, but nobody dared say what they were all thinking:

This city was about to bleed.

Chapter 30

Police Station – Interrogation Rooms – Night

The hallway buzzed low with tension. The lighting was cold, fluorescent, almost surgical. Outside three separate interrogation rooms, officers huddled, files in hand, strategy thick in the air.

OFFICER 1 glanced at his team, voice low but sharp.
"Let's go. Divide and conquer."

Without hesitation, they split off, each one peeling away toward a door.

INTERROGATION ROOM 1

The door creaked open. OFFICER 1 walked in, dropped a thick folder on the table like a hammer. Across from him, BEAL aka SPIKE, mid-20s, street-hard, leaned back in his chair, wiping his greasy fingers on a napkin. He chewed lazily, almost amused.

OFFICER 1 didn't waste time.
 "Your boys are putting all the break-ins, killings, and shootings on you. Said you're one of the ring leaders."

Beal snorted, tossing the napkin aside.
"Man, that's a damn lie. Conehead shot three people. That shooting at Dill Ave BP? That was all him."

The words dripped out of him like poison, casual as breathing.

INTERROGATION ROOM 2

OFFICER 2 entered slowly, observing JAMES aka CONEHEAD, a stocky fireplug of a man, ripping into a chicken leg like he didn't have a care in the world.

The officer leaned against the wall, arms crossed.
"So, Mr. James... I hear you were the mastermind behind the pawn shop heist."

James didn't even glance up. Keep chewing.

OFFICER 2 pushed a little more, casual.
 "While your friends are making deals, I hope you got money for a good lawyer."

James paused mid-bite, finally lifting his head. His eyes narrowed, something cold flashing there.

"Man, please," he muttered. "Chubby, Slime, and Blackie put that together. I ain't got nothin' to do with it."

He went back to eating like the conversation never happened.

INTERROGATION ROOM 3

In another cramped, windowless room, YOUNG aka OUTLAW sat stiff, his eyes burning with distrust. OFFICER 3 stood against the wall, silent at first, letting the pressure cook.

Finally:
"Word is, you're the shooter. The one giving all the orders."

Young leaned forward, his voice even but lethal.
"Man, y'all playin' games. Either do what you gotta do... or let me out. I need to talk to my lawyer."

The officer exchanged a glance with his partner, smirking.
"Alright. Have it your way."

POLICE STATION – HALLWAY

The officers regrouped just outside the interrogation rooms, files tucked under their arms. Captain Woods, grizzled and stone-faced, approached. His very presence straightened their backs.

OFFICER 1 spoke first.
"We got enough. They're pointing fingers at each other."

OFFICER 2 nodded.
"Beal gave up Nut on that BP shooting. Nut flipped on Chubby and Slime."

OFFICER 3 added,
"Young ain't talking... but he's rattled."

Captain Woods listened, absorbing every word. He sighed, heavy and knowing, scanning the notes.

"Let the DA know," he said flatly. "Pick them all up. And check out that hangout spot in the West End. I want every last one of them."

No questions. No hesitation. They moved out.

BLU'S HOME – NIGHT

The house was dim, half a porch light barely keeping the shadows away. Inside, BLU sat hunched on the couch, rugged, broken, still wearing the bruises and battle wounds of his survival. Bandages wrapped his torso, each breath a reminder of how close he came to death.

D-BO leaned against the wall, the cherry of his blunt glowing like a small, angry eye.

Blu shook his head slowly, voice raw.
 "Man... they slashed my tires. Then blindsided me as soon as I bent over. Tried to take me out... but I fought back."

D-BO exhaled, his voice low.
"Damn, bro. You are lucky to be here. Word is, one of them YN niggas just got smoked."

Blu's laugh was hollow, bitter.
"Good. Ain't no sympathy from me. But, man..." he rubbed his side, grimacing. "I ain't the same no more. Can't even walk right. Pain nonstop. Pissin' through a damn tube."

D-Bo flicked ash into a bottle.
 "Just take it slow. One day at a time."

Blu chuckled darkly.
"One day at a time? Man, my luck went from sugar to straight-up shit. Got gunned down with my sidepiece, my lady found out, ran off with my bag. Came home to nothing but what I had stashed."

D-Bo stepped closer, his voice quiet but firm.
"You know I got your back. Just don't let it break you."

Blu nodded slowly, hollow eyes staring at nothing. In the distance, the city buzzed with sirens and anger—indifferent to any one man's pain.

APARTMENT COMPLEX – LATE NIGHT

Back behind a beat-down set of apartments, the night was thick, humid. Trash littered the alleys. Street Lights flickered overhead.

EDDIE B moved through the darkness like a shadow in a hooded jacket. Cold fury in his blood.

Ahead, two YNG enforcers—COLD HEART and SHADE TREE—were busy roughing up a small-time dealer, rifling through his pockets for whatever crumbs he had left.

Eddie approached without a word. Close. Calm.

The Glock appeared in his hand like magic.

He pressed it against SHADE TREE's temple.
"Lay down."

Cold Heart and Shade Tree froze. Eddie cracked the butt of the Glock across Shade Tree's head—hard enough to drop him.

"I said... lay the fuck down."

They hit the pavement like sacks of bricks.

Eddie kicked them both, ribs cracking under the blows. The small-time dealer scrambled into the darkness like a rat.

From a parked car nearby, Chrissy and Tab watched, nerves snapping tight.

Tab whispered,
"You think he's gonna kill 'em?"

Chrissy didn't even get to answer.

POW! POW!

Two clean, merciless shots.

Silence swallowed the night whole.

Eddie turned, walking back toward the car like it was just another Tuesday. He slid into the passenger seat, eyes dead.

"Drive."

Tab didn't ask twice. Tires screeched as they peeled away, disappearing into the bloody, breathless night.

NIGHTCLUB – NIGHT

The bass rattled the walls like thunder. Lights strobed across a packed, sweating crowd. WILD MONEY, a rap group on the rise, commanded the stage, bodies moving like waves under the hypnotic pull of the beat.

At the end of their set, P. BROWN—host of the night—grabbed the mic.

He roared over the beat.
"Y'all give it up one more time! They just shut this bitch DOWN!"

The crowd exploded in cheers. Wild Money dapped each other up, making their way toward their section. Bottles popped like fireworks. Weed smoke curled in the air.

In the VIP lounge, TOM TOM, T-MONEY, and DEE lounged, clinking glasses, rolling up.

Tom Tom lifted his drink.
"Y'all rocked that shit."

T-Money grinned, taking a pull off his blunt.
"Hell yeah. Stage presence was on point."

Wild Money leaned in.
"Appreciate that, bro."

Tom Tom nodded toward the future.
"Let's toast to big moves—this is just the beginning."

Glasses clinked. The vibe was electric. Atlanta nights at their finest.

But the energy shifted fast.

Across the club, a small group pushed in, whispering urgently. A woman's voice cut through the bass.

"Cold Heart and Shade Tree just got killed."

The words hit like a fist to the gut.

A guy in the group shook his head.
"Man, I'm sure they were on some bullshit."

T-Money stiffened, locking eyes with Dee.

"You hear that?"

Dee nodded slowly, his face darkening.
"Yeah... someone taking them out one by one."

Tom Tom leaned in, serious now.
 "We need to find Eddie B. Fast."

The tension crawled up their spines.

Shots of liquor suddenly arrived at the table, sent over from P. Brown's section. He grabbed the mic again, trying to keep the mood alive.

"Tonight just got official! DJ, run more of that Wild Money! This is a goddamn showcase!"

The DJ dropped another beat, and Wild Money hyped the crowd back up. Women rapped along, climbed onto tables, danced wild.

Tom Tom caught the wave, bouncing with the rhythm. T-Money pulled out his phone, recording, his mind still calculating. Dee rocked in his chair, head nodding, eyes distant.

Outside that club, the streets of Atlanta were changing. Fast.

Inside, the music kept playing.

But everybody knew—

The real show was just beginning.

Chapter 31

Fabo's Spot – Night

Smoke hung thick in the air, clinging to the faded walls like ghosts from old arguments. The room pulsed with low energy—half tension, half boredom. A beat-up TV mumbled in the corner, but nobody paid much attention to it.

At the card table, three women sat playing Spades, their laughter sharp, their shots of tequila sharper. They stole glances at KAREEM and MELBO, who sat across from FABO on a worn-out leather couch.

Kareem leaned forward, his stare drilling into Fabo.

"So when are you gonna have my money?" His voice was calm, but there was no mistaking the warning buried underneath. "It's been two weeks."

Fabo exhaled heavily, rubbing his hands together like he could wipe the stress off.
 "I got you. I keep it real. A few people ran off, so I had to flip what I had. But you gon' get all your money."

Kareem shook his head slowly, unimpressed.

"That's the problem with y'all," he said, voice dropping lower. "Always taking matters into your own hands—with other people's money."

At the card table, the women kept playing, pretending not to hear. But their eyes flickered between the men with growing curiosity.

VOODOO DOLL nudged her friend.
 "Sin City, you gotta take that shot," she said, grinning.

Sin City eyed the glass, wrinkling her nose.
"Y'all tryna have me messed up before work," she said, laughing. "I ain't tryna be falling on stage."

Fabo leaned back, offering a greasy, confident smile.

"Man, you always been solid with me," he said to Kareem. "I got you. Dead ass."

Melbo scoffed, arms crossed over his chest.

"You keep saying that—but no action."

Kareem leaned in even closer, his voice dropping to a deadly whisper.

"Next time we roll through," he said, "have something for me. Or it's gonna get ugly."

For a moment, nobody moved. The only sound was the clink of a card being slapped down.

A tense beat passed. The women knocked back their shots.

Kareem and Melbo pushed back their chairs, standing up.

Right then, the flickering TV cut to BREAKING NEWS.
 The screen lit up with yellow tape, flashing police lights, and wide-eyed crowds gathering at a familiar corner.

The reporter's voice crackled through the speaker.

NEWS REPORTER (V.O.)

"We have another double homicide tonight on the Southside..."

Sin City turned to watch, shaking her head slowly.

"Watching the news in Atlanta," she muttered, "is like watching *First 48*."

Voodoo Doll laughed dryly, raising her glass again.

"You ain't never lied. If I wasn't from here and saw this on TV... no way I'd move—or even visit."

Kareem and Melbo exchanged a look—grim, knowing.

Without a word, they headed for the door, disappearing into the humid night.

YNG HANGOUT – NIGHT

The room was dim, the thick smell of cheap weed and sweat settling into the torn furniture. A broken fan whirred overhead, trying and failing to push the heat away.

Around the room, BLACKIE, SLIME, TRICE, and a few others sat frozen, the TV throwing a harsh blue glow across their hardened faces.

The news played on—grim headlines about the streets they walked every day.

The emotion in the room was suffocating: anger, grief, betrayal.

Blackie stood, her voice low and rough, the words scraping out of her

"We losin' our top guys left and right," she growled. "We gotta get to the bottom of this."

Slime's teeth clenched so hard his jaw twitched. He didn't take his eyes off the TV.

"When the block cleared off from the police," he said through gritted teeth, "we run through. Kill everything moving. Somebody knows something."

The front door swung open hard enough to rattle the windows.

NUT, KK, and SPIKE stumbled in. They stopped dead at the heavy air, sensing the shift before a word was said.

Spike's eyes darted around, uneasy.

"What we miss?"

Blackie turned, voice cold enough to freeze the room.

"Cold Heart... Shade Tree... gone."

Nut stiffened, hands balling into fists.

"As in dead?"

Blackie nodded once.
"Yeah. Dead."

The room sagged under the weight of the news.

Spike swallowed hard, his voice barely above a whisper.
"How? Where?"

"Gunned down," Blackie said. "Off Old Nasty."

Anger flared across the group like wildfire—jaws tightening, muscles flexing.

Slime snapped his gaze to Spike and Nut.

"And the police just let y'all go? What happened?"

Spike shifted in his stance, guilt flashing across his face.

"They pressed me about the pawnshop heist. Tried to play me against Conehead. Vice versa."

KK rubbed his chin, piecing it together.

"Yeah..." he muttered. "Somebody talking. They know too much. I think they got Chubby's phone."

The realization hit hard. Everyone could feel it—like the air had gotten thicker, harder to breathe.

Slime cursed under his breath, pacing.

"Damn. We shoulda grabbed his phone. We all could be in danger."

A heavy silence fell.

KK looked up, eyes colder than steel now.

"Can't lie..." he said slowly. "If it goes down, I'm goin' out in a blaze of fire. Takin' some with me."

One by one, the others nodded. No words needed.

War was already here.

The streets had rules. Blood rules.
Break them, and the ground swallows you whole.

YNG thought they were untouchable—loud, reckless, moving like kings without a crown. But their house wasn't built to last. Their top soldiers were dropping like flies, one funeral after the next, and loyalty was leaking through the cracks like a busted pipe.

And while they scrambled to hold their empire together, Eddie B was out there—somewhere in the shadows—moving silent, moving savage.

He wasn't playing chess.
 He wasn't playing checkers.

He was flipping the whole board over.

One body at a time.

And the scariest part?
Nobody knew who he'd come for next.

Chapter 32

Tab's Spot – Night

The room was heavy with smoke and something darker—defeat. Dim lights barely cut through the haze, casting long shadows across the cracked walls.

EDDIE B sat like a ghost in his own body, planted deep in a tattered armchair. Next to him, TAB and CHRISSY sprawled out, high as satellites—cocaine dusted on their lips, half-empty pill bottles rolling across the floor like forgotten dice.

Eddie didn't move. Didn't blink. His mind was miles away, somewhere only he could see.

He finally spoke, voice so low it was almost a growl.

"I'm gettin' rid of all the enemies. One by one," he muttered.

TAB cackled like it was the funniest thing she'd heard all year, her body swaying like a drunk in the wind.

"My brother says they out havin' a party," she slurred. "Even the old folks are happy."

Eddie didn't laugh. Didn't smile. He just picked up his phone, thumb trembling slightly, and walked off and hit the dial.

T-T picked up on the first ring, hope flickering in her voice before she even said a word.

"Hello?"

The warmth of her house bled through the phone—children's laughter, the clatter of pots and pans, the comfort of family. A life Eddie had once belonged to.

On his end? Only silence. A dead, hollow silence.

"Eddie..." T-T's voice softened, a breaking heart trying not to shatter. "Just come home. I don't care where you've been. I don't care who you are with."

Still nothing. Eddie's breathing was the only response.

"You hear your girls?" she said, lifting the phone closer to the kitchen.

Through the speaker came tiny, joyful voices:

"Love you, Daddy! Come home! Mommy cookin'!"

Eddie closed his eyes, squeezing the phone until his knuckles went white. For a moment, just a moment, the walls around his heart cracked.

T-T whispered, almost pleading. "Thanks for calling'... just letting' us know you good. Always know the door—"

Click.

The line went dead.

T-T stared at the screen, blinking back the tears.

"My baby alright..." she whispered to herself, forcing a smile no one in the room believed. "He will be home soon. Some things just don't change."

Across the room, YAYA and RED exchanged heavy looks.

"You're strong, T-T," Yaya said softly. "I'ma stay in prayer."

"Yeah, girl," Red nodded. "We're definitely gonna pray."

And in the house that smelled of fried chicken and broken dreams, silence swallowed them whole.

CAR LOT – NIGHT

Under the flickering fluorescent lights, the lot felt like a war room. The smell of oil and rubber lingered in the cool night air.

BAY and WHITE BOY sat hunched over a chessboard, deep in strategy. Buck leaned against a black Charger, scrolling through his phone like he was waiting for bad news.

"Nephew be in town in a few days," Buck said, eyes still on the screen. "Told him we got half."

BAY cracked a hopeful grin. "Hope he got good news on some work."

"That's why I said half," Buck muttered. "Next time he comes round, maybe he'll have something solid."

Across the lot, Kareem's phone buzzed. He stepped away from the group to answer.

"Yo," he said to the receiver.

On the other end, T-T's voice, strained but steady.

"Eddie B called. He is good. Ain't say much, probably gettin' high somewhere."

Kareem exhaled, relieved and frustrated all at once.

"Aight. Keep me posted. Are you good? Need anything?"

"Nah, I'm straight," T-T replied. "Guess he knew he was 'about to flip out—left me stacks on the nightstand."

Kareem chuckled. "Sounds like him. Be safe."

He hung up, turning back to the others.

"That was T-T," he said. "Eddie's good. Somewhere gettin' high. Bet he knocked them two YNs off on some old nasty."

Bay scoffed. "Sounds about right. We gotta find him."

The conversation paused as SAMMY pulled into the lot, stepping out of a slick black Benz. He moved with the kind of weight that made grown men straighten their backs without realizing it.

Sammy smiled, easy but sharp. "Fellas, what's good? Looks like y'all about ready for business. How are we feeling?"

"Excited," T-Money said, nodding.

Sammy scanned the faces around him, then leaned in like he was about to share a state secret.

"See, here's the thing," he said. "Other communities? They keep their money circulating for thirty days or more. Us?" He shook his head. "Three days. That's it. And it's gone."

The words hit like body blows. No one spoke.

Sammy kept going, voice calm, dangerous.

"But y'all? Y'all got the power to change that. To build something bigger than a hustle. Something permanent."

Buck nodded, serious now. "We've been thinking about expanding once this runs on autopilot."

Sammy's smile widened. "Good. Because I got moves lined up. Broker. Real estate agent. Financial strategist. I want y'all rubbing elbows with Atlanta's top dogs—from Mayor Devonta to black millionaires running the city under wraps."

"We down," T-Money said without hesitation.

Sammy's eyes gleamed.

"It's a silent auction fundraiser. Black tie. Tuxedos. Gowns for the ladies. Grown-man business."

Dee laughed. "Man, what you tryna turn us into?"

Sammy didn't miss a beat.

"Young billionaires," he said. "The type they can't touch."

T-Money laughed, but it faded fast. "Damn. You skipped millionaires?"

"Hell yeah," Sammy said. "If you ain't already a millionaire in the streets, what are we talkin' for? We pushing' past the moon and the stars."

Whiteboy tapped the table with a knuckle. "Talk that talk, Sammy. Them big B's."

Sammy laughed, but the steel never left his voice.

"Once I put y'all onto compound interest, stock flips, passive income streams?" He shook his head, like it was already written. "You gon' see your money doing gymnastics."

Ash leaned forward, eyes glittering with ambition.

"You got my full and undivided attention," he said.

Sammy grinned.

"That's what I like to hear," he said. "Remember—the key? Make your money work for you. Make it your slave. Never the other way around."

And for a long, heavy moment, the car lot wasn't just a place of oil stains and broken dreams.
It was a throne room.
And every man standing there was a king about to take his crown.

Chapter 33

The summer heat clung to the streets like a second skin. Even the asphalt seemed to sweat.

FLASHBACK – AUTO SHOP – DAY

Buck and John John rolled up to a run-down auto shop tucked behind a cluster of abandoned warehouses. The heavy bass from nearby speakers rattled the shop windows.

Inside, the greasy air smelled of burnt rubber and gasoline. NEPHEW and AZ sat on beat-up chairs, half-watching a music video on the small TV mounted in the corner. Curvy women danced across the screen, but their eyes stayed sharp, scanning every person who entered.

John John and AZ headed toward a backroom without a word, leaving Buck and Nephew making small talk about music, cars, and Atlanta traffic.

Moments later, John John reappeared, holding a heavy duffel bag slung casually over one shoulder. Buck took it without hesitation. Deals like this weren't discussed—they were understood.

They slid into Buck's car, the bag settled between them like an extra passenger.

INSIDE CAR – BEFORE PULLING OFF

John John glanced sideways, his voice dropping to a serious tone.

"See Buck," he said, "three key things to the game. One—stack your money. The plug only respects your buying power. Two—find you a good Mexican connect. Three—say what you mean, do what you say, and stand on your business."

Buck nodded slowly, the weight of the words sinking deeper than the humid Georgia air.

JOHN JOHN'S WORK SPOT – LATER

John John leaned against a scratched-up table, arms folded, watching Buck with a hint of pride and caution.

"I like how you and your boys movin'," John John said. "But if you really wanna get ahead... don't tell them what I'm charging you. Always make yourself an extra five hundred to a stack."

Buck shook his head, face firm.

"Naw, John John. We boys. Brothers for life. I charge them what you charge me."

John John smirked, chuckling low.

"I hear you... but trust me, that's how the game goes. They wouldn't do the same if the shoe was on the other foot."

Buck said nothing, grabbing his package and heading out. Loyalty was a rare currency—and it cost.

THE YOUNG FIST HANGOUT – EVENING

The smell of chicken wings and loud conversation filled the cramped living room.

T-Money and Dee were locked into a serious chess match in the corner, barely speaking except to slap down their next moves. Bay, Ash, and D-Bo devoured wings at the kitchen table, fingers greasy, mouths full.

Across the room, Tom Tom, Kareem, WhiteBoy, and Eddie B battled over Monopoly—but this wasn't plastic money. Stacks of real hundreds sat on the board.

The door swung open and Buck walked in, clutching a gym bag like a winning lottery ticket.

Tom Tom looked up, grinning wide.

"Bet they're glad to see you," he said, slapping the Monopoly money down. "I got all the bread on the board."

T-Money didn't even glance up from his chessboard. "Today is just your day."

Dee chuckled dryly. "That's all it is."

Kareem leaned in eagerly.

"How is the work lookin'?"

Buck cracked a slow grin.

"Good. We bought two bricks—and he fronted us one."

A collective "Hell yeah!" rang out from every corner of the house. This was the kind of news that lifted the weight off everybody's shoulders.

But the moment didn't last.

The front door burst open again. Melbo and AG stumbled in, breathless, wide-eyed.

Melbo panted, hands on his knees.

"Damn! Glad we caught you. John John's spot just got raided."

Buck froze, bag still in hand.

"Nah... you playin'. I just left there."

AG shook his head hard. "We were at some girls' house in the same hood. Rode past. Alphabet boys were *everywhere*."

The room fell into stunned silence. You could almost hear everybody's heartbeat thudding in their chest.

Buck let the bag slide to the floor.

"Damn... what are we gonna do?" His voice cracked. "After we move this out... our plug is gone."

Eddie B, sitting cross-legged on the floor, shrugged like he was suggesting what pizza to order.

"Didn't you say he let you ride with him to their shop?"

Buck nodded slowly.

"Yeah..."

"Then pull up," Eddie said coolly. "Talk to them. Tell 'em what happened. See if they rock wit' you."

Bay clapped a hand on the table.

"All they can say is yes or no."

A long, heavy moment passed as Buck sat there, weighing loyalty, fear, and survival in the balance.

PRIVATE AIRPORT – DAY

A sleek black SUV sat parked on the tarmac, its engine humming like a caged animal. Buck and Fireball watched as a white-and-chrome private jet glided down from the sky, touching the ground like a whispered promise.

The door opened. Nephew stepped out, a woman in dark sunglasses trailing behind him. She peeled off toward a waiting car without a word.

Nephew made his way to Buck, offering a half-smile.

Inside the SUV, the tension softened a little.

"ATL, Buck," Nephew said, slapping him on the shoulder. "Good to see you, my friend. You one of the few keepin' it real in crazy times."

Buck returned the smile.

"Y'all been nothin' but good to me. I gotta keep my word."

Nephew nodded.

"Unk's turning everything over to me now. I'm lookin' for two new buildings—that's why I brought her down. Realtor."

Buck leaned in, hopeful.

"You got a timeline? We need to make a new *check*."

Nephew laughed, pulling a gym bag from the floor.

"Workin' on it. Unk took some big losses. He is ready to get back in action."

Buck handed over the partial payment.

"This is half. Other half is coming soon. Been moving' light."

Nephew nodded, no pressure.

"All good. I'll be in touch."

He stepped out of the SUV, tossing the gym bag into the waiting car. Buck watched both vehicles peel away in opposite directions—just like paths in this life.

SCHOOL – DAY

Westside Buck walked hand-in-hand with his young son, smiling as the little boy recounted his day. Across the street, hidden inside a black SUV, a DEA agent raised a camera, snapping frame after frame.

Buck and his son climbed into their car. The SUV waited a beat... then pulled out, tailing from a distance.

OFFICE COMPLEX – DAY

Buck pulled into a crowded parking lot. Unaware, he and his son disappeared inside an office building.

Across the lot, two agents moved quickly.

One crouched low, slipping a GPS tracker beneath Buck's rear bumper, glancing around like a fox near a chicken coop.

Inside the SUV, the agents reviewed the latest files.

"How many cars he got?" Agent Whitemore asked, scanning the building entrance.

Agent Kingsley flipped through a folder.

"Six."

Agent Whitemore grinned.

"We got our hands full. What about the CI?"

"Buy's set up—five keys with Big Rich. Team's watching."

Agent Kingley leaned back, cracking his knuckles.

"Calm before the storm."

They shared a look that said everything the case files didn't.

RAINBOW'S HOME – NIGHT

The TV blared from the corner. Razor and Rainbow sat sprawled on the couch, a half-empty bottle of Henny on the floor between them.

"I want you to get Tan drunk one night," Razor said, not even looking away from the TV.

Rainbow smirked, lighting a blunt.

"That's easy. She likes to smoke and drink."

"Good," Razor said, finally glancing over. "I'll let you know when."

Suddenly, the screen flashed *BREAKING NEWS.* A grim-faced reporter stood outside a taped-off crime scene.

"Later today, the Mayor, Chief, and Captain will address the crime wave sweeping through Atlanta. From Cleveland Ave to Old National... multiple shootings... several dead..."

Razor chuckled darkly, blowing smoke toward the ceiling.

"These young dudes outta control," he said, laughing without humor. "I really could've made something outta them."

Rainbow just nodded, her eyes cold and distant.

YNG HANGOUT – DAY

The grimy apartment reeked of stale smoke and cheap beer. Blackie, Slime, Spike, and Nut huddled around a scarred table.

"We gon' be breaking' news 'til they respect us," Blackie said, voice like gravel.

Slime leaned back, a wicked grin on his face.

"They gon' have to send the National Guard when we done."

Spike leaned in, hungry.

"What's next?"

Slime's eyes gleamed, feral and eager.

"Fourth of July light show. City ain't gon' know what hit 'em."

Nut laughed, raising his plastic cup.

"My kinda party."

Outside, the fireworks were already being loaded—only this time, it wasn't just sparks they planned to light up.

It was the whole damn city.

Chapter 34

The weight of the city pressed down on everyone. Fear in the air. Hustle in the veins. And time—running out.

CITY HALL – DAY

Inside the grand but crumbling building, anger roared louder than the overhead fans.

The Mayor stormed back and forth, red-faced and breathing heavily, while the Chief, the District Attorney, and a handful of tense Officers braced themselves like soldiers before battle.

"I thought y'all had this under control!" the Mayor bellowed, voice cracking through the thick tension. "Now my city looks like World War III, my numbers are down, are y'all tryna sabotage me?!"

The Chief stayed calm, hands clasped behind his back, a lifer used to political firestorms.

"Sir, we're meeting with our CI today. We're planning to hit their hangout," the Chief said evenly.

The Mayor jabbed a finger toward him.

"This needs to happen sooner rather than later."

The District Attorney leaned forward, voice smooth like silk over a blade.

"Trust me, sir. When this is over... you're gonna look good. One of Georgia's biggest RICO cases ever."

The Mayor hesitated. His jaw tightened. But ambition gleamed in his eyes.

"Good," he muttered. "My people need to feel safe again. Should I push the press conference?"

"Keep it brief," the Chief advised. "Promise results—soon."

The Mayor forced a plastic smile, straightened his tie, and nodded stiffly.

"Alright," he said. "Let's make it happen."

The room emptied quickly, tension lingering in the stale air like gunpowder.

T-MONEY & ZURI'S HOME – EVENING

In contrast, peace lived here.

The living room glowed under soft light. A small mountain of gift bags covered the coffee table. The smell of scented candles floated through the air.

Zuri, Summer, Savannah, and Tamika sat cross-legged on the floor, wine glasses in hand, laughter bubbling up between serious talks.

"You're gonna be an amazing event planner," Summer said, grinning wide.

Zuri smiled, cheeks flushed with pride.

"That's the goal. Been doing my research—and I finally set up my LLC."

"What's the name?" Tamika asked, peeling a sticker onto a gift bag.

"Bright Lights," Zuri said, proud.

Savannah nodded, sipping her drink.

"I'm feeling that."

"Yeah, that's dope," Summer added.

But the mood dipped slightly when Tamika sighed, her glass pausing midair.

"I feel bad for T-T," she said. "Eddie still ain't come home. She said he called... but..."

Summer shook her head slowly.

"I don't know what The Fist gonna do with him. Man's on a collision course."

Zuri leaned back, drawing a slow breath.

"We just gotta keep them in prayer. Be there for T-T. Hold her up."

She grabbed another ribbon and smiled faintly.

"Have y'all men mentioned that silent auction event?"

Savannah smirked.

"Yeah... but I don't know what the hell they're getting into."

Zuri laughed softly.

"That's where all the big names are. Good place for connections. Maybe our men are finally getting a mindset shift."

Renay cackled, setting down her drink.

"Buck gon' be selling dope from a wheelchair, like Snoop on Training *Day*."

The whole room exploded into laughter, tears sparkling in their eyes. For a minute, just a minute, the weight lifted.

DEA OFFICE – TEXAS – NIGHT

Back in the real world, the war room buzzed.

Dim lighting. Coffee-stained files. Tension thicker than fog.

Several agents huddled around a battered wooden table, the faces grim and focused.

"Our CI says AZ is deep underground," Agent Jobs said, tapping a grainy photo pinned to the wall. "We need a local connection. Someone who knows who they call Nephew. He's running day-to-day."

Agent Robbins frowned, scribbling notes.

"All we got is a name? 'Nephew'?"

Agent Jobs nodded sharply.

"For now. But we're digging."

"What about Atlanta?" Agent Sharp chimed in.

Agent Jobs pulled out another file.

"They've narrowed it down to two suspects. One's ID'd and under surveillance. Control buys are coming soon."

"Good," Agent Robbins said. "I'll send some boys to the ground. We find this 'Nephew'—we cut the head off the snake."

RESTAURANT – EVENING

The upscale restaurant hummed with quiet conversations and the clink of silverware. Business deals brewed over wine and steak.

At a corner table, Tom Tom and T-Money leaned forward, eyes sharp. Across from them, two rugged Mexican associates sat stone-faced, their translator Carlos smoothing the conversation.

"We need a solid product at the right price," Tom Tom said. "Plenty of money to be made."

Carlos translated quickly, Spanish rolling off his tongue.

The Mexican associate nodded, lips pressed tight.

"No problema," he answered in Spanish. "I'm assembling my team. Thirty to forty-five days."

Carlos relayed the message.

Tension hung in the air.

"Let him know," Tom Tom said, voice low, "time's of the essence."

Carlos spoke again, and the Mexican man's expression darkened. He responded with a growl.

"There's a war at home," Carlos translated. "Routes and tunnels blocked. But he promises—soon, everything will move again."

T-Money and Tom Tom exchanged a hard look.

They didn't like depending on promises.

But in this life? You either waited—or you bled.

Tom Tom leaned back, smirking faintly.

"Guess we don't have a choice but to wait."

He raised his glass slightly in a silent toast—not to success. Not to survive.

To the hustle.
To the fight.
To the madness they all knew too well.

The city tightened its grip. Fear prowled the streets.
The Fist fought to expand.
The YNG prepared for war.
And the clock ticked louder with every passing second, counting down to the next betrayal, the next body, the next fall.
In a world where loyalty crumbled faster than concrete and power shifted with every bullet fired, everyone was hustling to stay one step ahead of the storm.
But deep down, they all knew—
The storm was already here.

Chapter 35

The streets had grown colder. Tighter. Fear and ambition moved hand in hand now—one wrong step, and the whole empire could crumble.

But tonight?
Tonight they weren't thinking about war.
They were stepping into something bigger.

Something that could change it all.

PARKING LOT – EVENING

Kev sat stiffly in his car, heart pounding against his ribs. His hands gripped a brown duffel bag like it contained his soul. Across the lot, a blacked-out Charger eased to a stop beside him.

Kev swallowed hard. His fingers trembled as he opened his door and slid into the passenger seat of Big Rich's car.

Across the street, hidden in the shadows, a faint click echoed—the cold eye of a camera capturing everything.

Inside the car, Big Rich glanced down at the bag Kev clutched against his chest.

"You lucky I mess with you," Big Rich muttered, voice low. "You know it's a drought out here. Ain't too many people working."

Kev nodded quickly, desperate.

"I know, man. I need this bad."

Big Rich's eyes narrowed slightly.

"You heard anything about Eddie B?"

Kev shook his head.

"Naw. Not since that night at the club."

Big Rich nodded once, thoughtful.

"Well... if you do, let me know. Got something nice for you."

They exchanged bags, hands quick and silent like professional thieves.

Kev stepped out, pulling his hoodie tighter around his face, and disappeared into the evening.

Big Rich watched him for a second before peeling off into the night, tires humming like a viper.

STRIP CLUB – NIGHT

The air was thick with smoke and sex. Basslines rattled the gold-trimmed walls. In a VIP section, Kareem lounged, drink in hand, smoke curling from the blunt hanging loosely from his fingers.

Sin City and Voodoo Doll danced inches from him—perfect bodies, shimmering under neon lights.

Kareem leaned forward, grinning lazily.

"How you get the name Voodoo Doll?"

Voodoo Doll's grin widened, hips still swaying hypnotically.

"Baby, I'm from New Orleans. But they call me that 'cause once I put this wet box on 'em... they can't leave me alone."

Kareem chuckled, deep and genuine.

"So that's how you got Fabo sprung?"

Voodoo Doll rolled her eyes dramatically, earning a laugh from Sin City.

"He's a joke," she said.

"We need a real man," Sin City teased, flicking her tongue over her front teeth.

Kareem smirked wider.

"What time y'all leaving the club?"

Voodoo Doll leaned closer, perfume sweet and dangerous.

"Tonight no good," she said, sliding her phone across the table. "But I'ma put your number in Sin City's phone."

"Cool," Kareem said, watching her type. "Can't wait to see what the hype about"

UNDERCOVER POLICE CAR – NIGHT

The inside of the car smelled like old leather and coffee. Spike shifted in the passenger seat, nerves crawling under his skin. Across from him, two plainclothes Officers watched like vultures.

"You sure I got full immunity?" Spike muttered, wiping sweat from his forehead.

"Yeah," Officer 1 said. "You signed the papers."

Spike exhaled slowly, shoulders sagging.

"Alright... Slime's planning something big this weekend. He calls it '4th of July.' Lots of fireworks. And I ain't talkin' bout no firecrackers."

Officer 1 leaned in.

"Where?"

Spike shrugged helplessly.

"He ain't revealed the spot yet."

"Fine," Officer 2 said, cracking his knuckles. "When y'all meet up at the hangout—text me. I need to know when everyone's together."

Spike nodded grimly.
 No turning back now.

CUZ'S HOUSE – DAY

Sunlight painted the cracked pavement golden. Cuz stood in his driveway, tossing a football with his young son, the two laughing, running routes, trying to chase back normal life.

Behind them, a mobile detailer scrubbed soap onto Cuz's Dodge Charger, suds sliding down the gleaming paint.

Across the street, an unmarked black car lurked like a spider.

Inside, two DEA Agents snapped photos with clinical detachment.

Agent 1 watched through the lens, voice dripping sarcasm.

"Waiting on his tax statements," he said. "Might be able to pressure him that way."

Agent 2 chuckled dryly.

"Yeah. They always live outside their means. We're gonna nail all of 'em. Break up the happy family."

Cuz crouched low, guiding his son's small hands into the right position.

"There you go. Plant your foot—boom! Explode out."

His boy ran the perfect route, giggling.
 Cuz's face lit up with pure pride—the kind you couldn't fake.

Inside the car, Agent 1's mouth twisted into a hard line.

"I smell the fear in him," he muttered. "We're gonna bust all their asses. Every. Single. One."

VARIOUS HOMES – NIGHT

A powerful montage unfolded across the city.

T-MONEY AND ZURI
Zuri checked her makeup in the mirror, adjusting the straps of a gold-sequined gown. Behind her, T-Money wrapped his arms around her waist, pulling her close.

"Damn," he whispered against her ear. "You gon' have every man in there jealous tonight."

She smirked, planting a kiss on his cheek.

BUCK AND RENAY
Buck wrestled with his tie, cursing under his breath. Renay, elegant in a deep blue dress, stepped up, fixing it with practiced hands.

"How you tough in the streets but can't tie a damn tie?" she teased.

"Hey," Buck said, grinning. "I got people for that."

DEE AND SUMMER
Summer leaned into the mirror, smoothing her eyeliner. Dee watched from the bed, head tilted in admiration.

"Take a picture," she said, catching his stare.

"I just might," Dee murmured.

BAY AND SUGAR
Sugar snapped selfies, hips popped to one side. Bay leaned in the doorway, arms crossed, grinning.

"Damn, woman, we supposed to be on time."

"And you supposed to be complimenting me," she fired back, flipping her hair.

KAREEM AND SAVANNAH
Savannah zipped up her dress with a wink over her shoulder. Kareem watched her from the bed, amused.

"You just gonna sit there?" she teased.

"Nah," Kareem said, rising. "Just waiting for you to say we ain't going no more."

ASH AND SKY
Sky slipped on dangerous-looking heels while Ash fastened his cufflinks, stealing a glance at her legs.

"You gonna be able to walk in those?" he teased.

"Baby," she said, flashing a grin, "I was born in these."

D-BO AND SHAN
D-Bo fixed his bowtie. Shan wrapped her arms around him from behind, resting her head against his back.

"Looking sharp, babe."

"I know," he smirked.

She playfully smacked his chest, laughing.

TOM AND Tamika
Tamika paced, frantic, checking her phone every few seconds.

"We are late, we late!" she cried.

Tom calmly laced his shoes, unfazed.

"We Black. We right on time."

WHITEBOY

Alone in his mirror, White Boy straightened his bowtie, popped his collar, and winked at himself.

"Still got it," he muttered.

The final shots stitched them together:

Each couple stepped into the night, dressed like royalty.
Cameras flashed. Engines roared. Tires kissed asphalt.

Tonight was bigger than business.
It was about respect. Image. Power. Legacy.

The city buzzed with silent tension as the players moved into position.
Deals were made. Betrayals whispered. Families armored themselves in tuxedos and silk.
Everyone is smiling on the surface.
Everyone knowing—
Behind the flash and glamour...
The next shot fired could change everything.

Chapter 36

Sometimes the streets teach you one kind of power.
Tonight, they were learning another.
The kind built in ballrooms, with smiles sharp as razors, and deals cut behind wine glasses.
A world where the highest bidder ruled, and legacy wasn't earned with bullets—but with checks.

INT. ELEGANT BALLROOM – NIGHT

The grand ballroom shimmered under the light of towering chandeliers, every inch dripping in wealth and polish. Gold-trimmed walls framed breathtaking artwork. The air buzzed—a low hum of laughter, murmured conversations, and the gentle clinking of wine glasses.

Atlanta's elite were out in full force tonight—business moguls, entertainers, politicians, old money, and new kings and queens rising.

At the podium, Mayor Devonta Smith lifted a crystal glass, flashing that politician's perfect smile.

"Ladies and gentlemen," he boomed, charm oozing from every word, **"thank you all for being here tonight. Your generosity will help shape the future of the Atlanta school system."**

Polite applause rippled through the room. Servers weaved effortlessly through the crowd, balancing silver trays, refilling glasses with champagne that cost more than some folks' rent.

Near the front, Sammy stood with The Fist beside him—T-Money, Buck, Ash, Tom Tom, and Dee—each one freshly pressed in tuxedos, trying to blend into a world they'd only seen from a distance.

Sammy smirked, nudging them lightly.

"See this?" he said low, voice steady. **"Power. Money. Legacy. This is where real moves are made."**

The young men nodded, their wide eyes drinking in the scene.
 It wasn't just a room full of rich people—it was an entire ecosystem of influence.

Across the stage, a sharply dressed auctioneer stepped up to the microphone.

"Alright, ladies and gentlemen, let's get this show started!" he called, voice booming.

The energy shifted—eyes sharpened, wallets loosened. The first item rolled onto the platform: a priceless painting, its frame sparkling under the lights.

BIDDING WAR #1 – SAMMY VS. MICHAEL

The auctioneer raised his gavel.

"We'll start at ten thousand dollars—do I hear ten?"

A hand shot up instantly.
The room tightened—this was the beginning of the dance.

"Fifteen!" another voice rang out.

Sammy raised his hand, smooth and deliberate.

"Twenty!"
MICHAEL—young, sharp, and cocky—smirked from across the room and joined the fray.

Sammy squinted slightly, sizing him up.

"Oh, he wants to play," he muttered under his breath.

The numbers climbed—twenty-five, thirty, thirty-five.
Back and forth like two chess masters bluffing at a poker table.

Finally, Sammy grinned wide and leaned back.

"I'm the Big Dog," he said loudly, withdrawing with swagger.

The crowd chuckled, some clapping lightly. Michael flashed a tight smile—proud, but clearly relieved.
Dignity intact. But everybody knew—**Sammy had owned the moment.**

BIDDING WAR #2 – RUSSELL VS. PINKY

Next up: a vintage Rolex, gleaming under the spotlight.

Russell, a clean-cut investment banker, tossed up his hand without hesitation. Across from him, Pinky—bold, beautiful, and unbothered—lifted her wine glass and smirked.

The auctioneer's voice rolled out like thunder.

"Fifteen. Twenty. Twenty-five!"

Pinky raised her hand lazily, mock applause following her move.

Russell straightened his tie.
Thirty.

Pinky giggled, licking her lips as she lifted two fingers.

"Thirty-five."

The room buzzed.
It wasn't just a bid—it was a battle.

Russell checked his own watch—a subtle flex—and without missing a beat, barked out:

"Forty."

Pinky held his stare... then smiled sweetly and bowed out.
The crowd erupted in laughter and cheers.

"A'ight, man. You got that one," Pinky said with a wink.

Russell tipped his glass, victorious.

BIDDING WAR #3 – FRANKLIN VS. JACKSON

The final war wasn't playful.
It was deadly serious.

The auctioneer unveiled the crown jewel: a luxury penthouse vacation package.
Starting bid: $50,000.

Jackson, a low-key billionaire, barely lifted his hand—like he was brushing off lint.

Franklin, a record label exec, smirked and raised without hesitation.

Sixty.
Seventy.
Eighty.

Whiskey glass in hand, Jackson moved like he had all the time in the world.

Franklin leaned forward, hungry.

Ninety.

The tension was thick enough to cut.

Finally, Jackson waved his hand again—nonchalant.

"One hundred and twenty thousand dollars."

Silence.

Franklin exhaled sharply. He was out.
The crowd exploded with applause.

Jackson didn't smile. Didn't gloat.
Just nodded slightly.
A lion among cubs.

THE FIST – TAKING IT ALL IN

Sammy turned to his young squad, eyes gleaming.

"Now you see?" he said quietly. "**This ain't about what you're buying. It's about *what you're showing*. It's about *who sees you*."

The Fist nodded, awe and ambition swirling in their eyes.

Tonight wasn't just about money.
 It was about learning a new kind of hustle.

One played with suits, not ski masks.

INT. AFTER-PARTY – NIGHT

The scene shifted to a more relaxed but no less impressive setting.

Smooth R&B rolled through the space. Laughter rose from different pockets of conversation. Fine whiskey and aged wine flowed like water.

Sammy leaned in conversation with a guest when Jackson approached, radiating effortless authority.

"Thanks for letting my granddaughter shadow you," Jackson said warmly. **"I told her you're the best in the business when it comes to finance and CPA work."**

Sammy grinned, clapping Jackson on the shoulder.

"Pleasure's all mine. She's sharp—sharp enough that *I* learned a thing or two."

Jackson chuckled, a proud glint in his eyes.

"She's got it. Maybe even better than me."

He turned to The Fist—now gathered like eager students.

"Gentlemen," Jackson said, shaking each hand firmly. **"You've got yourselves a hell of a mentor. Listen closely. Apply it. Information is free—application is rare."**

The young men nodded solemnly.

Suddenly, the DJ grabbed the mic.

"Alright, y'all! Time to break a leg and sweat!"

The beat dropped hard.

"Swag Surfin'" blared through the speakers—and the whole room moved in unison, bodies rocking side to side, arms swaying above their heads.

Wild energy.
Laughter.
Victory.

The DJ flipped it to "Bankhead Bounce," the rhythm contagious.
Then Yung Joc's "It's Goin' Down" took over—people strutting and dancing, reliving the good times.

Finally, as the energy softened, Outkast's "Sorry Ms. Jackson" crooned through the speakers.

– THE ROOM
A sea of Black excellence.
Dancing. Smiling. Building.

Not just chasing a bag.
Chasing legacy.

Tonight, something shifted.

Not in the streets.
Not in the clubs.
But right here—under gold chandeliers, with clean money and sharper minds.

And tomorrow?
The city wouldn't know what hit it.

Tonight wasn't just about money.
It wasn't even about power.
It was about awakening.

For the first time, The Fist stood in a world where bullets and backdoors didn't rule — *balance sheets did.*
Where silent nods replaced street wars, and the right handshake could flip a life faster than a Glock ever could.

They had learned how true kings moved:
Not with noise, but with strategy.
 Not chasing clout, but building empires.

The air in that ballroom was different — thicker, sharper.
It smelled like old money and new opportunity.
It tasted like the future.

And in the back of their minds, they all felt it:
The streets they came from were getting hotter.
The walls were closing in.
But if they played it right—
if they stayed patient, moved smart, and listened—
then maybe, just maybe, they'd live long enough to sit at tables like this...
and not just survive the city — but own it.

Tomorrow would bring enemies, betrayal, and blood.

But tonight?
Tonight was a glimpse of the promised land.

And they were hungry for more.

Chapter 37

The night was thick with smoke and suspicion.

CAR – NIGHT

Slime and KK sat parked outside the YNG hangout, smoking, the car windows cracked just enough to let the smoke bleed into the humid air.

KK exhaled a cloud, his voice low, heavy.

"I'ma be real... I think Spike or Nut snitchin'... maybe both."

Slime raised an eyebrow, pausing mid-puff. "That's a big allegation. You sure?"

KK leaned back against the seat, thinking out loud. "Think about it. Ever since we got pulled in for questioning, things have been moving strange. They had us in them rooms separately, drillin' us."

Slime nodded slowly, contemplating. "Yeah... things have been offbeat. Well, after tonight, we gon' be on world news. We snatch them up, see who is saying' what."

KK glanced sideways. "What about Blackie? You know how she feels about Spike."

Slime shrugged. "That's her brother... but if he ain't right, he gotta pay."

A long, tense beat hung between them. No more words were needed.

BLACKIE'S MOM'S HOME – NIGHT

Blackie paced the living room, agitated. She called out, impatience laced through her voice.

"Come on, Spike! You got us late. What's taking so long?"

In the bathroom, Spike hunched over his phone, typing fast.

ON SCREEN – TEXT MESSAGE:

SPIKE: Go now. 4th July happens tonight.

A vibration. A reply buzzed back.

OFFICER (REPLY):

Everyone there? The top leaders?

Spike's thumbs flew across the screen.

Yep. All in place. Hurry up.

He stared at the phone for a long moment before pocketing it. His face hardened, a forced grin breaking across it as he stepped out.

"Forcing a laugh," he called down the hallway, "Here I come, sis. Stomach actin' up."

Blackie smirked. "Oh, the Fourth of July surprise got you with the bubble guts? You scared? Go to church."

Spike gave a hollow chuckle. His eyes flickered—uneasy, unreadable.

Another buzz on his phone:

ON SCREEN – TEXT MESSAGE:

ON THE WAY.

Spike inhaled deeply, whispering to himself, "I was born for this."

He straightened his back and followed his sister out.

YNG HANGOUT – NIGHT

The night erupted in chaos.

Dark vans and unmarked police cars screeched into position, doors bursting open. SWAT and plainclothes officers stormed in, shouting commands.

Gunfire cracked the silence.

BAM! BAM!

YNG gang members scrambled, pulling weapons, returning fire blindly. Officers ducked behind cover, answering back.

It was a full-blown warzone.

STREET NEARBY – NIGHT

KK and Slime watched from a parked car, wide-eyed as the firefight unfolded.

"Told you something wasn't right," KK muttered, shaking his head.

Slime exhaled hard, his gut twisting. "If we hadn't stopped to eat, we'd be in there."

Another car screeched to a stop next to them. Blackie and Spike sat inside, stunned. Blackie stared at the chaos.

"Damn, bro... looks like your bad stomach saved us," she said under her breath.

Spike clutched the wheel tighter, silent.

OUTSIDE YNG HANGOUT – NIGHT

A news van skid to a stop, reporters tumbling out with their cameras ready. Lights flared. Microphones pointed toward the action.

A female reporter stood in front of the wreckage, speaking live to the city.

"We've been told this is a major takedown of the YNG gang—suspected in car thefts, pawnshop heists, and multiple murders across the city."

Behind her, the night flashed with sirens and gunshots.

YNG HANGOUT – NIGHT

Inside, the smell of gunpowder hung heavy.

Cops moved methodically, handcuffing battered and bloodied gang members. Weapons were strewn across the floors. Blood slicked the broken tiles.

Captain Woods strode into the carnage, scanning the wreckage like a field general.

"Status?" he barked.

An officer approached, flipping through notes.

"Two wounded officers. Four suspects were injured. Three dead."

"What did we recover?" Woods asked.

"Over 200 firearms. Thousands of pills. Thirty-three arrests."

Woods nodded, satisfaction cold on his face.

"Any sign of the ones they call Slime and Blackie?"

The officer shook his head. "Not sure. We'll know when we fingerprint each other at the station."

Woods smirked, knowing a win when he saw one.

"Good work. All thanks to our CIs."

The officer handed over a file. Spike's name was circled in red.

"Two of 'em. They gave us everything."

Woods tucked the file under his arm, straightening his uniform.

"The Mayor and Chief are gonna love this," he said. "Let me go smile for the cameras—might be the only time they let me shine."

YNG HANGOUT – NIGHT

Captain Woods stepped into the glow of the news cameras.
Behind him, cuffed gang members were loaded into transport vans. Doors slammed shut with an echo that filled the night air.

Bystanders gathered on sidewalks, some whispering, others shaking their heads.

"About damn time," one muttered.

"Ain't gonna change nothing'," another said, bitter. "More just gon' take their place."

The reporter pressed closer.

"Captain, what's next? Will there be more arrests?"

Woods didn't hesitate.

"You bet."

The tension crackled like static as the last prisoner van rolled away into the darkness.

STRIP CLUB – NIGHT

The neon glow of the club pulsed like a slow heartbeat.
A group of women—Tan, February, Rainbow, and Hawaii—stumbled out, laughing, their heels clicking against the pavement.

Tan, slightly ahead, made her way to her car, her keys jingling.

From the shadows, Razor emerged, low and predatory.

Gun drawn, he whispered, "Get in the car. Now."

Tan froze. The world seemed to shrink.

He nudged her forward, forcing her into the passenger seat. The door slammed shut. Tires screeched as they peeled off.

Rainbow, chatting with security, caught the tail end of it—the car disappearing into the night. Her stomach twisted with a feeling she couldn't name.

T-MONEY'S HOME – MORNING

Morning sunlight slanted across the living room.

T-Money and Zuri sat on the couch, watching the news in silence. Footage of YNG members getting dragged into jail cells looped on the screen.

T-Money shook his head. "I can't lie... last night had me up thinking. We just rubbed elbows with real billionaires."

Zuri nodded. "Me and the girls were talking. We need to step our game up—get on some real black power."

T-Money leaned forward, elbows on his knees. "That's what Sammy has been on. If we weren't convinced before, we are now. He's been trying to pull our coattails."

Zuri grabbed her keys. "Yeah, he's in the loot-loot.
Look, I gotta go pick up the kids from Mommy. I'll call you later."

T-Money watched her leave, the words hanging between them like a silent vow.

CAR LOT – DAY

The heat pressed down on the cracked pavement.

Buck, Dee, Bay, Tom Tom, and Kareem lounged around, the tension from last night still crackling in the air.

Tom Tom shook his head. "Man, last night was mad real. They were spending our re-up money on paintings.
We gotta tighten up."

Bay nodded. "I was thinking the same thing. Maybe we should take Sammy more seriously."

Buck cracked a grin. "He's come a long way...
and now he's in the same rooms as billionaires."

Dee nodded, hearing Jackson's words replay in his mind:

"We all get information, but how you use it makes all the difference."

Kareem pushed his hat back. "Yeah, we gotta lock in.
But first, we need to figure out our next check—we're low, low on product."

Buck smirked. "Nephew said he's taking over the business for AZ.
He's setting up as we speak."

Tom Tom added, "Me and T-Money talked with Carlos' plug.
He said he needs about two months."

Bay looked around, serious now. "Y'all heard about YNG getting busted?"

The group exchanged heavy glances.
They all nodded.

The streets had shifted.
 And whether they were ready or not, a new game had begun.

Chapter 38

Dea Office – Texas – Day

The office buzzed with quiet urgency.
A handful of DEA agents sat around a conference table littered with folders, laptops, and coffee cups. Fluorescent lights buzzed overhead.

Agent Jobs held up two photographs, studying them carefully.

"Our CI gave us these," he said, voice steady. "One's from about five years ago, and the other—him with the lady—less than a year old."

Agent Robbins leaned forward, squinting. "You running them through our database? See if we can get a name or last location?"

Agent Jobs smirked. "Already a step ahead. Just waiting for the lab report."

Across the table, Agent Wynn tapped his pen against a notepad.

"Atlanta DEA's making good progress," he said. "One of the Atlanta Buck control buys went through."

Agent Jobs nodded, satisfied. "Good. As soon as I hear from the lab, I'll update you.
This 'nephew' character... he's our way to bringing down one of the biggest drug cartels."

The room fell silent, the weight of that possibility sinking in.

OUTSIDE A RESTAURANT – DAY

On a dimly lit outdoor patio, Slime and Blackie sat at a table, half-eaten plates and sweating drinks between them. A slow, heavy breeze blew through the alley.

Slime leaned in, voice low. "I think Nut and Spike are working with the police."

Blackie stiffened, setting her drink down slowly. "What makes you say that?"

"Simple math," Slime said, lighting a cigarette. "Both of them knew not to be there. Both got picked up and questioned."

Blackie narrowed her eyes. "Then why didn't you include KK? He got questioned too—and wasn't there either."

Slime smirked, smoke curling from his lips. "Because KK wasn't there 'cause I asked him to roll with me and grab something to eat. What did Spike say?"

Blackie thought for a moment. "Said he had a stomach virus."

Slime chuckled, dark and humorless. "Yeah... because he knew."

Blackie exhaled through her nose, a slow, deliberate breath.
"Alright, then. We gather them all up.
Put them in a life-or-death situation. See who cracks."

Slime nodded. "Cool. But we gotta lay low. I'm sure they're looking for us. We need a money move—fast.
Until then, we stay in the shadows."

Their eyes met, an unspoken agreement made under the dying afternoon sun.

WESTSIDE SPOT – NIGHT

A dimly lit room swallowed in heavy silence.
Stacks of cash, guns, and loose papers littered a table.

Westside Buck sat back in a chair, deep in thought. Suge leaned against the wall, arms crossed.
A phone buzzed on the table. Buck snatched it up.

Big Rich's voice came over the line, casual but firm.

"Man, the drought has been good. I charged Kev thirty-four, and everybody else thirty-three. Run through them things quick."

Buck nodded to himself. "Yeah, they moved fast. Big Tony comes home tomorrow. Any word on Eddie B?"

Big Rich didn't miss a beat. "Man, ol' girl damn near livin' with his lady. The nigga ain't been home in weeks."

Buck's eyes narrowed. "You sure she ain't playin' both sides?"

Big Rich chuckled. "Trust me, she wants that extra five grand like a bum wants five dollars."

Buck leaned forward, the weight of the streets heavy on his shoulders. "Cool. When you coming by?"

Big Rich replied smoothly, "Be there in an hour."

Buck hung up and tossed the phone onto the table.
The room buzzed low with a dangerous energy.

ATLANTA DEA OFFICE – NIGHT

The tension was palpable.
A row of desks, cluttered with wiretap monitors, buzzed under fluorescent lights.

Agent Harrington and Agent Parker sat side-by-side, headphones on, reading live transcriptions scrolling across the monitors.

"We might be hearing about a murder about to go down," Agent Harrington said, eyes locked on the screen. "I need to run this up top, see what they say."

Agent Parker nodded. "We need to find Eddie B. Could kill three birds with one stone."

Agent Harrington jotted a quick note, already moving.
"Good thinking. I'll run that by them—things are heating up.
I gotta get with Kev."

The office buzzed with urgency. The walls were closing in.

HOTEL ROOM – NIGHT

The suite was wrapped in a hazy glow—dim lighting, smoke lingering, loud music vibrating the walls.

It was a wild night in progress.

Kareem sprawled across a plush bed, drink in hand, his tie undone.
Two women—Sin City and Voodoo Doll—were draped over him, naked, tipsy, indulging in each other, their laughter mixing with the bass.

Kareem chuckled, shaking his head. "Damn, y'all the bonfire truth.
I gotta add y'all to my heavy rotation."

Voodoo Doll winked, her voice sultry. "Told you, Daddy.
All we wanna do is please you."

Kareem raised his glass, grinning wide and picking up his cell phone fake dial number .
 "That, y'all do— hello put your mommy on the phone look here bitch I'm never coming home"

They laughed, bodies tangled in the low light, the night slipping deeper into beautiful, dangerous chaos.

The city roared outside, but up here... nothing else existed.

Chapter 39

THE OFFICE – NIGHT

The small, cluttered office buzzed with low conversation and the heavy scent of hot wings and smoke.
A flickering TV played in the background, its glow casting long shadows across worn-out couches.

WhiteBoy and D-Bo sat at a small table, locked into a slow, grinding chess match. Nearby, Buck, T-Money, Tom Tom, and Ash lounged, devouring wings, eyes occasionally flickering toward the TV.

The door swung open with a burst of night air.
AG, Melbo, Snow, and Fireball strode in, each carrying heavy gym bags. Without a word, they dropped them onto the counter with a dull thud—the sound of money.

Snow grinned, shaking his head as he wiped his hands on his jeans.

"Work's running low, low. We'll be out in a few days."

AG leaned back against the wall, casual but serious.
"Truth be told, we could've been out already. Just been choosy about who we're selling to."

T-Money nodded slowly, his expression unreadable.

"We milked the game good," he said. "But it's time for a new check."

Tom Tom leaned forward, elbows on his knees.
"What's the word on the streets? Dry or still moving?"

Melbo shrugged. "Work's been showing up, but numbers ain't changed. Westside Buck was working."

WhiteBoy narrowed his eyes, setting his chess piece down.

"Speaking of Buck... we need to find Eddie B. He's been missing long enough."

D-Bo shook his head, clicking his tongue. "I spoke with him briefly. He outta his mind... the drugs got him."

T-Money exhaled, a dark cloud hanging over the room.

"Damn," he muttered. "We need to put together a search party—find our brother before it's too late."

The room fell into heavy silence, the weight of loyalty pressing on all of them.

T-T'S HOME – NIGHT

Laughter bounced off the walls of the cozy living room, mixing with the low hum of music and the lazy swirl of smoke in the air.

Yaya, Red, and T-T sat around a worn table, playing cards and sipping from tall glasses, the smell of weed hanging thick.

Yaya threw her head back, laughing as she slapped a card down.

"Girl, I went over to Bo's house, and when I tell you—he had me cummin' three, four times.
I had to soak for an hour afterwards."

T-T groaned dramatically, tossing her card down.

"Please, don't talk about sex.
I'm going through double withdrawals. Missing Eddie... and him beatin' my back out."

Red chuckled, raising her glass. "You heard from him again?"

T-T nodded, her smile small but hopeful.

"Twice. It's about time for him to come home.
Keonna's birthday is coming up—he ain't gonna miss that."

Red lifted her glass higher.

"We drink to that. He does love his kids."

T-T smiled, a little sadness slipping through.

"He loves his family," she said softly. "Just got a few problems.
 Your play, Yaya."

The cards shuffled, the laughter returned—but beneath it all, a quiet current of worry remained.

SAMMY'S HOUSE – NIGHT

The house was warm with low light and rich with the smell of burning sage and rolled blunts.
A small chess table sat in the middle of the room where Sammy and T-Money played, heads bent over the board.

Tom Tom and Ash lounged nearby, passing a blunt between them, the night soft and serious.

Sammy made a slow move across the board, speaking without looking up.

"See, my dad always told me—making money ain't the hard part.
The key is how much you can keep."

Ash snorted, exhaling smoke.

"Man, I keep hearing you say shit like that."

Sammy grinned.

"'Cause it's true. How many times have y'all been broke or down bad?"

T-Money shook his head, a wry smile on his lips.

"Too many to count.
But this system you put in place—'leave no man behind'—it changed the game for us."

Sammy nodded, moving another piece.

"Exactly. Once we understand the power of strength in numbers? As a whole? The Black race would be untouchable."

Ash leaned forward, tapping his fingers against the table.

"You think we'll ever really come together like that?"

Sammy looked up, serious now.

"We did. Back when segregation was a thing.
We had Black Wall Street.
If we wanna be here a hundred years from now, we gotta move smarter—
'cause that window of opportunity? It's closing."

T-Money nodded, lost in thought.

"I can't lie... I had this book *Rich Dad, Poor Dad* sittin' on my shelf.
Wasn't even reading it. But after going to that auction?
Made me pick it back up."

Sammy's smile widened.

"Good book. Read it twice."

He moved another piece, trapping T-Money's bishop.

"Y'all remember Jackson?"

Tom Tom sat up straighter.

"The billionaire? Hell yeah."

Sammy's eyes gleamed.

"He wasn't always rich. Dropped outta high school just to help his family survive."

He paused, savoring the moment, letting the lesson hang there.

"Started working construction. Learned the game. Built his own business.
Got his GED. Took four years of business college."

T-Money moved his rook, trying to keep up.

"Damn," he muttered. "He really is the GOAT."

Sammy nodded, sliding his queen across the board.

"And it doesn't stop there. Built an empire, invested in a few fast-food franchises...
then one day, decided to sell most of it off."

Tom Tom leaned in, blunt dangling from his lips.

"Wait—why'd he sell everything?"

Sammy leaned back, his voice dropping low.

"Two things: stress and health.
 Cost him two marriages, trying to run all them businesses, always on the move.
 That's when I talked to him about passive income—the white man's game."

T-Money frowned. "Passive income? What's that?"

Sammy chuckled, tapping the side of his head.

"See, rich folks don't work for money.
They make their money work for them all about the right investment. ETF best alphabets you can learn."

He started ticking points off with his fingers.

"Smart investments.
Stocks.
Real estate.
Dividends.
Getting paid without lifting a finger."

Tom Tom laughed, shaking his head.

"Sammy, man, you talkin' alphabet soup. Only letters we know stand for FBI, DEA, and DA."

The group exploded into laughter.

Sammy lit a fresh joint, grinning.

"A'ight, lemme break it down easy."

He took a pull and exhaled a slow cloud of smoke.

"ETFs—like a basket of strong companies stocks you invest in all at once like Apple Home Depot Coke."

"REITs—real estate investments where you get paid like a landlord without owning property."

"IPOs—getting in early on companies before they blow up."

The group nodded, starting to catch the rhythm.

Sammy moved his final piece across the board.

"And... checkmate."

T-Money stared at the board, stunned.
The others laughed, clapping him on the back.

"Damn," T-Money said, shaking his head. "You tricked me.
Had me caught up in that rags-to-riches story."

The laughter filled the house, thick with hope and fire for something bigger than the block.
The night stretched on—talk of money, life, and legacy dancing in the smoke.

The night inched toward morning, but the lessons still burned in their chests.
In a world where bullets spoke louder than ambition, and fast money crumbled just as quick, the real game wasn't played in the alleys—it was played in rooms filled with patience, knowledge, and power.

T-Money, Tom Tom, Buck, Ash, and D-Bo weren't just hearing stories anymore—they were starting to understand the rules.
It wasn't about who flashed the most cash at the club, or who had the freshest whip.
It was about who could outlast, outthink, and outbuild.

Sammy didn't just school them on stocks and strategies—he gave them a glimpse into a world most never lived long enough to reach.
A world where your last name held more weight than your street name.
Where you didn't just hustle for a chain—you hustled for a legacy.

And sitting around that chessboard, with smoke swirling and laughter cutting through the heavy air, something shifted.
Something real.

The Fist wasn't just fighting for a corner anymore.
They were plotting for an empire.

An empire that couldn't be raided, busted, or gunned down.
An empire that could only be toppled if they let it.

Outside, the streets of Atlanta kept breathing their usual chaos—sirens, heartbreak, and betrayal around every corner.

But inside Sammy's house, a new fire had been lit.
And for once, it wasn't destruction on their minds.

It was destiny.

Chapter 40

The classroom was dim, smelling faintly of old books and disinfectant. A battered chess board sat at the center of the room, pieces scattered like soldiers awaiting orders.
At the front stood Duke—a rugged, wise man who spoke with the kind of authority earned, not given.

T-Money raised his hand, sharp curiosity in his eyes.
"How does the Queen move?" he asked.

Duke smiled, sliding the Queen smoothly across the board.
"She moves any way she wants. Straight, diagonal, whatever path she chooses."

Buck leaned forward. "What about the Rook?"

Duke shifted the Rook in a straight line, his movements firm and precise.

Ash piped up next. "And the Knight?"

Duke lifted the Knight, showing its strange, deliberate L-shape.
"The only piece that can leap over others," he said with a wink.

Kareem chimed in, "How 'bout the Bishop?"

Duke glided the Bishop across the board diagonally, like a blade slicing through defenses.

Eddie B, grinning, leaned back in his chair. "I'm a soldier. What about the Pawns?"

Duke hovered his hand above the smallest pieces on the board. His expression grew serious.

"The Pawns get slept on a lot 'cause they move small and slow. But most times... the one with the strongest Pawn game wins the whole damn thing."

The young men exchanged looks, that one line sinking deeper than any textbook ever could.

T-Money tilted his head. "What's the point of chess, anyway?"

Duke crossed his arms, his voice dropping low, like he was handing over a secret.
"It's a thinking man's game. Strategy. It teaches you to see not just the next move, but two, three, four ahead. To weigh every option... just like life."

Bay, sitting in the back, nodded slowly.
"So it's basically the game of life."

"You hit it dead on," Duke said, smiling.
"Every piece has a role. Some are bigger than others. But if you play 'em right... you get your checkmate."

The chessboard sat still between them. Small pieces. Big consequences.

The hot Georgia sun blazed down on the cracked asphalt of the juvenile yard.
T-Money, Buck, D-Bo, Ash, and Tom Tom walked side by side, low conversation passing between them.

"When we get out," T-Money said, his voice serious, "we are making moves. No more stealing cars. No more kicking in doors."

Buck nodded. "John John has been talking. He might put us on."

D-Bo clenched his fists. "We overdue. All or nothing now."

Ash smirked. "Time for chess moves."

Tom Tom laughed. "Checkmate."

Suddenly, White Boy came sprinting up, breathless, wide-eyed.
"Eddie just beat up Low from Techwood! Now they tryna jump on him!"

The crew exchanged one glance. No words.
They broke into a sprint, headed for the gym.

The juvenile gym was a powder keg ready to explode.

Eddie B stood alone at center court, fists balled at his sides, blood trickling from his lip.
Across from him, a wall of angry faces closed in—Techwood boys, looking for blood.

A single guard stepped between them, tension quivering in the stale air.

The doors flew open.
T-Money and the rest stormed in, positioning themselves behind Eddie without hesitation.

Kareem's voice cut through the noise, calm but lethal.
"Y'all don't want this problem."

The room froze. For a heartbeat, violence hung like humidity.
Nobody made a move.
Nobody dared.

Later that night, the world outside buzzed with life—music, laughter, chaos.

Inside a quiet bedroom, Eddie B sat at the edge of his bed, a stack of photographs in his hand.
Pictures of his daughters.
A smiling T-T.
Him and The Fist, back when loyalty was all they needed.

He stared down at the worn photos, his thumb brushing over cracked edges.
His chest tightened.
The world had changed, and somehow he hadn't changed fast enough.

In a dark, unfinished basement, the silence felt heavier than concrete.

Slime, Blackie, KK, Nut, Trice, MD, Ten, and Spike circled each other, the last remnants of a dying crew.
Fear was thick. Everyone felt it, but no one said it.

MD shoved Nut hard, pressing a gun to his forehead.

Nut's hands went up immediately, trembling. "Man, chill! What's up with all this?!"

Slime stepped forward, face like stone.
"You think you slick? I got people at the station. We know somebody talked."

Nut's voice cracked. "They were gonna pin it all on me! I had no choice! I'm sorry, Slime!"

Blackie's voice was cold, final.
"Too late for that. Say your prayers."

In a desperate move, Nut pointed a trembling finger.
"Wait! Your brother Spike—he's the one! He dragged me in!"

Every head snapped toward Spike.

Spike backed up fast, panic washing over his face.
"Come on, Sis—blood thicker than—"

Bang.
Blackie pulled the trigger without a blink.

Spike's body hit the floor hard, blood pooling fast.

Bang.
Slime shot Nut, ending the last of the betrayal.

They didn't say another word.
One by one, they slipped into the night, ghosts of the streets they once ruled.

At the DEA office, the mood was icy calm.

Four agents sat across from their boss, a man whose suit was pressed sharper than his morals.

Agent Parker spoke first. "Sir, Rich is plotting to kill Eddie B. He's with Southside Buck. Do we step in?"

The boss agent leaned back in his chair, steepling his fingers, his lips curling into a smirk.
"Let it go as far as it needs to."

A pause.
Then the real poison slipped out.

"They're drug dealers... and they're Black. They're doing society a favor."

The agents exchanged silent glances.

No argument.
No conscience.

Just smiles.

The game was no longer just about money or power.
It was about survival in a world where the system didn't just want you locked up—it wanted you erased.

The Fist thought they were players.
Now, they were realizing...

They were Pawns, too.

And the board had just flipped.

Chapter 41

The cigar bar buzzed with life, heavy with smoke and the low hum of laughter. Velvet chairs cradled Atlanta's power players, each one nursing a glass of aged whiskey or a thick cigar between calloused fingers.
In one corner, the velvet tones of Jazmine Sullivan's *"Let It Burn"* floated from a woman on stage, her voice dripping honey and heartbreak.

At a corner table, the real show unfolded. Mayor Smith sat flanked by Jackson, Sammy, and Pinky—the lone woman among the inner circle. Their drinks sweated under the weight of conversation.

Mayor Smith leaned back, exuding smug satisfaction.
"Since we picked up those YNG members, my numbers have been climbing," he said. "Gives me an edge."

Pinky nodded, sipping her drink with careful calculation.
"That's good to hear. This election? It's bigger than a title. There's a lot at stake."

Sammy tapped ash from his cigar, his tone calm but carrying weight.
"Might be the biggest contract era in Atlanta history. Billions on the table. We need somebody we trust calling shots."

The singer's voice soared, pulling a few glances from the room, but the real gravity stayed anchored at the table.

Jackson added, "Expanding the airport, finishing the BeltLine—Atlanta a Black city. We need Black faces at the table."

Mayor Smith lifted his glass.
"I'll drink to that. And I appreciate y'all's support. Means everything."

A group of women approached, grinning wide, excitement dancing in their eyes.
"Mr. Mayor, can we get a picture with you?"

He smiled, always the politician, slipping into position as Sammy snapped the shot.

From the stage, the DJ's voice boomed:
"Ayy, we got the Mayor in the building tonight! Y'all make sure you vote—he understands us better than anybody!"

The bar erupted in cheers.
Mayor Smith flashed a perfect grin, soaking in the glow of manufactured love.

The music rolled on, and deals, bigger than any election, sealed themselves in laughter and smoke.

The night thickened elsewhere, far from velvet chairs and staged photos.

Inside Razor's bando, the world was a different kind of dark.

The rundown apartment stank of old smoke, sweat, and something more dangerous.
Music blasted from a battered stereo, loud and chaotic, off-beat with Razor's wild energy.

Tan sat in a rickety chair, stripped down to her bra and panties, shivering. Her body trembled not from cold, but pure fear.
Across the room, Razor snorted a line off the scarred coffee table, his movements jerky, his mind gone.

The music cut without warning.
Silence swallowed the room whole.

Razor turned, a shark scenting blood, his eyes zeroing in on Tan.

"This is how this works," he said, voice low, deadly calm. "You're gonna show me where Buck stays."

Tan's voice cracked, desperate.
"I—I don't know! I have never been to his house. I'm just a side piece!"

Razor's boots scraped the floor as he closed the distance between them, stopping inches from her face. His breath, hot and ragged, mixed with hers.

"Better tell me something' worth my time," he said, unbuckling his belt, "if you wanna live."

Tan's chest heaved. Tears blurred her vision.
Then, a spark of survival.

"I can show you where his sister is staying!"

Razor's mouth curled into a slow, cruel grin.
"Now we're getting' somewhere."

He shoved her to the floor.
The camera of life tilted, shadows dancing against cracked walls.
Fabric tore.
Tan's choked sobs filled the room, drowning under Razor's heavy breathing.
The music started again, louder, a cruel soundtrack to survival's price.

Daylight hit the gym with a vengeance.

Inside, the Fist pushed themselves harder than the weights they lifted. Treadmills hummed under pounding feet, and a high-energy aerobics class rattled the windows, led by a seventy-year-old powerhouse who refused to acknowledge age.

T-Money wiped sweat from his brow, panting.
"Man, we need a new line fast. Or we're gonna be paying local prices."

Ash grunted in agreement.
 "Don't remind me."

Tom Tom chuckled, bouncing lightly on the balls of his feet.
"I got faith. My man'll come through."

Buck, calm as ever, folded his arms.
"We gotta learn patience."

Bay leaned on a machine.
"You heard back from Nephew?"

Buck nodded.
"Meeting in a few days. Once I drop the rest of the money, we are good."

Across the gym, their women were locked in battle with the aerobics instructor, each refusing to be outworked.

Summer gasped between reps.
"Girl... how is she pushing like that? I know she is close to seventy."

Zuri grimaced, muscles burning.
"Push. We ain't lettin' Granny beat us."

Later, in the locker room, the group cooled down, towels draped over their shoulders, bodies slick with victory.

"Mr. Everything's calling my name," T-Money said, clapping Buck on the shoulder. "Time to chew."

"I can taste that salmon wrap already," Buck added.

Ash smirked.
"Y'all looked like Granny was chasing you."

Skyy snapped back, laughing.
"Don't get twisted. She is the real MVP."

Buck's phone buzzed.

He read the message, face tightening.
"Eddie's been with Tab and Chrissy. Been throwing house cocaine parties."

Bay cursed under his breath.
"We need to pull up."

"Waiting on the Addy now," Buck said, already moving.

Down in a cold basement across town, yellow tape fluttered in stale air. Blood stained the cracked concrete.
Two bodies—Nut and Spike—lay sprawled, vacant eyes staring at the ceiling.

Captain Woods stood over them, his jaw clenched so tight it looked painful.

"We have a problem," he said grimly.
"Our two best witnesses? Dead."

A younger officer shifted uneasily.

"The Chief, DA, and the Mayor—" he started.

"I know," Woods cut him off.
"They were our keys to locking half this city up."

Another officer approached, face pale.
"Building owner says he walked in, found 'em like this."

Woods shook his head slowly.
"Sierra... I didn't think she'd let her own brother get killed."

He turned toward the tape, his face hard as granite.

"We keep this hush-hush. Last thing we need is a media circus. Lock it down tight."

The basement swallowed their words.
Another war was brewing.

And this time, it was far from over.

In a city where survival was a chessboard and loyalty could be bought for the right price, the real pieces weren't the kings and queens—they were the pawns willing to die for a seat at the table.
But the game was shifting.
And death... had just made its next move.

Chapter 42

T-T and Red sat together on the couch, deep into conversation when T-T's phone rang sharply, cutting through the smoke-laced air.
She grabbed it fast, hope lighting up her face.

"Baby!" she answered, almost breathless. "Are you ready to come home?"

Across town, inside Tab's house—

Eddie B sat slumped on the edge of a battered couch, rubbing his face with both hands. A duffel bag sat at his feet, heavy with regret. His voice came tired, worn.

"Yeah," he muttered. "Can you come get me? I'm beat... Sorry for putting y'all through this. I just had to make sure there wasn't no problems when I stabbed that nigga."

T-T tensed immediately.
 "Where are you at? We are good here," she said carefully. "I'm sure y'all can work this out."

Eddie sighed, the sound dragging across the line.
"I doubt it... but it is what it is. 2323 Walker Road, East Point."

T-T turned to Red, urgency flashing in her eyes.
"Wait, write this down."

"Appreciate you," Eddie mumbled.

"I'm walking out in five minutes," T-T said, her voice warm and thick with relief. "Love you."

"Love you too," Eddie answered before the line went dead.

T-T stood up, a grin blooming across her face.
"Yes! My baby is coming home."

Red grabbed her keys, smiling.
 "I gotta go help my mama. Thank God he found his senses."

T-T nodded, glowing.
"It's gon' be a minute before I talk to you. Me and my boo are locking in till our baby's birthday party."

Red pulled her close for a quick hug, then headed out, climbing into her car. As she pulled away, she picked up her phone and dialed a number.

Rich's voice snapped through the line.
"You better have good news."

Red leaned in, voice urgent.
"You better move fast—2323 Walker Road, East Point."

"Gotcha."

Rich hung up without another word.
He turned to his crew, a predatory grin cutting across his face.
"Let's roll. Just found out where Eddie at."

They rushed out. An unmarked car slid from the curb, following closely behind.

On the streets that night—

Inside the tailing car, two federal agents watched the dance unfold.

"We lost him," Agent 1 grunted.

"Get the base to track his phone," snapped Agent 2.

Tension wound the city tight.

Meanwhile, at Mr. Everything Restaurant—

Laughter filled the air as The Fist ate and drank with their women, the table alive with jokes and easy smiles.
Buck's phone buzzed. He answered quickly.

"Yeah?"

Wade's voice came sharp through the receiver.
"I'm sending you a location. Eddie B's there."

Buck nodded, his entire body shifting.
"Good. I'm on my way."

"I'll meet you there," Wade added before the call ended.

Inside Tab's House—

The air was thick with weed smoke, the music turned up so loud it shook the cheap walls. In the back room, Eddie zipped his duffel bag shut. His face was pale, but determined.

Tab leaned against the doorframe, arms folded.
"You heading out?"

Eddie nodded.
"Party's over. Gotta get back to my family."

Tab smiled sadly.
"I get it. Don't be a stranger."

"Never," Eddie promised, throwing the bag over his shoulder.

He moved through the house like a ghost, slipping past the smoke and chaos. People called out to him, laughing, offering drinks. He ignored it all. His eyes were fixed on the door—and the future was waiting just outside it.

Outside Tab's House—

Everything moved in slow motion.

T-T pulled up first, heart pounding with excitement.

Rich's car rolled to a silent stop across the street.

Eddie stepped out onto the porch, locking eyes with T-T. A smile broke across his face, small but real, blooming like hope.

Then—

Gunfire erupted, shattering the moment.
Rich lifted his gun, unloading a full clip.

Bullets slammed into Eddie's chest.

T-T screamed, diving for her gun, returning fire. She hit Rich, dropping him instantly.

Screams rang out as people poured from the house.
DEA cars screeched into view, lights flashing, but it was too late.

T-T fell to her knees beside Eddie, gathering him into her arms, sobbing. Their eyes met one last time—full of love, full of regret.

And then... Eddie was gone.

From the safety of a nearby car, the undercover agents watched, faces blank.

"Call 911?" Agent 1 asked, hesitating.

Agent 2 shook his head grimly.
"We can't blow our cover. The case is still unsealed."

T-T rocked back and forth, screaming Eddie's name to a sky that offered no answers.
Buck and the rest of The Fist rushed toward her, but it was already too late.

The streetlights blurred in her tears as sirens wailed closer.

Across town, inside Blackie's house—

A dimly lit living room sat heavy with grief.
Mommy J perched on the couch, hands wringing nervously in her lap. Blackie stood at the window, staring out into the dark, body taut like a coiled spring.

"I don't understand..." Mommy J's voice cracked. "Why would someone kill your brother? And do you know who that other person was—the one they found with him?"

Blackie's jaw tightened.
"Yeah, Mom. I'm gonna do everything in my power to find out who did this."

Mommy J shook her head. Tears welled in her eyes.
"I never wanted him hangin' around you. When he got shot... I tried to send him away."

Out the window, headlights flared.
Two unmarked police cars pulled up to the curb.

Blackie stiffened.

"I gotta go," she whispered. "Don't tell them I was here."

She grabbed her backpack and slipped out the back door, vanishing into the night just as the front door knocked.

Mommy J wiped her face, steadying herself. She opened the door.

Two detectives stood there, flashing badges.

"We're looking for your daughter, Sierra Jones," the first officer said.

"What's the problem?" Mommy J asked, her voice tight with pain.

"We think she might know something about your son's murder," the second officer said gently.

Mommy J's face twisted in agony.
"So y'all the reason my son's gone?" she whispered.

The officers shifted awkwardly.

"Have you seen or spoken to her recently?"

Mommy J shook her head slowly.
"No. She moved outta here a long time ago."

The detectives nodded, unconvinced but unable to press further.
They stepped back, leaving Mommy J standing in the doorway, grief and rage knotting her soul.

INT. DEA Office – Day

Inside the sterile white walls, seven agents sat facing a large cork board. Pictures of key players stared back at them—some with big red Xs slashed across their faces: Eddie. Big Rich.

Agent Harrington Harrington stood, scanning the board grimly.
"This didn't turn out well. Our case against Westside Buck is falling apart. And now that Big Rich is dead, we can't use any of our evidence."

Agent Parker Parker shook his head.
"Who tipped Rich off? Do we have a name or a number yet?"

Agent Kingsley Kingsley leaned in, tapping a file.
"They're working on it now."

The room hung heavy with disappointment—and the promise that the war was far from over.

In a city where loyalty was paid in blood and trust was nothing more than a pawn on a crumbling board, the streets whispered a cruel truth—
Every victory cost a soul, and every soul lost only sharpened the hunger for revenge.

And the next move was already being made.

Chapter 43

Int. Police Station – Interrogation Room – Day

A cold, sterile room buzzed under a flickering overhead light.
T-T sat stiffly at the metal table, her hands folded tight in her lap. Beside her, her lawyer adjusted his tie, eyes sharp and unreadable.
Across from them, two officers leaned in, skepticism heavy in the air.

"My client was defending her husband," the lawyer stated, voice steady. "He was gunned down in front of her. She's not a felon, and she carries a legal firearm. I have multiple witness statements backing this up."

One of the officers leaned forward, his gaze hard.
"Why were you there, T-T?"

T-T's voice cracked slightly, but she didn't flinch.
"Eddie called me," she said. "Told me to come pick him up."

The second officer jotted something down.
"So, you were waiting outside? He stepped out—and all hell broke loose?"

T-T nodded slowly. Her eyes brimmed with tears, her jaw locking tight.
She wasn't just telling her story—she was reliving her nightmare.

DEA OFFICE – LATER

The air inside the office was thick with defeat.
Agents sat slouched in their chairs, staring at computer monitors and empty coffee cups.

"We're back to square one," Agent Harrington grumbled, his hand raking through his hair. "The boss is pissed."

"We got a man posted at East Point station," Agent 2 offered. "Listening in on Eddie's wife's statement."

"We're gonna have to throw Kev in with Westside Buck," Agent Kingsley added. "Get him close. Get that number. Make 'em feel safe enough to start doing business again."

No one disagreed. They were in salvage mode now.

CAR LOT – NIGHT

A heavy fog clung to the ground under the sickly yellow parking lot lights. The Fist stood together in a loose circle, their faces hollow, grief clamping down on them harder than any enemy ever could.

T-Money broke the silence first, voice heavy.
"We failed our brother."

White Boy shook his head, looking lost.
"I never saw it ending like this... Where do we go from here?"

Buck stepped forward, his eyes rimmed red but hard.
"We stay strong—for T-T, for the kids."

Kareem looked down at the ground, scuffing his boot against the concrete.
"We saw the signs. The writing was on the wall."

Ash leaned against a car hood, his voice low and empty.
"I'm just numb. Burying our own... it doesn't feel real."

T-Money exhaled hard, trying to center himself.
"The grand opening is in a few days. He was supposed to be here for it."

D-Bo, always the realist, shook his head.
"Eddie lived wild. Y'all can mourn, but I'm thinking about the good times."

Bay lifted his drink slightly.
"No question—we gotta make sure T-T and the kids are straight. If we're good, they're good."

The group nodded, an unspoken oath sealing between them.

WESTSIDE BUCK'S SPOT – NIGHT

A haze of cigar smoke curled around the low-lit room.
Westside Buck sat slouched in an old leather chair, a glass of dark liquor in hand. Across from him, Jack Boy and Tutu drank in silence, tension threading the air.

"How'd he get away?" Buck asked, his voice low and simmering.

Jack Boy shook his head.
"Man, as soon as he got off the phone, he flew out the house. Peeled out before we had time to catch him."

Tutu added, "All he said was, 'We got action. I know where Eddie B is.' Then he was gone."

Buck stared into his glass, his face unreadable.
"This one hits home," he muttered. "He was like a brother to me."

He raised his glass. Jack Boy and Tutu followed without hesitation.

"To Big Rich," Buck said.

Their glasses clinked softly, the toast echoing across the dark room.

Across the city, at the car lot, The Fist raised their own drinks to Eddie B.

Two sides. Two toasts. One war is brewing in the streets.

KANDI'S HOUSE – MORNING

Sunlight bled through cheap blinds.
Kandi stood in front of the mirror, adjusting her outfit—a skimpy uniform for another shift at the strip club.
 On the dresser, her phone sat on speaker mode, Keith's voice crackling through from a federal prison line.

"Bae, when are we gonna hear something from them folks?" she asked, tightening the straps on her top.

"It takes time..." Keith answered, voice weary. "Have you seen any members of the Fist at the club lately?"

Kandi frowned, thinking.
"Last time I saw them was at Westside Buck's party. Eddie B stabbed Big Tony up."

"Damn," Keith cursed. "Wish you woulda told me that sooner. Who all was there?"

"Kareem, Eddie B, and Whiteboy," Kandi said.

"Keep an eye open for them."

Kandi hesitated, then added, "How about this—Tan's missing. She used to mess with Southside Buck. He just got her a condo in Midtown."

Keith went silent for a beat.
"You need to talk to them. Let 'em know what you just told me."

"Aight," Kandi agreed. "Love you."

"Love you too. Stay sharp."

The call ended with a mechanical beep.
Kandi stared at the phone for a long second, then slipped it into her purse, grabbed her keys, and walked out into the Atlanta heat—carrying secrets heavy enough to break bones.

The streets weren't just shifting anymore—they were breaking apart, cracks spidering through every crew, every hustle, every so-called family. Eddie's blood wasn't the last that would soak the sidewalks.
It was just the beginning.

Chapter 44

OUTSIDE THE SKATE RINK – NIGHT

The parking lot glowed dimly under flickering lights.
 Smoke from blunts curled into the cold air as the YNG group—Slime, KK, Trice, and Blackie—huddled together, flashing wads of cash, firearms tucked carelessly in waistbands.

Pills clicked out of small plastic bags, disappearing into eager mouths.
It wasn't just a gathering—it was a recruitment drive.
A new generation was pledging allegiance to the streets.

Blackie, counting a thick stack, grinned wide.

"We did good tonight," she said proudly. "Got close to twenty getting down with YN."

Slime nodded, exhaling a lazy cloud of smoke.
"We gon' light it up," he said, flashing a smile. "We don't die—we multiply."

They all laughed, throwing up gang signs as someone snapped a picture—another trophy for social media, another page in a story spiraling out of control.

T-T'S HOME – NIGHT

Inside T-T's house, the energy was thick—a strange cocktail of laughter, food, grief, and resilience.

Family and friends packed the rooms, plates stacked high with ribs, wings, and mac and cheese. Kids zigzagged under tables.

It was a gathering of love and loss, a bittersweet celebration to hold Eddie B's spirit close.

T-T sat on the couch, shoulders tense, her voice low but sharp.

"They were asking me all kinds of stupid questions," she muttered.

Zuri, leaning in close, her eyes flashing, shook her head.
"You know they always wanna make us the suspects... even when we are the victims."

Auntie Taylor, soft and gentle, reached over and squeezed T-T's hand.
 "Baby, God heals all things in time."

T-T's mouth tightened. She wasn't sure she had that kind of time.

"I'm still having my baby's party at the skating rink," she said, stubborn and strong.

T-Money nodded, fist tapping the table.
"As you should. We gon' keep everything moving—like Eddie is still here."

T-T's gaze dropped.
"That's easier said than done," she said. "These girls are already asking for their daddy."

Buck stepped closer, his hand heavy on her shoulder.
"We'll get through this," he said. "One day at a time."

At the food table, Summer took a giant forkful of potato salad and groaned happily.
"Who made this? This shit bustin'."

Tamika laughed, nudging her.
"Girl, all you do is eat—and don't gain a damn pound."

Brenda, proud, lifted her glass.
"You know I put my foot in it."

Across the room, Kareem grabbed the mic, swagger in his step. He turned on the stereo—2Pac's "Str8 Ballin'" flooded the house.
Heads started nodding. Smiles cracked tired faces.

Kareem raised his glass.

"One thing for sure—my brother was the life of the party. So we gotta keep that same energy! This was his favorite!"

The music lifted the heavy air. People rap along. Women grabbed the mic, men stomped their feet. T-T let herself smile for the first time in days.

 Renay pulled her into the center of the room, and together they danced.

FLASHBACK SEQUENCE

On the TV, grainy footage plays.
Old camcorder clips.
Memories of Eddie B.
Raw. Real. Forever burned into their hearts.

ON SCREEN:

—*Future's "March Madness"* plays.
Young Eddie B darts through the block, laughing, a black hoodie swinging around his waist.
T-T is behind him, chasing with a water balloon, both of them breathless with laughter.
"Dirty soda in a Styrofoam, spend a day to get my mind blown..."
"Dress it up and go to NASA, two hundred miles on the dash..."
The screen freezes on Eddie's wide grin — pure freedom.

—*T.I.'s "24's"* bumps.
The video shifts to a gritty dice game on a cracked sidewalk.
Eddie B, Kareem, and Buck crouch low, piles of cash between them.
Dice fly — they laugh, shout, shove each other playfully.
"Money rollin' in, my partner's on twenty-four inches..."
"Still smokin' plenty indo, throwin' elbows, up out the window..."
A shot lingers on Eddie picking up a thick stack, throwing his head back, victorious.

—*2 Chainz's "Feds Watching"* hits.

Inside a dusty Cutlass parked on a quiet street, Eddie and T-T sit low, paranoid but laughing like fools.

He raps into a blunt like it's a microphone; she films him, cracking up.
"I'm be fresh as hell if the Feds watchin'..."

"Drop top, head boppin'..."
The screen catches T-T reaching over, kissing his cheek mid-rap.

—*Outkast's "Git Up, Get Out"* fades in.
Back in Eddie's childhood bedroom—walls covered in rap posters—
teenage Eddie B stares into a cracked mirror.
He raps fiercely, every word a prayer for a better future.
T-T leans in the doorway, arms crossed, a soft smile on her face.
"You need to get up, get out and get something..."
"Don't let the days of your life pass by..."
The video wobbles as Eddie turns and playfully tackles her onto the bed,
both of them laughing uncontrollably.

—Final memory.
The garage.
All The Fist—Buck, T-Money, Ash, Tom Tom, Kareem, Whiteboy, D-Bo,
and Eddie B—together.
Old speakers blast *2Pac's "Str8 Ballin'"*.

They crowd the tiny garage, arms draped over shoulders, bottles in hand,
rapping at the top of their lungs:
"Pushin' a bucket but I ride it like it's a Benz..."
"Willing to die for all my soldiers up under the pen..."
The camera pans across their faces—young, fearless, invincible.

A freeze-frame—Eddie in the center, mouth wide in mid-verse, throwing
up a fist.

BACK TO THE LIVING ROOM:

T-T wipes her face, holding the remote like it's a lifeline.
The Fist stares at the screen—silent, some fighting back tears, others
letting them fall.
The kids don't fully understand yet. But the energy in the room—the love,
the pain—it's heavy enough to crush steel.

T-T whispers, barely audible.

T-T

(whispering)
He's still here. Every time we move... he's still here.

A room full of survivors.
A family stitched together by memories, love, and loss.

The memories bled together—raw, messy, beautiful.

For a moment, no one moved.

Then—clapping.
First slow, then louder. A standing ovation for a man who refused to be forgotten.

Tonight, they weren't just mourning Eddie B.

They were celebrating him.

WAFFLE HOUSE – MORNING

The sky was pale blue, the streets half-awake.
Outside the Waffle House, a black DEA car sat idling.

Inside, Agent Harrington and Agent Parker watched the parking lot through tinted windows.
Kev sat in the back seat, bouncing his leg nervously.

He glanced at the agents.
"What's next?" he asked. "I don't really have any ties with Westside Buck."

Agent Harrington leaned back, unbothered.
"Don't worry. We're gonna put you in the same spot as him. Let y'all bump into each other naturally. You work your magic."

Kev hesitated, gnawing his lip.
"He real funny about who he deals with."

Agent Parker smiled coldly.
"We believe you gained their trust through Big Rich. Speaking of—what's the word on the streets?"

Kev shrugged.
"Not much. Both sides are quiet."

Agent Harrington's phone buzzed. A new text popped up on the screen. It was from Kandi.

KANDI (TEXT MESSAGE)
We need to talk.

Agent Harrington tapped out a quick reply.

AGENT 2(TEXT MESSAGE)
Meet me in two hours at Sam's Club parking lot.

KANDI (TEXT MESSAGE)
Okay.

Kev opened the car door.

"I'm waiting on y'all," he said, stepping into the morning light.

The agents watched him go, stone-faced.

"Kandi wanna meet," Agent 2 said. "She must have some new information."

FEBRUARY'S HOUSE – DAY

The air inside February's house felt tight, like something was about to snap.
February, Buck, Kareem, and Ash sat around a cluttered table, untouched drinks in front of them.

"Tan just vanished," February said, voice strained. "Like...thin air."

Buck leaned forward, his eyes dark.
"When's the last time you saw her?"

"We were all at work, having drinks," February said. "We left together. That's the last time I saw her."

Kareem leaned back, suspicion flickering.
"Who all was there?"

"The girls from work—Rainbow, me, Tan, and Milkway."

Buck's jaw flexed.
"She never just disappears," he said. "If I call, she always calls right back."

He pushed away from the table, the chair screeching across the floor.
"I'm gonna ask around. See what I can find out."

The three men headed outside. The night air slapped them in the face, thick and heavy.

"Something ain't right," Buck muttered.

"Are you thinking about foul play?" Ash asked quietly.

Buck nodded grimly.
"It's just not her character."

Kareem shrugged, trying to lighten the mood.
"Maybe she found a man and left town. Tired of being your side piece."

They chuckled briefly—but the laughter faded fast, swallowed by something darker.

They all felt it.

Something was moving.

Something bad.

The city was changing again.
Old wars reignited. New enemies whispered in the dark.
For The Fist, for Eddie's family, for everyone tied to these streets—

The real fight was just beginning.

Chapter 45

EXT. REPASS – DAY

A week later.

A montage of pictures and old videos of EDDIE B plays on a large screen. Clips flicker—him laughing, rapping, playing with his kids—moments now frozen in memory.

Mourners move around the yard, eating plates of barbecue, sipping drinks, while kids bounce wildly in a brightly colored inflatable house.

Across the street, hidden inside an unmarked vehicle, DEA agents discreetly snap photos of every license plate parked outside the house.

BACKYARD

A cluster of men—the FIST—gather behind the house, standing in a tight circle. Smoke coils from blunts. The mood is low, heavy.

DEE broke the silence first.

"We gonna work it out with T-T?"

D-BO took a drag, nodding toward the house.
"We know she ain't good with money. She ran through it last time when Eddie did that bid."

T-MONEY crossed his arms, speaking evenly.
"Eddie left close to three hundred grand. Not even counting what she still might have tucked away."

ASH leaned against the fence.
"What are you thinking?"

DEE shifted, voice firm.
"I say we let Snow become a Fist. He has been down the longest."

KAREEM glanced at Dee.
"Dee, does your LT even have buying power?"

T-MONEY didn't hesitate.
"Knowing Snow? Definitely. Say we use half of Eddie's money, Snow puts up the other half. He pays T-T forty percent of the profit. Until when—that's the question."

BUCK took a slow pull on his blunt.
"Three to five years. Plus, she is still eating off the car lot and the tow trucks."

DEE nodded.
"He'll be good with that. Still puts him in the million-dollar race."

T-MONEY spoke again, thinking two moves ahead.
"I'll talk with Sammy about where to put the other half of the money— for the girls."

WHITE BOY raised a brow.
"What about Wade?"

BAY shrugged.
"He works under Snow."

T-MONEY scanned their faces.
"Anybody got objections?"

No one spoke.

"All in favor?"

Every hand in the circle lifted.

Just then, T-T walked out the back door, wiping her hands on her jeans, looking around.

"Thanks, y'all," she said, smiling sadly. "Y'all really laid y'all brother to rest right. I was just inside talking about—"

The group nodded respectfully.

KAREEM stepped forward, voice steady.
"T-T, now that you're out here, we need to share something with you."

They exchanged looks. Then T-Moneye broke it down.

"We got close to three hundred grand of Eddie's money. Now, we can come up with a plan, but let me ask you—do you want to take it all or keep flipping it?"

T-T's eyes widened.

"To be real," she said, "I thought all I had was thirty-two grand in a shoebox and whatever was in the bank. But if you ask—no doubt—flip the money. I trust y'all with all my heart."

T-MONEY nodded.
"Here's the play: Snow moves up to Eddie's position. He puts in half, you put in half. He'll pay you forty percent off every flip."

T-T tilted her head.
"Why forty if we're going half?"

T-MONEY explained, patient.
"He's the one moving it. Plus, it still comes with maintenance. Trust us— you're gonna be eating good every three or four days."

BUCK added, "First, we gotta get a new plug in place. Can't say what the margins gon' be just yet."

T-T shrugged.
"That's cool. I'm with it."

T-MONEY continued.
"The other half of the money—we're gonna invest it for the girls. I'll get with Sammy, then we'll set it up with you."

T-T took a breath, then leaned closer.
"But let me share something with y'all... My friend Red? She was acting funny."

The group stiffened.

" The reason I'm telling y'all?" T-T said. "She was messing around with Big Rich. She's the one who wrote down the address where Eddie was."

DEE frowned.
"When you say 'off,' what do you mean?"

T-T's voice dropped.
"At first, she made excuses not to come to the funeral, but Yaya made her. Now, she always used to be on my line—now she can't be found."

The Fist exchanged knowing, grim looks.

WHITE BOY clenched his jaw.
"We'll get to the bottom of it."

STREET – NIGHT

A dark, empty street.

RAZOR and TAN cruised slowly past BUCK's sister's house. Razor leaned over, staring hard at the windows.

He soaked it all in, memorizing the setup.

Then, without a word, they pulled off into the night.

NEW YNG HANGOUT – NIGHT

The new spot was lit—bare bulbs, rattling speakers, and walls thick with smoke.

Lil Baby's track thudded like a heartbeat against the cracked sheetrock.

Against one wall, BLACKIE, SLIME, and KK stood tall, surveying their recruits.

Kids—half-high already, guns tucked, pills popping like candy.

CLICK.

KK killed the music. Silence punched the air flat.

SLIME stepped forward, his voice slicing through the tension.
"By show of hands—who's down forever?"

The recruits froze—then fists shot up, bold and hungry.

BLACKIE grinned wide, sharp as a blade.
"That's what I like to see. Y'all ready to go all in?"

Murmurs, then louder affirmations.

SLIME raised his voice, chest heaving.
"Nah, nah. We ain't playin'. We go hard—or we go home. You wit' us or what?!"

CREW (shouting)
"HELL YEAH!"

In one blurred moment, GUNS lifted to the sky.

The new soldiers screamed into the night.
Ready to burn down the world or die trying.

T-T'S HOUSE – DAY

The house was still. Too still.

T-T moved slowly, folding Eddie B's clothes into neat stacks, placing each into boxes.
Every shirt, every shoe—every piece of him.

She pressed a shirt to her face, inhaling the memory, closing her eyes.

FLASHBACK – BEDROOM – NIGHT

T-T and Eddie B tangled under the covers, laughing like kids.
Whispers of plans for the future, promises that now floated like broken prayers.

BACK TO PRESENT

A LOUD CRASH jolted her.

Her heart thundered in her ears.

T-T (calling out)
"Erin! What was that?"

ERIN (O.S.)
"Ella knocked over the lamp!"

Footsteps raced down the hallway.

ERIN (10) and ELLA (5) hurried into the room, wide-eyed and uncertain.
They stopped near their mother, the packed boxes towering around them.

The weight of loss was thick between them.

ERIN (voice cracking)
"Mama... Daddy's never coming home again, is he?"

T-T knelt down, fighting tears.

"Daddy's with Grandma now," she said softly.
"He's watching over us."

ELLA sniffled, wiping her nose.
"I wanna go with Daddy."

T-T brushed Ella's hair back tenderly.

"One day, baby," she whispered. "But not yet."

ERIN clenched her fists.
"It's not fair! Daddy promised he'd be here for my birthday! He
promised!"

T-T tried to form words, her throat too tight.

DING-DONG!

The doorbell rang sharply.

T-T hesitated, wiped her eyes, then moved toward the door.

She opened it—

Standing there was YAYA, her expression hard to read.
Heavy. Seriously.

And T-T knew—something else was about

to hit them.

Chapter 46

DEA OFFICE – NIGHT

The office is dim, tension thick in the air. Several DEA AGENTS stand clustered around a table cluttered with case files, surveillance photos, and maps.

AGENT Harrington held up a file.
"We got a name—Lori Smith. Street name: Red."
(pauses, flipping through more documents)
"She's got ties to Big Rich. And get this—she's real tight with Eddie B's widow."

BOSS AGENT leaned forward, interest sharpening his features.
"We play her. She can lead us to Southside Buck and the rest of The Fist."
(beat)
"She's knee-deep in that double homicide."

AGENT Harrington nodded.
"We're tracking her location now. Updates coming soon."

CAR LOT – DAY

The lot buzzed with low energy.

A group of men sat inside —BAY and BUCK locked in a serious chess match while others scrolled through their phones. A TV played quietly in the background, the sound of a sports talk show filling the gaps.

KAREEM leaned forward.
"Our grand opening's tomorrow. Time to make the donuts."

DEE nodded.
"Yep. Our first business kick-off."

T-MONEY smirked, moving a pawn on the chessboard.
"Many more to come. I hollered at Big Vick—he said twenty-seven."

WHITEBOY whistled.
"That high? Man, our backs against the wall."

BAY shrugged.
"It gotta work till we get a new plug. Folks still paying twenty-nine, thirty."

BUCK studied the board, moved his piece with calm precision.
"Check. Next two moves—checkmate."

T-MONEY glanced up.
"We need a new check. I'm grabbing ten."

D-BO added,
"Count me in."

KAREEM eyed T-Money.
"He got a hundred to sell us?"

T-MONEY nodded.
"Yeah. He is ready when we are ready."

ASH leaned back, casual but serious.
"Then set it up."

OUTSIDE – PARKED CAR – NIGHT

BLACKIE, SLIME, rappers LV and BABY THUG, smoke curling up from their blunts. LV leaned casually against the hood, scanning the street.

BABY THUG spoke first, his voice slick.
"Look, we wanna put y'all on our payroll."

SLIME arched a skeptical eyebrow.
"What exactly do you expect us to do? And what's the pay?"

LV smirked, nodding toward Baby Thug.
"We know YNG runnin' these streets. When we have a problem or an issue—you handle it."

BABY THUG jumped in.
"Two hundred K a year. Plus bonuses. A dope-ass hangout spot. And y'all get to travel with us, from time to time."

Blackie and Slime exchanged glances—a silent conversation passing in one look.

Then—SLIME grinned.
"Y'all problem just became our problem."

They dapped up, the deal sealed without another word.

T-T'S HOME – NIGHT

T-T paced the living room, her nerves frayed to the edge.

T-T (gritting her teeth)
"Girl, I felt she was acting shady... but my sixth sense was off dealing with everything."

YAYA scoffed, rolling her eyes.
"Yeah, she's always been jealous of you anyway. All she used to say was, 'If it wasn't for Eddie B, T-T be a broke bitch from the hood.'"

T-T smirked darkly.
"We gon' see about that. She gon' be seen ASAP."

YAYA's face tightened.
"It took everything in me not to kick her ass when I found out."

CAR LOT – NIGHT

AG, CHI-CHI, MELBO, and COUP strolled in, gym bags slung over their shoulders. They dropped them onto the floor—each thud heavy with the weight of cash.

T-MONEY looked up from his phone.
"Big Vick said he would be ready in an hour."

BUCK's phone buzzed. He answered, putting it on speaker.

BUCK (on phone)
"John John, what's up, Big Homie?"

JOHN JOHN's voice came through, rough but upbeat.
"I'm good. Heard about Eddie B—had to call, see what happened."

The rest of the Fist leaned in.

THE FIST (in unison)
"What's up!"

BUCK spoke quietly.
"He got into it with Big Tony. Sliced him up pretty good. Big Rich wanted revenge... caught him slipping."

JOHN JOHN sighed.
"Damn. Sorry to hear. Y'all holding up?"

BUCK nodded.
"We have to keep it pushing. How are you, though?"

JOHN JOHN
"I'm good. Putting in another motion. They loosen up on the crack laws—might have a chance of getting out early."

BUCK smiled.
"That'd be super dope. I'ma stop by your sis' spot, give her some money for you and the kids."

JOHN JOHN
"Appreciate you. You kept it real the whole bid."

Just then, T-T burst through the lot doors, her face a storm of fury.

DEA OFFICE – NIGHT

Tension filled the air like static.

Two agents sat across from each other, stacks of paperwork between them.

AGENT Harrington leaned in.
"We got an address for Lori. Boss wants us to get a warrant before we move—box her in. Play no games."

AGENT Parker cracked his knuckles.
"Good. She might be the one to crack the code on "The Fist."

AGENT Harrington grinned grimly.
"Accessory to murder. Pressure busts pipes."

CAR LOT – NIGHT

T-T stood in the middle of the lot, her voice cutting through the air like a blade.

T-T
"Red gave Big Rich the address. Yaya heard her talking to Jack Boy."

KAREEM didn't hesitate.
"She gotta go. And I mean today."

BUCK (calling out)
"Show of Fist!"

Every hand in the room—T-MONEY, BUCK, D-BO, ASH, KAREEM, BAY, WHITEBOY, and even T-T—shot up into the air.

D-BO cracked his knuckles.
"I'll give Skinny a call. Tell him it's 911."

T-T smirked coldly.
"I'll see y'all tomorrow."

ATLANTA POLICE STATION – NIGHT

The station buzzed quietly under low fluorescent lights.

CAPTAIN WOODS sat behind his desk, his frustration barely contained.

A young officer, POLICE 1, stood before him, shifting nervously.

CAPTAIN WOODS
"Anyone from the bust talking?"

POLICE 1
"Sir, we believe they're all scared—especially after learning Spike and Nut were found dead."

CAPTAIN WOODS's jaw tightened.
"Without a new informant, we've got nothing on Blackie and Slime."

POLICE 1 shrugged.
"We pressed them, but no one's talking."

CAPTAIN WOODS snapped.
"Set up one-on-one interviews with all of them. The Chief, DA, and Mayor are breathing down my neck."

WESTSIDE BUCK'S HOUSE – NIGHT

WESTSIDE BUCK leaned back in his chair, phone pressed to his ear. MICHELLE, his sister, laughed through the receiver.

WESTSIDE BUCK (smiling)
"Dad loves bowling. Let's do his 66th there—get five lanes."

MICHELLE
"Okay, I'll put it together and send out invites. How are my nephews?"

WESTSIDE BUCK
"Good—killing it in sports and school."

MICHELLE
"And Big Tony?"

WESTSIDE BUCK
"He's getting better every day."

DEA OFFICE – NIGHT

AGENT Harrington and AGENT Parker sat back at their desk, maps and photos spread out in front of them.

AGENT Harrington
"We can get Kev to bump into Buck at the bowling alley once we find out the time and date. Checkmate."

AGENT Parker nodded.
"When do we get the warrant for Lori?"

AGENT Harrington
"Boss said first thing on Monday. We're picking her up."

OUTSIDE A BUILDING – NIGHT

NEPHEW stood outside a sleek new building with three beautiful women at his side. A SALE LADY handed him a folder of paperwork.

NEPHEW nodded approvingly.
"Yeah, this is the one. We'll have the paperwork and deposit ready tomorrow."

SALE LADY
"Great! I'll be waiting for your call."

NEPHEW and his crew climbed into a waiting SUV.

NEPHEW grinned.
"Let's go party—our mission's complete. Buck's meeting me tomorrow with the rest of the money."

BIG VICK'S HOUSE – NIGHT

BIG VICK lounged on his worn leather couch. T-MONEY stood nearby, drink in hand, a quiet understanding between them.

T-MONEY
"Appreciate it, homie."

BIG VICK chuckled.
"Man, you know how far we go back. I'm sure there'll be a time I'll need to holler at you."

T-MONEY shrugged, casual.
"Yeah. Things been off since Eddie B went down and our plug went on the run. But until then, I'll be hitting you up."

BIG VICK leaned forward, nodding.
"I'm here—whenever you need."

T-MONEY gestured toward the corner.
"Y'all can grab them bags over there."

TWIN, COUP, and WADE moved toward the pile, scooping up the heavy duffel bags, slipping out into the humid night.

The city breathed in smoke and suspicion.
From the car lots to the police stations, from dim-lit back rooms to family cookouts stained with grief—every move carried weight now.
The Fist was no longer just playing for money. They were playing for memory, for legacy, for survival.

Eddie B's shadow stretched long across every conversation, every decision.
Some built in his name.
Some betrayed for a dollar.
And somewhere in the cracks of the streetlight and concrete, bigger forces watched—DEA agents weaving their quiet web, politicians pressing for headlines, enemies plotting the next checkmate.

Deals were made in smoke.
Loyalty was measured by blood.
And in the cold corners of Atlanta, it was clear:
The game wasn't over.
It was just getting deadlier.

Chapter 47

Grand Opening Moves

The sun beamed down over the newly opened car lot, casting a golden glow over rows of freshly waxed vehicles. A DJ posted up near the entrance blasted bass-heavy tracks that thumped through the speakers, setting the vibe. Families milled around, drawn by the smell of sizzling food from the grill, while the laughter of kids floated over from the bounce house set up near the back fence.

Street 94.5 broadcasted live from a booth on the lot, interviewing locals and hyping up the grand opening. People line danced in unison on the blacktop, flashes from cameras capturing every smile, every hustle, every moment of celebration.

Near a long folding table, Zuri, Summer, Skyy, and Renay moved quickly but gracefully, handing out raffle tickets and managing gift bags like seasoned event planners. Their energy was contagious—focused, proud, unstoppable.

Across the lot, The Fist posted up, watching everything like hawks while blending in with the crowd. Some leaned against new cars, joking with customers. Others nodded politely at familiar faces from the neighborhood. This wasn't just a sale. It was a statement.

Buck scanned the packed lot from near the DJ booth, his arms folded across his chest, a slow grin spreading across his face.

"Man, Zuri really put this together well," Buck said, turning to T-Money beside him. "This turnout is crazy."

T-Money, equally pleased, nodded. "My baby worked her ass off. Couldn't have done it without the rest of the ladies, though."

Buck chuckled, his eyes tracking the dance circle that had broken out near the grill. "We might actually make this thing legit one day."

T-Money smirked. "As long as we follow Sammy's lead—he knows the way."

Buck scoffed but nodded toward another group further across the lot. "Speaking of... look at your boy."

Across the blacktop, Kareem and Tom Tom danced with Savannah and Tamika to Lil Jon's "Snap Yo Fingers," the crowd around them clapping along. The whole event buzzed with energy.

Just then, Dee rushed over, out of breath but grinning wide.

"We've sold four cars already!" he said.

T-Money clapped him on the back. "Good start. If this game's taught us anything, it's that nothing happens overnight. But you stay consistent— you win every time."

The energy shifted as Sammy made his entrance. He walked in flanked by two sharp-dressed men, every step radiating quiet authority. Heads turned. Conversations paused. People instinctively made space.

"Damn, this turnout is solid," Sammy said, his voice cutting through the air. "Who put this all together?"

T-Money, standing a little taller, nodded proudly toward Zuri. "My lady."

Sammy smirked. "I got some business for her, then."

He gestured to the two men beside him. "This here is Mr. Brooke—VP of Brooke Stone. And this is Mr. Wells. Runs his own brokerage firm."

Handshakes were exchanged, names murmured with the heavy undertone of future opportunities. The smell of deals hung just as thick in the air as the barbecue smoke.

As the afternoon wore on, the raffle drew closer.

Near the DJ booth, the crowd pressed together, tickets clutched tight in sweaty palms. The DJ pulled a slip from the spinning drum and leaned into the mic.

"And the winner of the $500 gift card is..."
A drumroll of whispers moved through the crowd.

"Ticket 728!"

A woman screamed with joy and sprinted forward, waving her ticket high above her head as the crowd cheered. Cameras flashed. People clapped. Energy soared.

Later, as the sun dipped low and a cooler breeze settled over the lot, The Fist gathered by the DJ booth.

T-Money took the mic first, his voice steady and confident, speaking over the heavy beat rolling under him.

"First off, we wanna thank everyone for coming out. This is just the beginning. We're on a mission—to keep our dollars in our community longer than a week."

Ash stepped up next, flashing a grin. "For us, by us. We're here for y'all."

Then Kareem. "Tell your friends, tell your family—we got the best payment system to fit your budget."

The crowd answered with applause, loud and real. This wasn't just a car lot opening. It was the planting of a flag. A movement was breathing to life right there under the Atlanta sun.

Later That Night

The mood shifted across the city.

In a dark sedan parked under a flickering streetlight, Agent Harrington and Agent Parker quietly, staring at Kev, who squirmed nervously in the backseat.

"Tomorrow," Agent Harrington said, "you and a lady friend go to Pin Strikes Bowling Alley. Westside Buck will be there."

Kev hesitated, licking his dry lips. "What time?"

"Get there before him," Agent Harrington answered. "Say around seven. His dad's party starts at eight."

Kev nodded slowly, the weight of betrayal sinking deeper into his chest. "I'll be there. And... "How's my situation looking?"

Agent Harrington glanced at his partner, then back at Kev. "I'll talk to the DA next week for you."

No promises.
No guarantees.
Just survival—or prison.

Kev exhaled hard, opening the door and stepping out into the night.
The sedan pulled away without another word, leaving him standing there under the sickly yellow glow of the streetlamp, swallowed by his own desperation.

Chapter 48

Smoke And Shadows

The sky deepened into twilight as Razor leaned under the open hood of his battered Cutlass, the hum of crickets filling the air. Across the driveway, Nikki pulled in quietly, her two kids asleep in the backseat. She climbed out, balancing grocery bags on both arms, sighing as she fumbled with her keys.

Razor wiped his hands on a rag, watching her from the corner of his eye. His mind wasn't on the car anymore. It was elsewhere—caught between regret, survival, and whatever scheme he had brewing. Nikki disappeared inside, the door closing softly behind her. Razor stayed where he was, lost in thought as the night settled in.

Across town, the atmosphere was far different.

Inside a dimly lit hotel room, Nephew paced back and forth, clutching his phone to his ear. On the bed behind him, two women lounged half-naked, laughing loudly over some inside joke, oblivious to the storm brewing just a few feet away.

"I just gave you ten thousand!" Nephew barked into the phone, frustration dripping from every word.

On the other end, Pebbles' voice came smooth, mocking. "Well, Miguel, I need ten more. What's the problem?"

Nephew gritted his teeth. "You think money grows on trees?"

Pebbles barely hesitated. "Are we really gonna go back and forth about this?"

The woman's laughter rose again, and Pebbles must've caught the noise through the line because she added with a smirk in her voice, "Ohhh... sounds like you out trickin'. Don't let them get all the money."

Nephew's grip tightened around the phone, veins popping in his arm. "Say anything else, and if I don't have the money by—"

Click.
The line went dead.

Nephew stared at the phone like it had personally betrayed him, then threw it onto the bed with a grunt. The women glanced over briefly, unfazed, before returning to their conversation. He wiped a hand over his face and cursed under his breath.

Meanwhile, in a different corner of Atlanta's underworld, a state-of-the-art recording studio throbbed with bass.

Thug Baby and LV bobbed their heads to a new beat rattling the walls, the rich scent of burning incense mixing with the vibrations in the air. They were lost in the rhythm until the door slammed open.

One Punch—sharp suit, harder eyes—strode in with two women draped on either arm like trophies. He stopped mid-stride, surveying the room with the cold efficiency of a general.

"How's it coming?" One Punch asked.

LV, grinning nervously, gave a thumbs-up. "Beats hard."

"Good," One Punch said. "I'll get Tay Tay to write y'all something."

Thug Baby shook his head. "We already started writing something."

One Punch arched an eyebrow. "We? What, y'all a group now? Something I missed?"

"Naw," Thug Baby said quickly. "We just vibin'. Liked the beat so much, we started writing."

One Punch leaned in, lowering his voice into a threat wrapped in velvet. "Look—don't get no big head 'cause y'all got a few hits on the radio. Always remember—I put this together. I run this."

LV sat up straighter, voice respectful. "Ain't like that, One Punch. Just sharpening our skills."

"I said what I said," One Punch snapped. "If I don't like it, Tay Tay will come through."

Thug Baby nodded, a forced smile plastered on his face.
Cool, he said, even as something in his chest hardened.

One Punch smirked, satisfied, then spun and strode out, his entourage trailing behind him. The heavy studio door slammed shut, leaving Thug Baby and LV in a silence thicker than smoke.

They exchanged a long look.
No words needed.

The real darkness, though, was just beginning to unfold.

At the edge of a crumbling suburban street, a battered house sat cloaked in night. Four DEA agents stood outside, weapons low but ready.

Agent Harrington knocked sharply on the peeling front door.
No answer.

The agents exchanged a glance. Agent Parker leaned in, whispering, "No movement inside."

"Try again," Agent Kingsley muttered.

Agent Harrington hammered harder with his fist. Still nothing.

"Screw it," Agent Whitemore said grimly.

With a swift kick, the door splintered inward, the agents sweeping inside with flashlights slicing through the gloom.

The hallway reeked of mildew and stale electricity. Their beams danced across cracked picture frames and broken furniture.

"Guys... over here," Agent Harrington called out.

The others hurried toward a bedroom, guns still raised. In the doorway, Agent 1 stood frozen.

Inside, dangling from a frayed rope, was Red.

Her lifeless body swayed gently, the chair she kicked over lying sideways on the floor.

The agents rushed forward. Agent Kingsley caught her weight while Agent Parker sawed through the rope. They eased her onto the sagging mattress.

But it was already too late.
Red's skin was cold.
Her body is stiff.

Agent Harrington swore under his breath.

"We were too late," Agent Parker said quietly, shaken.

Agent Kingsley thumbed the radio. "We need forensics in here—now."

Silence pressed in around them, thick and suffocating.

Agent Whitemore, scanning the room, spoke the thought none of them wanted to voice. "Was it suicide?"

The question floated, poisonous and heavy.

A slow, creeping noise—like a floorboard moaning underweight—echoed through the empty house.

Every agent froze, turning sharply toward the sound.

Weapons raised.
Hearts pounding.

In the streets, the dead don't rest easy — they linger in whispers, unfinished conversations, and promises broken before the sun can rise again.

Eddie was gone. Red was gone.

And now, the ones left breathing had to carry the weight of it — the lies, the betrayals, the choices made in the shadows when nobody was looking.

Loyalty was no longer a given. Family didn't always mean blood. Sometimes it meant who would bleed for you when the lights went out.

In basements, studios, car lots, and broken-down homes, the city moved like a silent beast. Everybody plotting, everybody praying, everybody pretending not to be afraid of what was coming next.

The Fist knew the rules had changed. The DEA knew the clock was ticking. And somewhere deep down, everybody understood one thing clear as day—

There's no mercy in unfinished wars. Only consequences.

Chapter 49

Skating Rink – Day

The birthday party buzzed with life. Kids zipped across the rink, shrieking and laughing, a referee trailing behind them with a whistle ready. The colorful lights spun overhead, casting a dreamlike glow over the polished floor.

At a nearby table, adults lounged, sipping sodas and exchanging easy conversation. But at a quieter table off to the side, a group of men leaned in close, their voices low and serious.

T-Money leaned forward first, his expression tight.

"Man, it's about time to re-up again. Any word from anyone?"

Tom-Tom shook his head. "Nope."

Ash leaned back, frustrated. "My folks are still talking about a few more weeks."

Bay chimed in. "Ol' dude said he'll hit me as soon as."

Buck, arms folded, let out a short grunt. "Nephew said he's gonna need a few more weeks too."

T-Money scoffed, a hollow sound. "Guess it's Big Vick again."

Dee nodded grimly. "Work tight. Numbers just higher than what we used to—especially buying a hundred dun."

White Boy blew out a breath. "Right now, no choice. Gotta keep a new check coming in."

"Right," D-Bo said, his voice low, almost resigned.

Kareem shook his head slowly. "We need to find a new plug."

The silence that followed wasn't uncomfortable—it was heavy. They all knew the stakes. No moves meant no money. No money meant no survival.

At a separate table, the women gathered, laughter lighter, but their eyes were vigilant, flickering toward their kids gliding by.

T-T sipped from her cup, her voice soft but edged with exhaustion. "Girl, just one day at a time for me. Living for my girls."

Savannah leaned over, squeezing her hand. "We are all here for you. And, girl, you look fabulous."

Skyy flashed a supportive smile. "Yeah, but you need a new hobby or something to keep you busy."

T-T allowed herself a small, tired laugh. "I've been thinking about opening a dance studio."

Zuri brightened. "That you can do. And your girls? That'd be a great family business."

The women gathered closer, the conversation warm and full of hope. Someone called for attention, and they all rose together, forming a tight half-circle around the birthday table.

Together, they sang:

"Happy birthday to you..."

Laughter echoed as they celebrated Erin's 10th birthday. The table overflowed with wrapped gifts, bright balloons floating above. For a moment, the weight of grief lifted — replaced by love, resilience, and the memory of Eddie B, stitched into every laugh, every hug.

BOWLING ALLEY – NIGHT

The energy shifted. At the lively bowling alley, the sharp crash of pins filled the air. Neon lights buzzed. KEV and MELISSA sat at the bar, drinks in hand, exchanging small talk.

The entrance doors swung wide.

Westside Buck entered with his entourage, their arms full—balloons, a birthday cake, and a few gift bags. Buck's energy was magnetic, commanding without even trying.

Kev's eyes followed him closely.

Buck spotted Kev and Melissa at the bar and made his way over.

Kev grinned, lifting his glass. "Buck, what's good, my dog?"

Buck nodded coolly. "I'm good. Out celebrating my dad's birthday." His eyes flicked to Melissa. "Hey, Melissa."

"Hey, Buck," Melissa replied warmly.

Kev leaned in slightly, his voice dropping. "Man, God must've answered my prayers. Been feeling lost ever since Big Rich has been gone. Think I can get your number?"

Buck studied him for a beat. A long enough pause to weigh trust.

Finally, he nodded. "Really been cooling, only dealing with a handful of people. Shit been off. Strange things are happening." He rattled off his number: "404-290-3254."

Kev tapped it into his phone, grinning. "Appreciate it. I'll hit you tomorrow."

"Bet," Buck said, nodding.

He glanced at Melissa. "Where has your cousin been? Been looking for her."

"She's been working overtime dealing with her kids. We haven't kicked it in a minute," Melissa replied.

"Tell her to hit me up."

Without another word, Buck drifted back to his family, who were bowling and laughing together like the world hadn't shifted underneath them.

Kev finished his drink, his mind racing.

"You ready?" he asked Melissa, standing up.

"I thought we were gonna bowl?" she said, raising an eyebrow.

"Next time," Kev muttered. "Some money just text."

Melissa sighed as he tossed a few bills on the counter. Kev was already moving, his body pulled by a gravity that didn't include her.

DEA OFFICE – DAY

The room was dim and heavy with the smell of old coffee and tired hopes. Maps of the city lined the walls, push pins marking strategic points like battle plans.

Three agents sat at a cluttered table, flipping through case files and surveillance photos.

Agent HARRINGTON leaned back, frustrated. "I'm having doubts that Lori hanged herself. Examining the crime scene will be tough, but proving it wasn't suicide? Even harder."

Agent PARKER tapped a pen against the table. "The real question—did The Fist find out she sold her friend out? Or is Westside Buck just covering their tracks?"

"My guess?" Agent KINGSLEY said grimly. "The Fist. If someone took her out, it gives Buck even more reason to move carefully. He just lost his right-hand man."

Agent HARRINGTON shook his head slowly. "Strong point. Still can't believe we have nothing solid on them—no paper trail, no witnesses willing to talk."

"Exactly," Agent PARKER said. "A crew moving that much product and staying under radar this long? We're missing something."

Agent KINGSLEY leaned forward, voice steady. "The Fist isn't just a gang—it's a lifestyle. If we want to bring them down, we have to move faster."

On a brighter note, Agent 1 pointed out, "Kev's in with Westside Buck. Our plan worked. He's setting up a deal."

"Good," Agent PARKER nodded. "And maybe it's time we check our old toolbox. Somebody we locked up might be desperate enough to cut a Rule 35 deal."

Agent 1 tapped the file folder meaningfully. "Solid thinking. I'll reach out to Keith—see if he knows someone willing to talk."

Outside the office window, the gray sky cracked with distant thunder. A storm was coming. And this time, everybody knew it.

Chapter 50

OUTSIDE THE YNG HANGOUT – NIGHT

A blacked-out car idled quietly outside the YNG hangout, headlights off, blending into the shadows. Inside, LV and Thug Baby passed a blunt back and forth, the smoke swirling between them like the tension neither wanted to name out loud.

LV exhaled, voice tight.
"One Punch has us by the balls. Eats more than us, makes all the decisions."

Thug Baby shook his head slowly, bitterness cutting through his words.
"Yeah, like he's pimping us. All our cars? His name. Our houses? His name. We're fucked."

LV nodded grimly.
"We need to figure something out."

A long beat of silence. Then Thug Baby spoke again, voice low, deadly.
"We need to get out… YN needs to kill him."

LV took a long drag, the words hanging heavy in the car, before handing the blunt back. He stared through the windshield, weighing a decision that could cost them everything—or finally set them free.

"That might be our only way out," LV murmured. "But it has to be clean. You know he's Blood. They ride for him."

Thug Baby smirked, cold.
"Them YN boys? They are ruthless. Give zero fucks. Look how we have them living now—they do what we say."

At that moment, Blackie pushed through the hangout door, striding toward the car. She leaned into the window, casual, unaware of the storm brewing.

"Y'all coming in?" she asked.

LV nodded. "Yeah, in a few minutes."

"Bet," Blackie said, walking back inside.

LV and Thug Baby exchanged a loaded look. No words needed. The future had already shifted.

BRUNCH CLUB HOUSE – DAY

The cowboy-and-cowgirl-themed brunch bustled with life. Music thumped from outdoor speakers as kids laughed and jumped in a bounce house, rode small ponies, or clambered aboard a colorful train weaving through the lot.

Inside, the scent of fried chicken and sweet tea filled the air. SIR CHARLES's "Pour Me a Drink" poured through the speakers as the blackjack table filled up, old heads slapping cards down with dusty wisdom.

Outside, under a white tent, a group of men—The Fist—stood together, arms crossed, watching the kids play. Business never paused for long.

Tom Tom cracked a grin.
"I'm going tonight to watch Wild Money perform."

T-Money nodded.
"You know I'm there."

Kareem, leaning against a post, lit a cigarette.
"What's up with the work?"

T-Money shrugged.
"He said tomorrow."

Bay shook his head, restless.
"Need it bad."

D-Bo glanced around, voice low.
"Work's flowing back through the streets. We need a better number."

"I was thinking the same thing," T-Money said, his eyes dark. "I'm gonna put pressure on him."

Dee blew smoke into the air.
"He'll bend."

T-Money lowered his voice even further, as kids squealed and ran past.
"I talked with Sammy. He's got something lined up—says it'll be the start of generational wealth for us."

White Boy grinned.
"I like the sound of that."

Ash nodded slowly.
"Sammy's made me a believer."

T-Money looked around at the children, the families, the future they were building.

"Think about it. Each of us has anywhere from 400 to 600K. Let's round it off at 500K apiece. That's five million in cash power we possess together."

The numbers hit the group like a hammer. The quiet stretched as each man did the math in his head.

"What's our endgame?" T-Money asked. "Two, five, or ten million apiece?"

Kareem chuckled, shaking his head.
"Man, I never really thought about it, but five sounds good. That's fifty million all together."

"Not even counting what we have invested," Tom Tom added, eyes gleaming.

Buck smirked.
"I could live with that."

Snow shrugged.
"Sounds real good to me."

T-Money's voice hardened.
"It's time we really lock in. Get our houses. Get ourselves in order."

A solemn agreement settled among them. The weight of dreams too long deferred, now finally feeling real.

CLUB HOUSE – DAY

Inside, the women lined the floor, line-dancing to "Country Girl" by a southern soul artist, laughter lighting up their faces. A few kids tried to jump in, adding to the chaotic beauty of the scene.

At the blackjack table, two old-school men and a woman slapped down cards, trash-talking like it was a contact sport.

Tamika smiled over at Zuri.
"Zuri, you're really good at putting events together. This is so nice."

Zuri, beaming, leaned in close.
"The real surprise hasn't happened yet."

Little Dee ran full-speed toward his father, face glowing.

"Daddy, can I spend the night at T-Money's house?"

Dee laughed, ruffling his son's hair.
"Ask T-Money."

T-Money, grinning, gave the green light.
"Yes."

The day was a tapestry of small, golden moments—family, fun, and hope stitched together in real-time.

CLUB HOUSE – LATER

Zuri clapped her hands, calling everyone inside. Music dimmed. Anticipation rose.

The room gathered tight as they sang Happy Birthday to Sky. Sky stood at the front, her two kids hugging her legs, Ash standing proudly at her side.

The song ended—and in a heartbeat, Ash dropped to one knee.

The gasp from the crowd sucked all the air from the room.

Ash held out a small velvet box, voice trembling slightly but sure.
"Sky, will you marry me?"

Sky's hands flew to her face, tears spilling over as she nodded fiercely.

"Yes! Yes! Yes!"

The room exploded in cheers, cameras flashing. Sky, overcome with joy, turned to the crowd, quoting from *The Color Purple*, laughter bubbling through her tears.

"I married now!" she said, holding her hand high.

More laughter erupted.

Tamika wiped her eyes, teasing through a grin.
"It's gonna rain on your head!"

Jagged Edge "Let's Get Married" hit the speakers. Sky and Ash danced together, spinning into a new beginning.

CLUB HOUSE – NIGHT

T-Money nudged Kareem as they stood watching.

"You know Ash just put all the pressure on us, right?"

Kareem laughed under his breath.
"Who you telling? But for real... we all got some good down ladies."

The two men shared a knowing look. The street life had shaped them, but it hadn't hardened them beyond redemption.

Not yet.

The day had been stitched together with smiles and celebration, but underneath the laughter, something deeper pulsed—a promise.

They weren't just building businesses, throwing parties, or raising toasts to each other's victories. They were fighting for a future their fathers never lived to see, laying bricks for a legacy too big to fit into old dreams.

In the shadows, enemies gathered. New wars brewed behind closed doors. But for now, the children's laughter drowned out the whispers of violence, and the weight of the streets rested, if only for one afternoon.

This was their new foundation—built on loyalty, sacrifice, and the quiet hope that maybe, just maybe, they could rewrite the ending.

And when the dust settled, they'd either be kings of it...
Or buried beneath

Chapter 51

INT. NIGHTCLUB – NIGHT

The club throbbed with life. Neon lights flashed across a packed crowd, smoke from hookahs and blunts swirling like mist under the pounding bass. Bottles glistened in VIP sections where status, women, and money flowed like rivers. On stage, an artist wrapped up a fiery performance, and the crowd's eruption blurred into a frenzy of cheers and conversation.

In a prime VIP section, TOM TOM, T-MONEY, WHITEBOY, DEE, ASH, and WILD MONEY sat draped in success. Models in skintight dresses leaned in close, sipping champagne, their laughter blending with the music.

OUTSIDE NIGHTCLUB – NIGHT

Across the street, a blacked-out car idled silently. Inside, ONE PUNCH leaned forward, eyes locked on the club's entrance. LOU sat beside him, calm and observant. Behind them, a Sprinter van lurked, its tinted windows shielding whoever waited inside.

ONE PUNCH
(shaking his head)
"See? This right here is why I keep my foot on their necks. Told 'em 11 sharp."

LOU
(calm)
"Punch, ease up. Artists are always late. Plus they're your Bread and butter, you press too hard, somebody's gonna get in their ear."

ONE PUNCH
(smirking)
"Man, I got 'em in a headlock. Ain't nothin' but suburban kids rapping like they real street."

LOU
"Are you doing a Group album or keeping them solo?"

ONE PUNCH
"Both. Milk the cow. And right now pushing Wet Wet gon' she give Big Mama and Sexy Red a real run for their money."

Before Lou could reply, two flashy cars peeled into the lot. Doors swung open.

Out stepped THUG BABY, draped in Bad Smith gear, chains glittering under the streetlights. Beside him, LV climbed out in full The Vault drip, his entourage dripping in diamonds and hunger.

NIGHTCLUB – VIP SECTION – NIGHT

The atmosphere shifted the second THUG BABY and LV walked in. Heads turned. Phones flashed. The DJ seized the moment.

DJ
(hyped)
"Ayy! We got Thug Baby and LV in the building! Home Run Records CEO One Punch in the house—y'all know what time it is!"

VIP bottles appeared, sparklers flickering as they snaked through the crowd.

ONE PUNCH approached The Fist's section with a wide grin.

ONE PUNCH
(grinning)
"What's good, my niggas?"

TOM TOM
(leaning in)
"How much for a feature with your artist?"

ONE PUNCH
(smirking)
"Love price. Fifteen for both. Easy 30-ball or better."

TOM TOM
"Bet." (pulling out his phone) "Your number still the same?"

ONE PUNCH
"You already know."

The deal was sealed with a dap, and the night pulsed on. But deep in One Punch's eyes lingered a predator's calculation.

MAIN STAGE – LATER

The crowd roared as WILD MONEY closed their set. Four dancers twerked in flawless sync, electrifying the stage. The music faded. Salutes exchanged between One Punch and The Fist—mutual respect, but laced with silent wariness.

Suddenly, the lights dimmed again.

THUG BABY and LV grabbed mics, commanding the stage.

THUG BABY
"Y'all know what time it is! Heat comin'! Group albums, solos—but tonight—it's about the queen of the hour!"

LV
"Give it up for the one and only—WET WET!"

The crowd exploded. WET WET strutted out, owning the stage as her hit "Wet Wet" dropped. Beside her, THUG BABY hyped the crowd into madness.

BY THE STAGE – LOUNGE AREA

BLACKIE and SMILE sat watching. Not fans. Predators.

LOU nudged ONE PUNCH.

LOU
"Who are these two hanging with Thug Baby?"

ONE PUNCH
(waving it off)
"Just strays they picked up."

LOU watched longer, squinting.

LOU
 "They look like they put in real work."

ONE PUNCH
(smirked)
"Man, they're all pussies."

But the unease stayed in Lou's gut.

GYM – EVENING

Outside the gym, ZURI, SUGAR, MEKE, SKY, RENAY, SUMMER, SAVANNAH, and SHAN laughed and chatted, carrying gym bags and fresh ambition.

SHAN
(grinning)
"Guess I'm finally joining the book club. Career moves next."

ZURI
 (cheering)
 "Boss moves only!"

SUMMER
"Behind every strong man..."

SUGAR
"And a stronger woman."

They laughed, sisterhood alive in every step.

ZURI
(Smiling)
"Sammy hit me—wants me to organize a black-tie dinner."

The women erupted in cheers.

WESTSIDE BUCK'S SPOT – NIGHT

A dim room, heavy with suspicion. WESTSIDE BUCK, BIG TONY, and KEV sat around a table, exchanging bags.

WESTSIDE BUCK
(eyeing Kev)
"You good?"

KEV
 (jittery)
 "All good."

BIG TONY
(gruff)
"Stay buster-free. Lotta fake love out here."

KEV rushed off, his nervous energy not lost on them.

WESTSIDE BUCK
"Kev acting off?"

BIG TONY
"Scary nigga. Probably nothing."

Westside Buck nodded but couldn't shake the feeling crawling up his spine. His instincts screamed louder every day since Big Rich's death.

WESTSIDE BUCK
"Feels like I'm being followed."

BIG TONY
(somber)
"Follow your first mind."

Westside Buck sat back, drowning in thoughts, knowing survival came to those who listened to the quiet warnings in their gut.

The nights were getting heavier, and the streets whispered different stories to every man left standing.

For some, the music was still playing. For others, the shadows were already moving.

Loyalty means nothing if it wasn't tested in the fire.
And in Atlanta's heat, the real ones weren't just built—they were baptized.

One wrong move now wasn't just a mistake.
 It was a tombstone waiting to be engraved.

Chapter 52

The night air outside Karen's house was heavy with the scent of fresh rain. Inside, Kareem sat at the dining table with Karen and Chad, deep in conversation. Half-drunk glasses of wine littered the table, and a stack of business papers sat untouched in the corner.

"My goal," Chad said, leaning forward, voice filled with passion, "is to open five stores locally, then expand nationwide. We'll cater to ball players, hustlers, and your everyday working man."

Kareem nodded thoughtfully, weighing the ambition in Chad's words. "I like the sound of that. How much do you need to finish the first project?"

"About a hundred and twenty-five grand," Chad replied without hesitation. "Some for inventory, some for promotions. I need twenty-five K just to finish the build-out."

Karen, sitting between them, grinned with encouragement. "Bro, the place is nice! You gotta come see it for yourself."

Kareem leaned back, his mind sharp and cautious. A beat of silence stretched between them.

"Let me ask you something," Kareem said, his voice low, his stare unwavering. "And don't lie. Do you have a gambling problem?"

The question sucked the air out of the room. Chad stiffened, his easy confidence wavering for a split second. He held Kareem's gaze, refusing to flinch.

"No problem, bro," Chad said finally, shrugging. "Maybe a parlay bet here and there, but no habits."

Kareem shifted his eyes toward Karen. Her smile faltered—just for a moment. Long enough for Kareem to catch it.

"He's good, bro," Karen said, recovering quickly. "Nothing like that. You know I wouldn't ask you to come on board otherwise."

Kareem studied them both, feeling the weight of the moment, the tension thick and unspoken.

"Alright," Kareem said after a long silence. "Because I take real penitentiary chances for my money. Don't play with it."

Chad straightened up, nodding firmly. "Understood, bro."

At the same hour across town, Kev stood in his living room, back turned, phone pressed tightly against his ear. The walls seemed to lean in around him. He spoke low, almost a whisper.

"Were you able to talk to the judge or DA on my behalf?" Kev asked. "I just got a court date."

There was a pause. On the other end, the voice of a DEA agent crackled through the phone.

"I'm handling that tomorrow," agent Harrington said. "Don't worry. Can you make another buy?"

Kev rubbed the back of his neck, anxiety bleeding through his skin. "Yeah. I can make another purchase. Buck trusts me now."

He didn't notice Melissa standing in the doorway, frozen. She had caught every word.

Melissa backed away slowly, her heart hammering in her chest. She grabbed her bag off the kitchen counter and made for the door.

Kev turned just as she reached for the handle. "Are you leaving? Thought we were gonna watch a movie."

"Something came up at my house," Melissa said quickly, avoiding his eyes. "I'll call you later."

Without waiting for a response, she slipped out into the night.

Kev stood there, watching the door close, suspicion creeping up his spine.

The following morning, inside Sammy's gleaming downtown office, the atmosphere buzzed with opportunity.

T-Money, Dee, Buck, and Tom Tom stepped inside, passing two sharp-dressed women typing away at computers. A third man nodded at them as they continued into the glass-walled conference room.

Sammy sat at the head of the table, composed, his hands folded over a thick folder. He smiled, rising slightly as they entered.

"Gentlemen," Sammy greeted. "Glad y'all could make it on short notice."

The men nodded back, taking their seats. Sammy pushed the folder across the polished table. Each man opened a copy, flipping through dense pages filled with numbers and maps.

"I've got an incredible opportunity for y'all," Sammy said, voice steady. "A massive project—A 2 billion dollars—tied to the Beltline expansion. I'm blessed to have a seat at the table."

The men leaned in closer.

"Here's the deal," Sammy continued. "You each invest a hundred grand. Within three to five years, you'll start receiving fifty thousand annually— for life. Or, we can sell the entire project later and look at a percentage of billions."

T-Money frowned, flipping back a page. "Break it down for me, bro. You know we don't speak this language. And that fifty—do we split it, or is that each?"

"Each," Sammy said, nodding. "We're building shopping strips, condos, entertainment venues, setups like Atlantic Station living and more. Eventually, we will expand into other states."

Buck leaned back, arms crossed.

"Is Jackson part of this?" he asked.

Sammy smirked knowingly. "That's who brought me in. I'm letting y'all eat off my plate. I'm setting up a trust so the money flows clean."

Tom Tom narrowed his eyes, still skeptical. "I love it, but why us?"

Sammy's voice dropped to a lower, heavier tone.

"Because I was y'all," he said. "My mom was on drugs. My dad hustled anything that moved. I saw y'all come up from nothing—T-Money's family getting evicted, Ash's family raided by the police."

He looked each man dead in the eyes.

"Y'all got grit," Sammy said, the weight in his words undeniable. "The kind that can move mountains. You just need the light."

Silence gripped the room.

"You believe in us that much?" Dee asked finally.

Sammy nodded. No hesitation.

"I'm in," Dee said, and one by one, the others nodded their agreement.

They shook hands—an unspoken pact solidifying between them.

"My end goal," Sammy said, his voice low and urgent, "is to show that when we as Black people really come together—no matter our backgrounds—nothing can stop us. Imagine if ballplayers, entertainers, lawyers, and businessmen really united? We'd be an unstoppable force. That's why I chose hustlers—to show our strength."

The weight of his words settled over them like a heavy crown.

Outside, the sun blazed as T-Money's phone rang.

"Yo," he answered.

Big Vick's voice boomed from the other end.

"Ready for you, my guy. Got better numbers."

T-Money grinned. "Cool. Give me a few hours."

"Bet. I'm pulling up."

T-Money hung up, pocketing his phone.

He looked up at Bay and Buck standing nearby.

"Just like that," T-Money said, a half-smile pulling at his mouth. "Reality. Big Vick is ready for us. Said the numbers better—exactly what I asked for."

Bay clapped him on the shoulder. "Good. We need work bad. That hundred K investment gonna hurt for a minute."

Buck nodded, serious. "Don't forget—we still house shopping too."

T-Money turned, already texting the rest of the crew.

"Meet y'all at the office soon as," he said.

Business wasn't just business anymore.
 It was legacy

In a world where trust was currency and loyalty was rare, the line between survival and betrayal grew thinner by the day.
Deals were made. Promises were tested.
And somewhere between ambition and desperation, the next move would decide who built an empire—and who got buried beneath it.

Chapter 53

The house was small but full of tension. Melissa stormed around her cousin Monica's living room, the fury practically radiating off her.

"I'm telling you, cuz," Melissa hissed, pacing like a caged animal. "That nigga's a bitch-ass snitch. Call Buck. I hate snitches. Got my daddy doing twenty years behind rats like him."

Monica stayed seated, concerned but calm.
"Are you sure you heard what you heard?" she asked carefully.

Melissa spun around, glaring. "Stop playing with me."

Monica sighed heavily, reaching for her phone. She dialed.

Across town, Westside Buck lounged in his SUV when the call came through. His voice, when he answered, was dripping with cocky charm.

"Are you finally ready for me to hit that wet pussy again?" Buck teased.

Monica rolled her eyes. "Boy, that's what's wrong with y'all niggas. Always thinking with the wrong head. Look—come to my house. Now. My cousin needs to talk to you."

Meanwhile, outside Nikki's house, a different storm brewed.
 Razor sat low in his blacked-out car, waiting.

Moments later, Buck pulled up, heading inside. When he emerged with a bag slung over his shoulder, Razor moved fast—gun in hand.

"Stop looking like you saw a ghost," Razor said, stepping out of the shadows. "If you want your sister to live, walk slowly."

Without a fight, Buck obeyed. Razor zip-tied his wrists and ankles, then shoved him into the front seat of a nearby car.

Inside the office, Kareem, Whiteboy, and D-Bo were lounging, half-watching TV. Dee entered with a gym bag, swinging it casually.

"Nothing like a new check getting made," White Boy said, grinning.

"We need it," Dee replied, dropping the bag onto the floor. "Way we spending money, it'll all be worth it later."

D-Bo nodded solemnly. "We are playing chess for real now."

Bay and Tom Tom entered next, each carrying bags of their own.

"'Bout to get a song with Thug Baby and Wild Money," Tom Tom said proudly.

Kareem grinned. "That's gonna be hard. He's hot-hot right now."

Back at Monica's house, the mood was heavier. Melissa paced, Buck leaned forward.

"What's the 911?" Buck asked.

Melissa took a deep breath, the words spilling out fast.
"I heard that nigga talking. He's a snitch."

Not far down the street, two DEA agents sat inside a nondescript car, watching Monica's house from a distance.

"You think it's a booty call?" the first agent asked.

"Second time he's been over there," the other said. "She's fine, though."

The first agent smirked. "If he keeps money there, we'll know soon enough."

In a damp, musty basement, Buck lay hogtied on the floor. Razor hovered nearby, black bags stacked against the walls.
Outside, Razor popped the trunk on his car, pulling Tan out roughly and dragging her down to the basement.

Tan's scream caught in her throat when she saw Buck lying helplessly on the floor.

At Monica's, Buck's jaw tightened as Melissa handed him her phone.

"He is texting me now," she said. "Told you."

Buck nodded grimly. "Play it cool. I'm about to break you off something real good. Give me his address."

Melissa scribbled it down, handing it over without hesitation.

Nikki's nerves frayed by the second. She paced back and forth, peering out the window at Buck's SUV still parked in the driveway.
She called his phone again—straight to voicemail.
Again.
Again.
Nothing.

Something was wrong.

Later that night, the office grew heavy with unease. Big Vick leaned against the wall, arms crossed as T-Money, Kareem, Bay, and Dee talked quietly.

"Something's off," T-Money said, tension sharpening his voice. "Buck knew we were meeting up."

"Last time something felt off like this," Kareem said, "Bay got kidnapped."

Bay grimaced. "Don't think like that."

Big Vick shifted impatiently.
"I need to roll. Got people waiting.l Leave the work—I'll catch Buck tomorrow."

Dee frowned. "He never puts pussy over business. Especially not when you coming."

T-Money nodded slowly. "Leave it. But we're riding by Nikki's. Tonight."

At a bar across town, Westside Buck nursed a drink next to Big Tony.

"That nigga setting me up," Buck muttered darkly.

"I checked with Sasha," Big Tony said. "He caught a case."

Buck slid a burner phone into his jacket.

"Put all the money up," Buck ordered. "I'm gonna need your wife to rent me a car. I'm catching a train to my sister's spot. Pull up on me there."

"What about the work?" Big Tony asked.

"Move it out of the spot. Now."

Big Tony nodded grimly. Buck's gut had been screaming for weeks—and in their world, the first mind was never wrong.

The two DEA agents walked quietly through the streets by bars looking for Westside Buck, casual but alert.

"We lost him," Kingsley muttered.
"Phone's off. He might be onto us."

"We'll figure something out," Whitemore said. "Circle back to the car. He's bound to slip."

Inside Nikki's house, the room was thick with tension. T-Money, Kareem, D-Bo, and Dee stood awkwardly.

"So he came in, grabbed the money, and left?" T-Money asked.

Nikki nodded. "Yeah. I went to the back for a minute, came back out— his truck still here. Called his phone. Straight to voicemail."

Kareem frowned.
"Have you noticed anything strange lately?"

Nikki hesitated. "Yeah… There was this old blue Chevy parked across the street. Some guy working on his car for few days, now it gone"

D-Bo's jaw tightened.
"We'll be in touch," he said.

"And Nikki," Dee added firmly.

" don't call the police"

The night was thick with questions and thin on answers. One by one, the walls around them were closing in—old betrayals resurfacing, new dangers circling like wolves. In their world, loyalty wasn't a word, it was survival. And as the streets shifted beneath their feet, everyone would soon find out: you don't outrun your past—you confront it or get buried by it.

Chapter 54

KARAOKE BAR – NIGHT

The karaoke bar buzzed with smoke, weed, and the slurred high of cheap drinks. KANDI, FEBRUARY, and RAINBOW lounged in their booth, hookah coiling around them like lazy snakes. Onstage, a woman sang "Call Tyrone" by Erykah Badu, the heartbreak notes cutting through the haze.

KANDI leaned over, concern lining her forehead.

"Girl, slow down. You okay?"

RAINBOW shook her head, hollow-eyed. "Not really. I'm stressed the fuck out."

FEBRUARY threw her hands up. "Who are you telling? I need some dick too."

Rainbow chuckled darkly, but the weight never left her shoulders. "It's not that — it's Razor."

Kandi blinked. "I thought he was dead."

Rainbow leaned in, voice lowering. "Nah. He's on some Makaveli shit. You know The Fist had him and his boys sodomized for kidnapping Bay. Took all their confidence... their swag."

The girls froze, stunned. Then—another round of shots.

Rainbow added, voice dropping to a whisper, "He killed his boys with an overdose, switched IDs, and left a promise of revenge."

Kandi shook her head slowly. "Damn. That's deep."

They clinked glasses, but the celebration had a crack down the middle now.

CAR LOT – DAY

T-Money, BAY, D-BO, SNOW, KAREEM, and BUCK gathered, the Atlanta sun pounding the pavement, heavy with unease.

"I stay up all night thinking... what if YNG is behind this?" T-Money muttered.

BAY rubbed the back of his neck. "I wonder if Tan being missing got something to do with Buck."

D-BO nodded grimly. "Right. I didn't even think about that."

T-Money eyed them all. "We all need to throw in and give Big Vick the rest of the money for the work."

"Make sense," SNOW said.

"Yep," KAREEM agreed.

BUCK's jaw tightened. "We gotta find our boy."

RESTAURANT – LUNCH

Across town, two DEA agents leaned into KANDI over half-eaten salads.

"So who all knows Razor isn't dead?" Parker asked, voice low.

"Not sure," Kandi shrugged. "I just heard about it."

The agents exchanged a look.

"We need to find Razor," Harrington said. "And get him to flip on The Fist."

BASEMENT – NIGHT

In the damp, mold-slick basement, BUCK lay hog-tied on the floor. TAN huddled nearby, eyes swollen from crying.

RAZOR stood over them, seething.

"I'm gonna do you like you had them do us," he sneered. "Took my homies' pride. Now it's your turn."

Buck stared up at him, hollow and broken.

Razor leaned down, snorting another line of cocaine off the back of his hand.

"Time to pay."

MAYOR'S OFFICE – DAY

The gleaming high-rise windows didn't wash away the tension. Janet stood before the Mayor, smiling wide.

"Numbers are good. People are feeling confident. We're running more ads starting Monday."

The Mayor nodded, pleased. "City tour. Factory. Business districts. Two schools. Lenox Mall. I want cameras everywhere."

"You got it."

The Chief and District Attorney entered next.

"How's the YNG case?" the Mayor demanded.

"Didn't get everything we wanted," the DA admitted. "Had to jump the ball to avoid blood in the streets."

"But it's under control," the Chief assured.

The Mayor nodded stiffly. "No surprises. We're eight weeks out."

HOUSE – NIGHT

WESTSIDE BUCK slid two keys across the table to PAT.

"One in my sister's name, one in Auntie's. $250K in each box. Plus deeds to a few houses."

Pat's hands trembled.

"I don't wanna lose you."

Buck touched her hand gently. "I need you strong. We gon' be alright. I just want everything in place."

Pat bit her lip. "What about your mom?"

Buck smiled sadly. "She's good. She got her own box."

Outside, the dark gathered like a coming storm.

FEBRUARY'S HOUSE – NIGHT

Tension sat thick like smoke.

FEBRUARY looked each man in the eye—KAREEM, ASH, DEE, BAY, T-MONEY.

"Razor's not dead," she said. "He's coming."

ASH cursed under his breath. "What the hell do you mean?"

"Exactly what I said. Be careful."

KAREEM's face darkened. "You're too late. Buck's missing."

FEBRUARY's voice cracked. "I just found out."

"Who told you?" T-MONEY asked.

"A dancer. Name's Rainbow."

"I know her," BAY muttered.

Silence.

KAREEM spoke first. "We find Razor. This time—we end him."

YNG HANGOUT – NIGHT

Smoke curled toward the ceiling. In the shadows, THUG BABY addressed SLIME, LV, BLACKIE.

"We need y'all to take out One Punch."

SLIME blinked. "That's your CEO."

LV grinned coldly. "We are having a company dinner. Do it after. In front of everybody. John Gotti style."

BLACKIE smirked. "World news, huh?"

"Chess, not checkers," Thug Baby said. "Our time now."

They clinked glasses. A silent death sentence.

RENAY'S HOUSE – DAY

The women gathered, leaning on each other in the sun-lit kitchen.

SUGAR took Renay's hand.

"Trust me. Buck's coming home."

T-T nodded. "The Fist don't play about theirs."

RENAY's eyes brimmed. "I'm holding on. Holding on because of y'all."

SUMMER whispered, "We gon' get through this."

Outside, kids laughed—unaware the city teetered on the edge of bloodshed.

THE OFFICE HOUSE – DAY

The Fist convened. Heads bowed. Plans sharpened.

D-BO broke the silence. "We got eyes on Rainbow. Just in case."

T-Money added, "Sammy's money's in. Big Vick's paid. Now—it's about Buck."

KAREEM clenched his jaw. "$125K invested with my sister. We need a new plug. Now."

DEE exhaled. "We've been dishing out money fast."

ASH said, "Something always works out."

TOM TOM added, "Just think—Buck could be down $260K. We need a miracle."

T-MONEY closed it out. "Right now, we find our brother. Alive."

RAZOR'S BASEMENT – NIGHT

Cigarette burns pocked the concrete floor. Dim light flickered over broken men.

TAN sobbed in the shadows.

RAZOR towered over BUCK.

"I'm not after money," Razor whispered. "I'm after your soul."

BUCK—helpless. Razor grinned.

The needle gleamed in his hand.

LOW-KEY SPOT – NIGHT

WESTSIDE BUCK handed COCO an address and twenty thousand in cash.

"Kill Kev," he said simply.

"No problem," Coco replied. "You'll see it on the news."

BIG TONY patted Buck's back.

"All the work's moved and safe."

Buck nodded grimly. "Now we wait."

RESTAURANT – NIGHT

ONE PUNCH laughed heartily with THUG BABY, LV, and others.

"Bigger than No Limit, Death Row, Bad Boy," he boomed. "This is the new dynasty."

They toasted, glasses clinking.

Outside—BLACKIE and SLIME crouched by the car, eyes locked on the door.

SLIME checked his phone.

"Thug Baby gonna text when they come out."

BLACKIE smirked. "This about to be a movie."

DEA OFFICE – NIGHT

AGENT Harrington stared at the board, connecting red strings.

"We have everything we need. Pick up Westside Buck."

AGENT Parker scribbled another name down.

"And Big John. Southside Buck's last ghost."

They shared a grim nod.

Game time.

Atlanta's streets had always run red—but this time, it wouldn't be blood alone. It would be loyalty. Power. Revenge.

Razor was moving. The Fist was hunting. The DEA was closing in.

And somewhere in the thick black smoke of it all—
Somebody's empire was about to burn.

OTHER BOOKS BY TIERRE FORD

DARRIN DEWITT HENSON
ROBIN GIVENS
TOBIAS TRUVILLION
AND KEITH ROBINSON
BASED ON THE NOVEL BY TIERRE FORD
THE PRODUCTS OF THE AMERICAN GHETTO
DIRECTED BY HENDERSON MADDOX
A DIFFERENT KIND OF AMERICAN DREAM

TIERRE PRESENTS
ALL FOR TEN MINUTES OF FAME